CW00865831

Caroline Hartley and the Dreadnought Battleship

Caroline Hartley
and the
Dreadnought
Battleship

By
D. J. Robinson

Book Two of the Four-Part Caroline Hartley Series

Caroline Hartley and the Dreadnought Battleship

iUniverse books may be ordered through booksellers or by contacting:

iUniverse
1663 Liberty Drive
Bloomington, IN 47403
www.iuniverse.com
1-800-Authors (1-800-288-4677)

ISBN: 978-1-5320-0848-1 (sc)
ISBN: 978-1-5320-0850-4 (hc)
ISBN: 978-1-5320-0849-8 (e)

Library of Congress Control Number: 2016917872

Print information available on the last page.

iUniverse rev. date: 02/14/2017

For my deceased parents

Also by D.J. Robinson

Caroline Hartley and the Magic Key

Book One of the Four-Part Caroline Hartley Series

Chapters

Central Europe

The story so far...

Just before the end of the school summer term, the postman had delivered a large padded envelope to Caroline Hartley's house in Welwyn Garden City. The mysterious envelope, addressed to *Ms C. Hartley,* had a Zurich postmark on it.

Caroline's mother had thought, the *Ms* should be *Mr,* and should be for her ex-husband Chris, who had a bank account in Switzerland. Knowing her children were due to go on holiday, with him, the following day, she had asked her daughter to give him the envelope.

The Hartley children had met their father at London-Stansted airport. They had travelled with him on Ryanair to Bratislava, in Slovakia, where he now lived. The next day, their father had opened the envelope in front of his kids. A large old key had rolled out that had been carefully-wrapped in an old pink piece of paper. On it, was a name – *Caroline.*

Caroline had wanted to know, who had sent her the key, who had written the word, and most of all, why would someone send her a key that according to her brother, was magical?

Their father took his children to a small castle in mid-Slovakia. Caroline and Martin had discovered its huge overgrown garden, which they had run around and explored. They also discovered the key fitted a door at the bottom of a stairway, at the castle. It was here, Caroline discovered, her key really was magical. Curious, the children had ventured up the attic stairs; where at the top, they were drawn forward by a mysterious white beam that had appeared, just before she had unlocked the upper attic door.

Caroline and Martin arrived, in 1912, where they met two children called Veronica and Manfred Strauss, who were the same ages as them. The Hartley children were thrilled to discover the castle garden, as it once was. They went on to have many adventures with their new friends, in it, as well as around the lake and forest that lay beyond.

The children also discovered, the magic key had a mind of its own. No one knew why it kept flashing different numbers, other than the fact that it allowed the Hartley children to travel backwards and forward, between their time period and 1912.

Disaster however soon struck. Following their last adventure to 1912, on returning to their own time, bad weather caused some serious damage to their father's flat, in Bratislava, forcing the Hartley family to have to unexpectedly return to the city.

The children were aghast at the thought of leaving the castle, so suddenly, without saying goodbye to their new friends from the past or present. Caroline still hadn't found out who had written her name, on the pink piece of paper. Nor had she discovered, who had sent it to her. Mortified, she realised she might, now, never find out the answer. Worse, was the thought that they might never return...

1

The Bar Terrace

Bratislava, Slovakia
Summer 2007

It was a typical hot summer's day, down by the river, in Bratislava. The temperature must have been more than 35ºC. There was a slight wind blowing along the river Danube that proved a blessing for those sitting outside, on the bar terraces of the new Eurovea Shopping Mall.

Caroline Hartley was sitting looking out across the river, at one such bar terrace. She was relaxing under a sunshade, while drinking her Coca Cola. Her brother, Martin, was sitting opposite her, sucking on his straw.

"Martin," said his sister. "Can't you drink it properly? It's so common to slurp, while drinking in public."

He stuck his tongue out at her.

"So, is that," she added.

"I'm bored," said Martin. "I want to go back to the castle."

Caroline looked at him.

"So do I," she replied.

"I want to go back to 1912, to see Manfred and Veronica."

"Me too! But we're stuck here, like lemons."

"I know, we are."

1

"All, because of that *ghastly* thunderstorm."

Changing the subject, Martin said, "What time is it?"

"Dunno. Someone called my brother, lost my mobile in a lake, remember?"

"Only asked."

Caroline looked over at the small clock tower that was next to the bar.

"It's just gone one," she said.

"I thought we were meeting Dad at one."

"We are. He's just late, as usual."

Caroline looked around her. Suddenly, she saw her father walking towards them.

"Look! There he is," she said, pointing and waving.

"Oh, yes," replied Martin. "And it looks like he's got Mr Slavo with him."

Their father saw his daughter waving and walked over to them.

"Sorry, I'm late," he said, embracing her.

"Oh, that's alright," she said. "We were just enjoying the view, weren't we, Martin?"

"The view," he replied, having been looking elsewhere. "Er, yes."

"I invited my former neighbour Slavo, to join us for a drink," said his father.

"Hello, Mr Slavo," said Martin, beaming.

"Hello, Martin, Caroline. How are you both?"

"Fine, thanks," they replied.

The two men sat down next to the children.

The waitress appeared.

"Do you speak English?" asked Chris.

She replied, "Yes, of course."

"Great! Could I order some drinks, please?"

"Yes, what would you like?"

Chris asked everyone what they wanted, then ordered the round of drinks.

Once the waitress had departed, Chris said to Slavo, "I must say, that was a good idea of yours to suggest a beer."

"I think we deserve one, after sorting out all your paperwork at the insurance company this morning. Anyway, a good Slovak beer, in this heat, is refreshing, Chris."

"Indeed!"

They all sat relaxing under the sunshades, looking out on the river Danube.

After a moment, Slavo said, "How is the new flat, Caroline?"

"Oh, fine thanks. It's much bigger than the last one. I even get my own bedroom."

"So do I," added Martin.

Slavo added, "I would imagine moving flats has been quite an experience for you both?"

"Er, yes. It has," replied Caroline.

"After all, it's not every day you move flats."

"Yes, that's true."

"Slavo," said Chris, smiling. "I don't think it was on Caroline's original top ten list of things to do on holiday."

"No, it wasn't," she said, laughing. "I definitely hadn't planned to spend two days of my summer holiday, helping my dad move flats."

Slavo replied, "It'll be something to tell your friends, back home."

"Er, yes, I suppose that's one way to describe it."

"We spent yesterday, cleaning up a bit of his damaged flat," said Martin.

"That's very good of you," said Slavo.

"Yes, I thought so."

"When I saw it the other day, it looked quite a mess."

"It still is."

"I don't know, what I would have done, without their help," said Chris.

"It's a good job we're here then, isn't it, Dad?" said Caroline, giving him one of her famous smiles.

"Yes, Sweetheart"

Slavo added, "I'm sure, being here in Slovakia, has been an interesting experience for you both."

The children looked at each other.

"You can say that again," replied Caroline.

"It has certainly been different," added Martin.

Chris then said, "You'll be pleased to hear, Caroline that the building workers, which the flat management got in, started fixing the roof this morning."

"Oh, that's good."

She added, "But what about your flat?"

"Well, as you know, this morning, Slavo was helping me with the translation, at the insurance company. They will pay for my personal damaged items. All we need now, however, is for the builders to come and repair the flat."

"I thought your landlord was sorting that?" said Caroline.

"He is, Sweetheart. Arthur rang me this morning. He's coming round this evening, to have another look at it."

"I see."

"What about my damaged computer game?" asked Martin.

Chris replied, "Ah, I think I'll probably have to buy you a new one."

"Yes, it's a pity about that, Martin," said Slavo. "Chris told me it got damaged in the flood."

The boy replied, "That's right. It did."

He added, "So what am I going to do, now?"

"You can play with your train set," said Caroline, smiling sweetly.

Martin gave his sister a filthy look. He stuck his tongue out at her.

She reciprocated.

"Oh, I see you two are on form again today," said their father. "Personally, I'm not into tongue sandwiches. Are you, Slavo?"

"Sorry, what was that, Chris?"

"Er, nothing"

"Ha, ha," said Caroline, sarcastically.

Chris decided to change the subject.

"With any luck, if everything is alright, and keeping your fingers crossed, we might be able to return to the castle, tomorrow."

His children looked at him.

"Really?" said Martin.

"Well, hopefully," said Chris.

4

"I don't believe it," added Caroline, sarcastically. "But it'll be great, if we can."

"It'll be *brilliant*," added Martin.

"Mind you," said Chris. "It'll only be for a week or so, as we'll need to return to Bratislava, because of a presentation I have to do, in Vienna, the following week."

"I suppose, anything is better than nothing, eh, Martin?" said Caroline.

"Yeah, that's true," he added.

The children were secretly delighted to hear the news, as it meant they would hopefully be able to see their friends at the castle again.

Slavo then said, "Chris tells me, you're missing the castle, Caroline. Is that true?"

"He's right. I am."

"Me too," added her brother. "It's boring here. All we've done is move flats and clean."

"Well, it has been an emergency, Martin," said Chris.

"I know, Dad."

"I mean, you'll be able to tell all your friends about your adventures, when you get home."

"I hardly think moving flats and cleaning a bit of your flooded flat, is an adventure, Dad," said Caroline.

"Well, try to think of it as such. After all, worse things have happened."

"Like what?" asked Martin.

"Erm, well," said Chris. "I can't think of anything, off the top of my head."

"I can," replied Martin.

"What?" asked Caroline.

"Dad's divorce from Mum"

Caroline gave him 'The Look'.

"Yes, I take your point," said her father, smiling.

The waitress arrived with the drinks.

Chris said to her, "Oh, thank you."

After he had paid, Caroline took a sip of her drink, and then said, "Dad, did you remember to buy me a new mobile phone?"

He looked at her in horror.

"Ah, the mobile phone"

Caroline looked at him in 'her way'.

She said, "You've forgotten it again, haven't you?"

"Erm," said Chris, apologetically.

He then said, "Yes, I forgot to buy you one again. Sorry, Sweetheart."

"Pity!" said Caroline, who added, "What are you, Dad?"

"Forgetful," said all three of them, laughing together.

"Sorry, sorry," he said. "Look, it'll probably be best, you buy another one, when you get home. You know, warranties and all that."

"Alright, Dad," she replied, disappointed.

"Tell you what. This afternoon, we'll go and buy you a new watch."

"Really?"

"Look, I know it's not the same as a mobile. But at least you'll be able to tell the time, with it."

"Okay," she replied, happily.

Chris took a swig of his beer.

"This is a really great place, Slavo," he said, putting his beer back on the glass table.

"Yes, I like it," he replied.

Slavo added, "It's where all the Slovaks sit. Have you noticed, all the foreigners tend to sit in the Old Town?"

"I hadn't. But now you mention it…"

"I think you really need to be with someone, to sit here to enjoy it."

"I could sit here all day on my own," said Caroline, who was enjoying the moment.

"That's *not* what you said earlier," added her brother.

"What did I say, earlier?"

"You said, you'd prefer to be at the castle."

"Yes, that's true, I did. I'd rather be sitting in the conservatory, in the castle, or better, in this weather, sunbathing on the lawn, outside it."

"Yeah, me too"

"Remember, Martin," said Caroline, sipping her drink. "It's *our* secret castle. So, I prefer to sit there and enjoy it, away from everyone else."

"And I like it, 'cause it's got that magical feel to it."

Caroline, who was sucking on her straw, gave Martin 'The Look' again.

He got the point, adding, "And I want to go back to the lake."

"Well," said Chris, "If everything goes to plan. Tomorrow, you'll be able to."

"Great!"

Caroline and Martin were delighted to hear the news. Both were desperate to get back to the castle, so they could try Caroline's magic key, one more time. Both children wanted to return to 1912; so that they could see the friends, they had previously met at the castle, in that time period...

2

The Landlord and the Builder

In the early evening in Chris's flooded flat, Caroline was sitting on some newspapers on the sofa, reading a book. Chris and Martin were also sitting on newspapers on their chairs. They were playing chess on Chris's laptop.

"It's still in quite a mess this flat," said Martin, moving his knight.

Chris laughed.

"Yes, that's one way to describe it," he replied, moving his bishop.

Caroline looked up.

"Good job we were at the castle, when the storm hit."

"Why do you say that?" asked her father.

"Well, judging on the mess in here, we'd have got soaked if we'd been here."

"Oh, I see what you mean. Yes, we probably might have done."

"What time is the landlord coming?" asked Martin, moving his rook.

After looking at the time, Chris replied, "Hopefully, any time now."

"Check," added Martin.

"Yes, so I see."

Just then, the doorbell rang.

"That'll be him," said Chris.

He got up and went to open the front door.

"Oh, hello Arthur. Thanks for coming."

"Good evening, Chris," he replied, adding, "I hope you don't mind. But I brought my builder with me."

"Not at all. Do come in."

The men entered the flat.

"This is Edward, my builder," said Arthur, introducing him.

"Pleased to meet you," replied Chris, shaking his hand.

"Good evening," said the builder, in Slovak.

Arthur was looking around.

"I see you've done a bit of cleaning up," he said.

Chris replied, "Yes, just a bit. I thought it might help. It was pointless doing too much, knowing the builders are coming in."

"Yes, of course"

"As you can see, we've moved everything of mine over to the new flat."

Arthur was looking around him.

"So I can see."

He added, "Is everything alright at the new flat?"

"Yes, it's fine, thanks. It was lucky no one was renting it. I don't know what I would have done without it."

Nor did Arthur. He was happy to let Chris have it, knowing it was far cheaper than a hotel bill that he might otherwise have incurred.

"Hopefully, it'll be alright for you, until we can sort this one out and get some new furniture put in here."

"Right"

The builder and Chris's landlord were looking up at the ceiling.

"Chris, you should have seen it, when the water was pouring in at two in the morning. The firemen got here, just before I did. They were in here, when I arrived. I tell you, it was a scary sight, I won't forget."

"I can imagine."

He then spoke to Edward, in Slovak.

"May my builder look around?" asked Arthur.

"Yes, of course," said Chris. "Do whatever you need to do."

The builder and Arthur then looked around the flat. They saw the damaged ceilings and walls in Chris's bedroom, the living room, the kitchen and bathroom, not to mention the floor and furniture.

During all this, Caroline had one eye on her book. Martin fiddled and looked at his still wet computer game gadget, that didn't function any more. He then played a game of solitaire. Both children were watching events with interest.

"Luckily," said Chris. "The one room that survived the ordeal, is my kid's bedroom. But the furniture in it and some of the bedding was still damaged by the flooding."

"So I saw," replied Arthur.

"Many of the walls in the flat are still wet."

"Yes, so I see."

Arthur said something to the builder, in Slovak, and then said, in English, "The builder will have to repair the ceilings. He'll need to re-plaster some of the walls and we'll need to lay a new floor."

"How long do you think it'll take, to complete?" asked Chris.

Arthur spoke to Edward, in Slovak, and then said, "About a month. Maybe, two."

"Two months!"

Chris was, actually delighted about the reconstruction time. He had heard stories that it could take many months.

"Sorry about that, Chris," said Arthur. "Still, you've got the other flat, rent free, till it's all sorted."

"Yes, thanks, for that"

"Once the building work is complete, I'll get the new furniture delivered and fitted. Is that alright, Chris?"

"Fine," he replied.

"Erm, you mentioned that you might be going back to your cottage?"

"Yes. All being well, we're going back tomorrow morning."

"Uh-huh"

Arthur translated this into Slovak.

Chris added, "I only came back, because of the emergency. I hadn't planned to be here, for another week or so."

"I am grateful you could come back so quickly, Chris. Thank you."

"No problem. By the way, when can the builder start?"

Arthur asked his friend, in Slovak, and then said, "Because he's a very good friend, he's agreed to start, next Monday."

"Oh, that's good of him."

"Yes, it is."

He added, "You know, getting hold of a good builder, during the summer, is not easy, as they are usually booked up months in advance. It just so happens, he's finishing a project a week early."

"I see."

Chris added, "Arthur, is there any chance you could get the internet connection transferred?"

"Sure! No problem. Leave it with me. I'll give the cable provider a call in the morning and get it all sorted for you."

"Thanks"

He added, "Erm, if you could get it done by the end of this week, it would be great, as I need it for my job. I've a presentation at the United Nations, in Vienna. And I need to connect with my boss, on a couple of issues, ahead of the actual presentation."

"Okay, I'll see what I can do. Oh, and we can have another beer, when it's all sorted."

"I'll hold you to that," said Chris, laughing and pointing his finger at his friend.

The landlord was an occasional beer drinking friend. So Chris knew he could live with the situation. He didn't like hassle and this seemed like a sensible solution.

Arthur got a set of keys out.

He said, "I got these cut for the builder. He'll need them, next week."

"Yes, of course"

The landlord said something, in Slovak, that Chris didn't understand, and then gave the keys to Edward, who put them in his pocket.

Arthur said, "The builder is asking, whether there is anything of yours, still in the flat?"

Chris replied, "No, as far as I know, it's all been removed."

"Just checking."

Arthur added, "Fine. Well, we'll be off."

He and Edward headed towards the door. Chris followed them.

"Thanks for coming," said Chris, shaking hands with them.

"Not at all," replied Arthur.

"Goodnight," said Edward, in his limited English.

"Goodnight," replied Chris, in Slovak.

Returning to his kids, he said, "Good. I am glad that's sorted."

"Will they really do it all in two months?" asked Caroline.

"Well, hopefully they will. You know what builders are like, Sweetheart. Sometimes they promise you the earth and you wait a year. Let's hope I'm lucky, eh?"

"Sure"

"Tell you what. Let's go and get something to eat, shall we?"

"Can we go to McDonald's?" suggested Martin.

"If you like."

"Great," said Caroline, getting up.

"Cool!" added Martin. "But what about finishing the game?"

"Later," replied Chris, adding, "Aren't you hungry, Martin?"

"Starving"

"Caroline?"

"Me too"

Chris added, "Okay, well let's go then."

As they walked out of the flat, Caroline said, "I fancy a Big Mac."

"So do I," said her brother.

Chris added, "Two Big Macs coming up. But don't tell your mother, I took you there."

The Hartleys departed their old flat. Chris took his kids downtown in Bratislava, to the McDonald's in the Old Town. In it, they wolfed down their Big Macs and ice creams. Later, the three of them returned to their new flat. Everyone spent the night watching a movie on TV together, before calling it a night.

Tomorrow would be another day. It would be when Caroline and Martin could return to 'their secret castle'. As Caroline got into bed, she looked at her magic key that she had placed on her bedside table, next to where she lay. She hoped and wished that it would work its magic, for her, one more time…

3

Return to the Secret Castle

The next morning, Caroline was woken by her father knocking on her bedroom door and entering her room. She had been in a deep sleep, dreaming about her previous adventures at the castle, both past and present.

"Morning, Sweetheart," said Chris. "I've brought you a nice cup of Rosy Lee."

"Ugh, thanks," she replied, turning over and trying to get back to sleep.

Her father put the tea on the bedside table, then went and opened the curtains.

"Oh, don't do that," said Caroline.

Chris replied, "Sorry, Sweetheart. But you need to get up early this morning."

His daughter sat up and took a sip of her tea.

She looked at him and said, "What time is it?"

"It's just gone seven thirty."

"Cor, that's early."

"Not really. I've been up since six. Anyway, we need to leave by eight thirty, at the latest, if you want to get to the castle and go to the lake."

"Alright. Well, give me five minutes, will you?"

"Sure, Sweetheart," said Chris, adding, "I'll take Martin his tea."

Caroline turned over again and then rolled over to the edge of the bed, where her tea stood on the bedside table. She leaned over, picked the mug up and sipped it.

Chris knocked on his son's bedroom door and went in.

"Good morning, Sunny Jim. I've brought you a cuppa."

"Morning, Dad," said Martin, yawning. "I was half-awake, anyway. I couldn't sleep."

"Well, don't forget, we're leaving early this morning. So you'd better fight it out with your sister, as to who gets in the bathroom first."

Martin took a sip of his tea, then leapt out of bed.

"I think, it'll be me," he said. "She takes forever in there."

Chris laughed: "Most women do."

Later, as they sat eating their breakfast in the living room, Chris said, "Have you two got everything packed?"

"Not yet," replied Caroline, finishing her tea.

"Don't worry," she added. "It'll only take me a minute or two."

"Martin?"

"I just need to pack my toothbrush."

"Yes, don't forget that. But don't forget to brush your teeth first."

"Yes, Dad!"

Chris looked up at the clock on the wall.

"Gosh! Look at the time," he said.

He added, standing up, "Right chop, chop, you two. We need to make tracks."

At the railway station, the Hartleys got off a tram and made their way up the escalator into the station concourse. The place was buzzing with people, mainly students, going here, there and everywhere, with many going nowhere, as they waited for their trains to depart.

"I see what you mean about it being busy, on a Friday," said Caroline, looking around her.

"What train are we getting?" asked Martin.

"Hopefully, the 9.15 to Zvolen," said Chris, as the three of them looked up at the train departures board.

Caroline decided to check the time.

Looking at her wrist in horror, she said, "Oh, gaud. I've left my new watch on the bathroom sill."

"What are you?" asked Chris, smiling.

The three of them then said, "Forgetful," and burst out laughing.

At the ticket counter, there was no one queuing for a ticket.

Chris bought three tickets to Zámočany.

"That makes a change," he said, putting them in the pocket of the jacket he was carrying.

"What does?" asked Martin.

"No queue"

"Uh-huh"

Chris checked the time on the station clock.

"Right," he said. "I'm just going for a Jimmy Riddle. Do either of you need to go?"

Both his kids shook their heads.

"Okay," said Chris.

He added, "Can you two wait here, for me?"

"Sure," replied Caroline.

Once their father had departed, Martin said, "Have you brought the magic key with you?"

"Of course I have, Nitwit."

"Where is it?"

"It's in my bag. Why?"

"I just wanted to see it."

"Martin, we can do that at the castle, when no one's around."

"Oh, go on. Let's have a look at it, now? No one's gonna know it's a magic key, are they?"

"Oh, alright"

Caroline rooted in her bag.

"Just a quick look, as Dad'll be back at any moment."

"I know that."

Caroline got the key out.

"There – satisfied?"

Martin looked at it.

"It's still showing a '5'," he said.

15

Caroline took it from him and looked at it.

"Yes, so I see."

Suddenly, the number '5' that was in the round circle on the magic key, flashed at her, in green.

"Oh my god, Martin. Did you see that? It just flashed at me."

"Yes, I did," he replied, delightedly. "I wonder what it means."

"I'm not sure. The key seems to have a mind of its own. It changed numbers when we were at the castle before. So, I don't understand why it's flashing at us now."

"Me, neither"

Caroline was thinking.

"If I'm right. I think it means, we stand a good chance of being able to go back to 1912 again."

"Brilliant!" added Martin, jumping up and down for joy.

Seeing her father approach, Caroline quickly popped the magic key back in her bag.

"You two look as happy as Larry. Is everything alright?" asked their father.

"Yes, I think so," replied his daughter, smiling sweetly.

Caroline was desperately trying not to show, how happy she was about the key.

Her father looked at her.

"I worry about you sometimes, Caroline."

He looked at his son.

"Are you two up to something?"

"No, no," replied Martin. "We're just messing about."

Chris looked at them both.

"Right! Well, come on," he said. "I think it's platform three this morning."

"Where's that?" asked Martin.

"It's down the stairs and up one of the stairways in the middle."

Emerging from walking up the stairs, Chris said, "We're looking for carriage number five."

Walking down the platform, Caroline said, "There it is."

"Right, hop on," said Chris.

His kids did.

After finding their seat, they sat down.

Soon after, the stationmaster waved his flag and blew his whistle.

As the train edged its way out of the station, Caroline said, "It looks like we've got the train compartment to ourselves."

"Looks like it," replied her father, smiling.

"Is it going to be a long journey?" asked Martin.

"It's the same as before," replied Chris, opening his book he had brought with him, to read on the journey.

"Oh, right," replied the boy, gormlessly.

Five hours and a change of trains later, the two wagon diesel train arrived at Zámočany's small railway station, its passengers alighting at the platform. Two local women and a man got off. Joining them were Caroline, Martin and their father, Chris.

"We're here," shouted Caroline.

"Great!" replied her brother.

"Yes, it's good to be back," added their father, smiling.

He walked on, ahead of them.

Turning round, he said, "Well, come on you two. I thought you wanted to go down to the lake?"

"We do," replied Caroline.

She waved at the ticket lady on the train, who was watching the stationmaster.

Today, it was actually a lady on duty, waving her flag.

The train slowly edged its way, away from the children, who watched, as it disappeared into the distance around the bend.

"Come on," said Chris.

"Coming," replied Caroline.

Martin hurried on behind. He was once again struggling with his bag. Caroline saw this and went to help him. She took one side of his travel bag.

"Here, let me, Martin," said his father, taking his side of the travel bag.

All three of them walked on, towards the pathway ahead of them.

As they walked up the road towards the castle, Martin ran for his life, when a dog, he feared, ran out and along the garden it was guarding.

"Martin, it won't bite you. It's on its chain in the garden," said Chris, reassuringly.

The boy stopped running and looked around.

"I thought it was going to kill me," he said.

Chris laughed.

"Don't worry about the dog, Martin," he said. "You need to show you are not frightened of it. Otherwise, it senses you are frightened and then it will go and bite you, if it escapes."

"I hope it never escapes. I hate dogs like that."

They walked on, towards the castle.

A bit further up, Martin forgot the dog, and yelled, "There's the castle, Caroline. We're back."

"Great!" she replied.

Martin ran on ahead of them, towards the castle. While he waited at the entrance gate for his father and sister to catch him up, he stood there looking at the castle.

Caroline was secretly delighted to be back. She couldn't wait, to run about and explore the garden again, and then go swimming in the lake.

Chris still had the keys Slavo had originally given him. Opening the gate, they walked in, across the grassed-over castle entrance.

"The place hasn't changed a bit," said Caroline, looking around.

Chris looked at her.

"We've only been gone, less than a week."

"Gosh! Is that all? It seems longer than that."

"I think the grass has grown," said Martin.

Chris was looking at it.

"Yes, it probably has," he replied, laughing, "Especially after all that rain."

He added, "Come on, let's go inside."

Leading the way, he walked towards the front door of the small decaying castle. In reality, it was more of an old run-down manor house. But, having said that, Chris knew from his previous visits that everyone called it a castle. It certainly felt like one. Its vast overgrown, unloved magnificent garden, was what made it special.

The Hartley family each had their own initial reason to be back at the castle. For Chris, it was the joy of spending time in the garden, after living in the confines of a flat. For the children, it was an opportunity to try to go back in time, once again...

4

The Secret Garden

After unlocking the front door of the castle, the children rushed in to the flat that Chris had rented. It was part of the castle, which in recent years had been split into different flats.

Caroline and Martin dumped their bags in the hall, then rushed through to the conservatory, where they looked out of the window. The long grass in the garden around the fountain had been cut. Caroline realised that parts of the garden were slowly beginning to look like a garden again.

She said, "It's still there, Martin."

"I know," he replied. "Isn't it great?"

"Isn't what great?" asked their father, who had followed them in.

"The garden"

"I didn't think you liked gardens?"

"I don't. But this one is special. I don't know of any garden like it."

"That's true," said Chris, as he looked out with them.

Caroline unlocked one of the doors that led to the garden.

"I'm going outside to look around."

"Fine," replied her father.

Chris knew his kids loved the garden. He did as well. It allowed him to relax and unwind, in between his web work. He called it his 'cottage garden', as it was so peaceful and in many places, it was still totally overgrown.

It was also a cheap way to spend a holiday, which, right now, was a godsend to him, as his teaching work was nil, till September. Chris wasn't that fussed, because his web work kept him well occupied, in a part time way.

Caroline and Martin ran down the steps into the garden. Caroline was delighted to be back in their secret garden, that no one else knew about and was theirs to explore.

The children ran around to all the places they had been before – the hidden overgrown pathways in the woods, the lower patio and the big circle at the bottom of the garden that led into the forest. They also went to the concert arena and the old abandoned summer house. It was their way of rediscovering the garden.

"This is brilliant, Martin," said Caroline, as she ran around it.

"Yeah, I know it is."

They ran on, burning their energy, until Caroline decided to sit down on one of the broken benches in the garden.

"Oh, I needed to do that," she said. "I feel much better, now I've had a good run around the garden."

"Me too," replied Martin.

After catching her breath, Caroline said, "You know, I can't wait to go back to 1912. I want to see Veronica and Manfred again."

"Oh, so do I," replied Martin.

"I just hope the magic key will still work. It will be a disaster, if it doesn't. Gosh, can you imagine, if it didn't work?"

They both sat there for a moment, thinking about it.

"Well," said Martin. "Let's hope, it doesn't happen."

After listening to the birds in the tree, Martin said, "I want to go fishing with Manfred again."

Caroline added, "I want to dress up as a lady again."

Martin paused and said, "You know, there's only one thing I don't like about 1912."

"Oh, what's that?"

"Those stupid shorts"

Caroline laughed.

"Yes, I must admit, you do look a bit silly wearing them."

"I feel really stupid. I much prefer wearing my jeans."

"Well," said Caroline. "If you ignore that fact, what we do is kinda special. I mean, how many other kids, our age, can time travel and go back to 1912?"

"Er, none," replied Martin.

He added, "I suppose, that's why I put up with wearing them."

Caroline got up.

"Come on," she said. "Let's go and explore a bit more."

"But I thought we were going down to the lake?"

"We are, Martin. But first, I want to get reacquainted with the garden again. We've got all afternoon."

"True"

As he got up, he said enquiringly, "When are we going back to 1912?"

"I'm not sure," replied Caroline, walking away from him.

Her brother ran after her.

As they walked towards the meadow, she said, "I thought we might spend a few days here first, then go back. To be honest, I like going down to the lake in this time, as well as the other lake, in 1912."

"Oh, so do I."

"Anyway, I'm not sure how long we are going to be here. So, depending on how long we are, depends on how many times we might go back to 1912."

"Uh-huh"

Martin added, "I thought it depended on the magic key?"

"Yes, of course it does. But you know what I mean."

As they walked along in the overgrown garden, Caroline was thinking aloud.

"You know, it's really weird, us, time travelling back to 1912. I mean, this garden is *so* different, back then. When we are there, I always think, it's impossible to believe the garden could become, like it is, now."

"Why does it get, like it is?" asked Martin.

"Because in our time, it looks like there's only Mr Slavo to cut the grass. And, according to Dad, he lives in Bratislava most of the time. So he can only cut it, when he visits the castle."

"Oh!" said Martin.

"Veronica said, they had about a dozen gardeners to look after it, in her time."

"Mr Slavo's got Dad to help him."

Caroline stopped and looked at her brother.

"It's hardly the same, is it?"

"True"

A bit further round the garden, Caroline decided to sit on another old weathered garden seat. Martin sat down, next to her.

"Listen to those birds, Martin," she said.

"I am," he replied.

"It's so peaceful here. That's what I like about the place. It's our own secret garden, whichever time period we are in."

"I think I prefer the garden in Veronica's and Manfred's time," said Martin. "It's prettier."

"Me too"

As they sat there, looking out on the nature around them, she said, "You know, Martin, there are many things about this castle, I would love to know the answer to."

"Like what?"

"Well," replied Caroline. "I don't know exactly, but knowing what we do know, makes me want to find out more. Are you with me?"

Martin was a bit confused.

"Er, I think so," he said.

Caroline got up.

"Come on," she said. "I think it's time, we went down to the lake."

"At last!" replied Martin, who followed her.

Together, they slowly ambled their way back across the grass, towards the castle.

Walking up the back stairs, the children entered the conservatory. They could see their father was unpacking his laptop.

"I need to charge it," he said.

While Caroline stood at the window looking out, Martin sat down on a chair at the table. He watched his father fiddling with his laptop.

After a moment, Caroline said, "I'm going to unpack my bag."

"So am I," added Martin. "I'm gonna to put my swimming trunks on, before we go to the beach."

"Oh, that's a good idea."

Once they had changed and got their small backpacks ready, the children returned to the conservatory. Chris was still fiddling with his laptop.

"We're off, Dad," said Caroline.

"Righty-Ho. Have a nice time, Sweetheart."

"Yeah, see you later, Dad," said Martin.

As they walked out of a side door of the conservatory, Chris said, "Er, Caroline. Aren't you forgetting something?"

She turned to look at him.

"Like what?" she said.

"The bikes"

He added, "We still need to collect them, Sweetheart."

She looked at her brother.

"That's a good point. We do."

"You see, your father's not just a pretty face," he said, smiling. "Of course, you could always walk."

"Walk," said Caroline, giving him 'The Look'.

"Just a daft idea, Sweetheart"

"Well, you can keep that idea."

"Tell you what," said her father. "Let's go and pick them up. Shall we?"

"Good idea"

As they walked round the castle, Chris said to his kids, "Luckily for you, when I was having my beer with Slavo yesterday afternoon, after you two went for a walk about, I got him to ring his friend up. I am pleased to tell you, he managed to sort everything out, for us, once again."

"That's very decent of him," said Caroline.

"Slavo is a very decent person."

"Yes, I know."

Chris looked at his watch.

"We're a little bit late. But, hopefully, the man will still be there, to give us the bikes."

"Great," replied Caroline, smiling.

At the house where the bikes were kept, Chris, Martin and Caroline opened the gate and walked up the drive. Chris rang the bell. The dog that was tied up went crazy when he heard them. A man came to the door.

"Good afternoon," said Chris, in Slovak.

In English, he said, "We've come for the bikes."

The man didn't speak any English. But he knew why they were there. He smiled, then beckoned them towards the shed, where he wheeled the bikes out; giving them to the children and Chris.

"Thank you," said Chris in Slovak, waving to him as they departed.

The man waved back.

Outside the gate, Chris said, "Right, well, I'll leave you two to it."

Caroline looked at him.

"I thought you were coming with us?" she asked.

"No, you don't need me with you. I'm sure you want to see your own friends down there this afternoon."

"Well…"

"Tell you what, Sweetheart. You go and have fun. And when I've finished what I've got to do, I'll cycle down there this evening. Then we can have something to eat at the lake, together, later."

"Now that's a good idea," said Caroline, getting on her bike. "Any particular time?"

"Umgh, let's say around six."

"Okey Dokey"

She added, waving, "See you later, Dad."

"Have a nice day," replied her father, waving at her.

"Don't worry. We will," added Martin, waving back.

5

The Witch's Cave

Caroline and Martin enjoyed their bike ride, along the quiet country road. They raced down the steep hill, which led them to the long straight road that they liked to speed along. At the fork, they veered left and then right towards the lake. The children charged down the hill. It gave them enough speed to climb up the much steeper and longer hill that took them to the top of the dam. On it, they stopped to look out across it and the mountains beyond.

"I do like this view, Martin," said Caroline.

"Yes, I do too."

"I still can't believe when we cycled here, in 1912, it was *so* different."

"Yeah, I know what you mean."

Just then, a small horn sounded, from across the dam.

As they looked across it, they saw two cyclists riding towards them.

One of them was waving at them.

"Look, Caroline," said Martin. "There's Mike."

"Oh, yeah," she replied. "And it looks like, he's got company."

The boy and a girl pulled up, next to them.

"Howz it going, Mike?" asked Caroline.

"I'm cool," he replied, copying her style of English.

"Watcha, Mike?" said Martin.

"Watcha, Martin," he replied, copying him.

Mike added, "Oh, this is Lucy. She's my neighbour's granddaughter."

"Oh, right," said Caroline.

Everyone said 'Hi' to each other.

"We were just coming to see you," added Martin.

"Were you?" replied Mike.

"That was the general idea," said Caroline.

"Where are you going?" asked Martin.

"To the witch's cave," said Mike.

"The witch's cave?"

"Yes, I wanted to show Lucy the witch's cave, I know of, that's in the forest."

"Is it a big cave?" asked Martin.

"It depends what you call big. Tell you what, why don't you come with us? Then you'll see."

"Well," said Caroline. "We were going to the beach. Erm, is it far?"

"No, it's about fifteen minutes from here, by bike."

"Uh-huh"

"Do you want to come with us, or not?"

"Erm, yeah, I wouldn't mind. Do you wanna go, Martin?"

"Yeah, why not? It could be different."

Both English children were now curious, to know more about this cave.

Caroline added, "But we'll need to be back at the lake, by six, Mike, as my dad's meeting us down there."

"Oh, don't worry. We'll be back, before that."

"Great! Well, in that case, I'll let you two lead the way."

As the children cycled along the quiet country road, Mike said, "So what happened, Caroline?"

"Sorry, what was that?" she said, cycling a bit closer to him.

"I haven't seen you and Martin, for a while."

"Oh, it's a long story. I'll tell you later."

"Okay, fine"

A bit further up the road, Mike said, pointing, "When we get to the rocks, halfway up the hill, we'll need to take a right. The forest track to the witch's cave, is about 100 metres after that."

"Okey Dokey," said Caroline.

Mike led the way, on his mountain bike.

In the forest, he led his friends, on their bikes, along a long windy narrow path.

"Wow! This is *real* mountain-biking," said Martin.

"Yeah, it is pretty cool," replied Caroline.

The children loved their bike ride, through the forest. They had to do some steep climbs and drops, and then more climbs. The terrain was perfect for their mountain bikes. As they cycled along, the English children wondered where their friend Mike was taking them and his friend Lucy.

The forest ended by a rock face. Mike followed the path, next to it. Suddenly, he pulled up. The others stopped, next to him.

"Is this, where the cave is?" asked Caroline.

"Hopefully!" joked Mike.

"Will we need a light?" asked Martin.

"Have you got a torch?"

"Er, no," replied Caroline. "Had I known we were going to a cave, I might have brought one with me."

"Have you got a torch, Lucy?" asked Martin.

"No," she replied, shaking her head.

"Don't worry," added Mike. "Once you're inside the cave, your eyes will soon adjust to the light."

A bit further up the path, he said, "We can leave the bikes here."

"Will they be safe here?" asked Caroline.

"Sure! No one's gonna steal them, if that's what you mean."

Mike walked towards the rock face. "If you look, over there, you can see a large boulder. This is the rock that once concealed the cave."

"It's quite a big rock," said Martin, looking at it.

"Yeah, it is," added his sister.

Mike then said, "There's a story about this particular rock that you might like to hear."

"Alright," replied Caroline.

"Lucy, the story I am going to tell Caroline and Martin, in English, is the one I told you, earlier."

"Uh-huh"

Curious, everyone stood there waiting for what Mike might now say.

Clearing his throat, he said, "Once upon a time, there was a good witch and a bad witch. The two witches, who were sisters, didn't get on. One day, the bad witch cast a spell on her sister the good witch that involved thunder and lightning. The bad witch got her wand, to power the thunder and lightning, across to her sister's cottage that lay on top of the hill, in the forest. Luckily, her sister happened to be out."

"Wait a minute, Mike," said Caroline, interrupting him. "Martin and I have heard this story, before."

Her brother added, "Yeah, Mr Slavo told it to us, on the night of the thunderstorm. Do you remember, Caroline?"

"You're right. He did."

"Well, let me finish the story," said Mike.

"Sorry"

"Erm, where was I?"

"You were talking about the good witch and the bad witch," said Martin.

"Right! Well, in revenge, the good witch cast another spell that powered the thunder and lightning over, to the bad witch's cave. It hit the rock, causing the giant boulder, you can see, to fall off the rock face and lock the bad witch in her cave. She was unable to escape and died inside it."

"I thought this was just a story," said Caroline.

"It is. It's local legend."

"Right!"

"Is she still there?" asked her brother.

"Don't be daft, Martin."

"Come on," said Mike. "Let's go in."

As he led them through a small slit in the rock, that led them into the cave, Martin turned to his sister, and said, "Caroline, you've forgotten something."

"Oh, what's that?"

"Your broomstick and black hat"

"*Funny!*"

Once they were inside the cave, the children's eyes soon adjusted to the darkness.

They looked around them.

"It's dark in here," said Martin.

"That's 'cause you're in a cave," replied his sister, in her dumb sounding voice.

"There's a bit of light, over there, in the corner," said the boy, pointing.

"That's a natural opening in the cave," added Mike. "It lets the light in and the smoke and smells out."

"Smoke?"

"You can light a fire in here, to keep warm. The smoke escapes through the natural opening."

"Oh!" replied the boy, gormlessly.

"It looks quite big, in here, Mike," said Caroline.

"Yes," he replied. "It is fairly big."

"I was expecting a much smaller cave, than this."

"Were you?"

"Yes," said Caroline. "As I imagined the bad witch lived in a small cave, with her black cat and broomstick. I thought her cauldron would have been in the middle of the cave, above a fire, where she would have cast her spells."

"You have a good imagination, Caroline," said Lucy.

"Yeah, possibly"

Martin then said, "Mike, ask a stupid question, but how does thunder and lightning leave this cave, if the entrance is as narrow as it is?"

"Simple! When the bad witch lived here, the cave had a big open entrance. It only got narrower, when the lightening hit the rock face and the rocks and boulder, blocked its entrance. Over time, the weather has changed the rock face and entrance. Trees kept it a secret for many years. The cave has actually been here for thousands of years."

"Has it?"

"Sure"

Caroline was walking around it.

"Hello, can you hear my echo?"

"Yes, I can hear your echo," replied Martin.

"And mine too," said Lucy.

"I am glad, you suggested coming here, Mike," said Caroline.

"I am happy, if you're happy," he replied, laughing.

"I'm happy," said Martin.

Mike then said, "You might be interested to know, that this cave has been used by the local people, in times of war."

"What do you mean?" asked Caroline.

"When the Turks attacked Hungary, in the fifteen century, their Ottoman Empire took over this region. Some of the local people hid in this cave, to escape from the Turkish soldiers."

"Did they really?"

"Sure"

He added, "More than 100 villagers, mostly women and children, lived in here, when things were really bad for them, sometimes for several months."

"Blimey! I wouldn't want to live in here, for all that time."

"Well, you would, if you didn't want to die."

"Yeah, that's true. Erm, did they survive?"

"Yes, I think so."

Mike added, "The cave was also used by the local villagers, during World War Two. It, once again, hid a lot of villagers, and, quite a few Jewish people were hidden, in here, from the Nazis."

"Really? So, the place has got a bit of history then," said Caroline.

"Just a bit"

Martin was getting bored with the history lesson.

He started to walk around.

"What's this, over here?" he asked.

The others walked over, to where he was now standing.

"It looks like a small wooden stage," said Caroline.

"It does," added Lucy.

"Why's it here, Mike?" asked Martin.

"No idea," he replied.

"Perhaps the people who lived here, entertained on it?" suggested Lucy.

"Yeah, they might have," replied Caroline. "Or perhaps, it might have been used for something else?"

"Uh-huh"

Caroline had noticed something.

"Mike," she said. "There are some candles and some matches here."

"Where?" said Martin, going over to see for himself.

"So there are," said Lucy.

Caroline lit a match and then some candles.

"That's better," she said.

"Maybe, there's someone living here, now?" suggested Martin.

"Yeah, maybe? But I don't think so. As there probably would have been a bed and other such stuff, in here. Now, we've got a candle each. We can look around and see."

"That's a good idea," said Martin. "We can go and explore."

Carrying his candle, the boy walked further into the cave.

"I can hear dripping," he said.

His sister added, "It sounds like water, dripping off the roof of the cave."

Martin stopped, to look at some strange objects, he could now see.

"What are those things hanging down and sticking up, Caroline?"

"They're erm…they're called stalactites and stalagmites. Oh, I always get them mixed up."

"Let me help you," said Lucy. "The ones hanging down are stalactites. The ones sticking up are stalagmites."

"There's your answer, Martin."

"The stalagmites are usually made from calcium carbonate. They are formed on the floor of the cave by the dripping calcareous water. The stalactites, Martin, are also made of calcium carbonate. These are shaped like an icicle. They hang from the roof of the cave and are formed by the dripping calcareous water."

"Gosh! Where did you learn that?" asked Martin.

"In school, why?"

"Just wondered."

"I'm good at chemistry."

"I'm not," said Caroline, laughing.

The children stood, looking up, at a natural air duct.

"I can see the sky," said Martin.

"If you look down, from above," replied Mike, "You'd never know, there was a cave, like this, below. That's why, it's such a good hiding place."

"How did you hear about it?" asked Caroline.

"Me? Oh, I've known about it, for a very long time."

"How long?" asked Martin.

"Erm, my father brought me here, as a boy."

"You are a boy," said Martin.

"When I was a small boy."

"Like you, Martin," said his sister, jokingly.

"*Funny!*"

Caroline then said, "Listen! I can hear voices."

They all listened.

"Someone's coming," said Martin.

The children could hear what sounded like people laughing and joking.

Lucy said, "Whoever it is, is at the entrance of the cave."

"Mike," whispered Caroline. "I thought you said, no one came in here?"

"Erm, they don't, normally."

Everyone was suddenly a bit scared, as to who was outside the cave. Caroline looked at Lucy, who looked at Martin, who looked at Mike. The children suddenly realised that they had nowhere to hide. For a moment, they stood there holding their lit candles, unsure what to do next…

6

The New Cave People

The four children were a bit alarmed at the thought of someone else coming into the cave, they were in, when they were in it. Safety was *always* one of Caroline's concerns. But before she, or the other children, could do anything, four people walked into the cave. The candles, the children had lit, immediately gave them away.

"Hello," shouted Lucy, in Slovak, in the semi-darkness, still holding her candle alight.

"Hi," replied one of the small group of people, also in Slovak.

"Do you speak English?" asked Martin, from where he stood.

A girl replied, "Yes, we speak English."

"Do you?" said the surprised boy, who wasn't expecting that answer.

Everyone made their way towards the central area of the cave, where the small stage area was. The children saw four students, who were a few years older than them.

"I see you found our candles," said one of them, in English.

"Oh, they're your candles, are they?" asked Caroline.

"Yes, they are."

"Oh, sorry! Had we known, we wouldn't have used them."

"It's okay. They are there to be used, by whoever comes into the cave."

"Oh, I see. Well, thanks."

She added, "By the way, I'm Caroline."

"Hello, Caroline, I'm Irena. This is Ivan. Over there is Karol and Lucia."

"Oh, that's my name," said Lucy.

"I thought your name was Lucy?" asked Martin.

"It is. But my name, in Slovak, is Lucia."

"Oh, I see."

Caroline then said, "Next to Lucy, on the left is Mike, and on her right, is my brother, Martin."

Everyone said "Hi" to each other.

"What are you doing in this cave?" asked Caroline.

"We've come to practise our music," said Ivan.

"Really?"

"We like to come here, for a jamming session. We can also make as much noise as we want, and chill out, without disturbing anyone."

"What type of music do you play?"

"This might surprise you. We play Central African and Australian aboriginal music," said Irena.

"You're kidding?" said Caroline, in disbelief.

"It's true."

"But, we're in Slovakia," said Martin.

"We like to be original," added Ivan.

"You sound as if you are English?" said Irena.

"We are," said Martin. "I come from Welwyn Garden City."

"Where's that?"

"Near London"

"Have you been to London?" asked Caroline.

"I was there last year. Great city," said Ivan.

"Yes, it is."

Irena then said, "You might also be surprised to know, that we've come all the way from Bratislava, to come to this cave."

"Now, you are kidding," replied Caroline.

"No, it's absolutely true. My boyfriend and I, and our other two bandmates, have rented a cottage, nearby. It makes a perfect few days, for us to come here and practise. We're performing next week at a concert, in Bratislava. So we do need to practise. Coming here, makes it all worthwhile."

"Wow! That's really cool."

"We think so," said Ivan.

"I thought you would have played Slovak music," added Martin.

"Oh, we do," replied Irena. "But some of us have travelled the world. And we wanted to create our own style of music, from what we have learnt, whilst travelling."

"Uh-huh"

"Can we hear some of your music?" asked Lucy.

"Sure!" replied Ivan. "Just give us fifteen minutes to get everything set up and we'll play you a few of our songs."

"Oh, that'd be really great," said Caroline, who had never expected any of this.

Whilst the band went to get more of their gear, that was located somewhere outside the cave, Caroline, Lucy and Mike, sat on the stage.

Martin was looking around it.

"Caroline," he said. "There are some benches here, we could sit on."

"Are there?"

Mike added, "Well, let's sit on them."

"I think we need to construct them first," suggested Caroline.

Once that was sorted, the children sat down on two of the benches.

"You know, Caroline," said her brother. "I've thought of a great bit of music the band could play us?"

"Oh, what's that?"

"Yab-a-dab-a-doo"

"Martin, I don't think they'd know how to play the Flintstone's theme."

"They might do. We're in a cave."

"Perhaps, they play rock music?"

"Yeah, they might."

Just then, a bat flew overhead.

"What was that?" asked Caroline.

"I think it's what you might call a bat," replied Mike.

"We're in the Batcave, Caroline," joked Martin.

"What's your name? Batman."

"No, he's out fighting the Riddler with Robin. I'm the Joker. Ha ha!"

"You're one big joke, Martin."

Ignoring her comments, he said, "I've just thought of another bit of music, you could play, in here."

"Oh, what's that?"

"Der der der der der der der der, Batman"

"Ha, ha!"

"I'm not sure, I understood all of that," said Lucy.

"Don't worry. Nor did I."

After a moment of silence, Martin said, "I could do with a drink, Caroline."

"Well, there's one in your backpack."

"Oh yeah, I'd forgotten about that."

"What are you?"

"Forgetful," they said, jokingly together.

Mike and Lucy looked at them, oddly.

"Old English joke," said Caroline, smiling.

"Oh!" replied Lucy.

Martin shared his drink, with everyone.

"Thanks," said Lucy, passing it to Caroline.

As they did so, Mike said, "Caroline, you said earlier, you were going to tell me where you've been, since I last saw you."

"Oh yeah, I did. Sorry, Mike."

"No worries"

"Where to start?"

"How about at the beginning?" suggested Martin, who was listening.

"Yes, okay"

She cleared her throat.

"We had to leave the castle in a rush on Monday and return to Bratislava."

"Oh," said Mike. "Why was that?"

"Because the roof of my father's flat, in Bratislava, was struck by lightning."

"Was it, really?"

"Yes," said Martin, who added, "The roof caught fire and the fire brigade had to put it out."

"Wow!" said Mike.

Caroline added, "It was the same thunderstorm that was here."

"Oh, that one. Yes, that was pretty bad."

"Apparently, the storm was even worse, in Bratislava."

Mike and Lucy were carefully listening to her.

"Anyway," Caroline added, "My father's flat, as a result of the storm damage and the fire engines water putting the fire out, got severely flooded. So we had to move flats."

"Really?" said Mike.

"Yes"

She continued: "It took us a while, to help my dad move flats. Once that was done, we had to help him clean up some of the mess in his old flat. The walls and ceiling have to be repaired and most of the furniture will have to be replaced."

"Gosh!" said Mike.

"The roof on the house is now being fixed. The builders started repairing it, yesterday. So at least, the flat shouldn't get any more rain coming in."

"I see."

"My dad's landlord is getting the flat repaired. The builders arrive next Monday."

"It sounds pretty bad."

"Yes, it was," said Martin.

"And you say, you changed flats?"

"Yes, that's right," said Caroline. "The landlord had a spare flat. Actually, it's a bit bigger than my dad's normal flat."

"Uh-huh"

Bored with talking about her dad's situation, Caroline decided to change the subject.

"Anyway," she said. "What have we been missing, Mike?"

"Not much. I met my friend Lucy again. She comes down to the beach, with me, most days."

Caroline was keen to talk to Lucy. She had noticed she hadn't said much, since they had first met.

"I noticed you speak some English, Lucy?" said Caroline.

"Yes, I learn it at school."

"Oh right. So, where are you from?"

"I'm from Martin."

When he heard the name, Martin's ears picked up.

"Martin," he said. "Where's that?"

Lucy replied, "It's a town in mid-Slovakia."

"I thought we were in mid-Slovakia?"

"We are," replied Mike. "But this is a different part of mid-Slovakia."

"I see," said Martin, not really understanding him.

Looking at the girl, he said, "So Lucy, I'm Martin, and you're from Martin."

He laughed at his comment. Lucy laughed at it, as well.

"What brings you here?" asked Caroline.

Lucy replied, "I came to visit my grandmother, for a few days."

"Oh, right," said Caroline, scratching her nose.

She added, "Have you been here, before?"

"Yes," replied Lucy. "I come here every year."

"Do you?"

Five minutes or so later, the Slovak music group returned with the rest of their instruments. Martin saw one that was rather unusual and big.

"What's that?" he asked, pointing at it.

"It's a didgeridoo," replied Ivan.

"Wow! Is it really?"

"Gosh! It's huge," said Caroline.

"Where did you get that from?"

"Australia"

"Really?"

"How did you get it up here?" asked Martin.

"In my car and then by foot," replied Ivan.

"Cor!" said Caroline. "That's amazing, as it's quite a hike from the road."

"Yes, it is, but we can bring the SUV vehicle, we came in, pretty close."

"Oh, I see."

"What other instruments do you play?" asked Lucy.

Irena said, "Karol plays bongo drums, Ivan plays the didgeridoo, I play the guitar and Lucia plays the balafon. All of us sing."

"Oh, that's pretty awesome," replied a surprised Caroline.

"What's a balafon?" asked Martin.

Irena laughed.

"This is a balafon," she said, pointing.

"Oh, right," said Martin.

The boy went to look at the instrument.

Irena added, "It's a bit like a glockenspiel."

"You know what that is, Martin?" asked his sister.

"Yes," he said, nodding. "We have one at our school."

"Oh, so do we," added Lucy.

"Er, Irena," said Caroline, looking up. "Is the cave suitable for playing musical instruments in?"

"Sure, it is."

"Oh!"

Ivan then said, "The acoustics in this part of the cave, make it just perfect for playing our instruments in, especially the didgeridoo. Give us five minutes and you'll see."

Whilst the band got ready, the children sat and watched.

Irena lit a lot more of the candles, which she placed around the cave.

"We like to get the feel of the place, when we play our music," she said.

"Wow! This is really great," said Caroline to Lucy.

"Yes, I never would have expected this, when Mike first invited me here."

"I didn't expect it either," he replied, laughing.

"What's the name of your band?" asked Caroline.

"We call ourselves 'The New Cave People'."

"Oh, that sounds interesting."

"Are you famous?" asked Martin.

"One day, we might be."

"Oh, right"

With everything prepared, the band was ready to play.

The four children sat a short distance away from the stage. So they could enjoy watching the band.

"It's a bit alternative," said Ivan. "But we hope you enjoy, what we play…"

At the end of three pieces of music, the children showed their appreciation, by clapping.

"I hope you liked our short performance," said Ivan.

"Yeah, it was really good," replied Caroline.

"It was awesome," added Martin.

"Thank you," said Lucy.

Mike added, "Yes, it was good. Thanks a lot."

"I hope your concert, next week, goes well," said Caroline.

"Thanks," replied Ivan.

Caroline stood up and stretched.

Looking at her friends, she said, "Well, I don't know about you, but I think we should let them practise, without us. We should head back to the lake."

"Oh, that's a good idea," replied Martin.

"Is that alright, Mike?"

"Yes, whatever you want, we can do."

Caroline walked over to the band.

"We gonna be going now. Thanks for making it a very special afternoon. I really enjoyed your music"

"It's a pleasure," said Ivan. "Enjoy your stay in Slovakia."

"Don't worry. I will. Thanks."

"See you later," said Martin.

Everyone said their goodbyes.

The children waved to the band members, as they departed the cave, with Martin saying, "Ciao," as he followed the others.

Outside the cave, the children adjusted their eyes to the bright sunshine.

"That was really-awesome, Mike," said Caroline.

"Yes, it was a bit different. Even I wasn't expecting that."

"Life is full of surprises," added Martin.

"Yeah, that's true," said Caroline. "Did you enjoy that, Lucy?"

"I did, thank you."

As they picked up their bikes, Martin said, "Have you got any other surprises, for us, Mike?"

"Er, well, let me think…"

Everybody laughed.

7

The Beach

The children enjoyed their mountain biking, through the forest and along the road that took them back to the lake. After stopping off at the dam, once again, to look out, they cycled around the shoreline of the lake. At the beach, they parked up, walked past the beach huts and along the green strip of land that was known as 'The beach'.

"We can sit, over there?" suggested Caroline.

"Alright," replied Mike, laughing.

Everyone got changed into their swimming wear and relaxed on their towels for a while.

Caroline was looking at Lucy. She couldn't fail to notice her new friend was a redhead. Curious, she said, "Lucy, can I ask you something?"

"Sure"

"Are you a natural redhead?"

The girl laughed.

"No, it's dyed."

"Oh, right," replied Caroline, feeling a bit like a lemon.

She reached into her bag and got out some suntan lotion, she had bought in Bratislava.

"Mike," she said. "It's a bit late in the day for this. But even so, could you put some of this sun lotion on my back, please?"

"Sure," he replied.

"Just a dab. Not too much"

Mike squirted some lotion on her back.

"Ugh, that's cold," she said, laughing.

As he massaged it in her back, he said, "Is that alright?"

She replied, "Yes, it's fine, thanks."

Once Mike had finished applying the suntan lotion, he got out his bag of mints, and said, "Mint anyone?"

He passed the bag round. Everyone helped themselves.

The four of them then laid there, for a while, lapping up the late afternoon sun.

Sometime later, Mike said, "I need to cool off. I'm going for a swim. Who's coming?"

The girls looked up.

"Yes, I'll come," replied Lucy.

"I'll join you," said Caroline. "I could do with a dip, myself."

The girls got up.

When Martin saw the girls get up and walk towards the water, he leapt to his feet and said, "Hey, wait for me."

A fun time followed, in the water.

When the four of them had had enough of splashing about, they returned to their sunbathing. Caroline got Mike to put some more suntan lotion on her back. Everyone relaxed.

A short while later, as the four of them lay there, Caroline sat up. She looked around her. As she did so, she saw someone she recognised.

"Martin, there's Dad, over there."

"Where?" replied the boy, sitting up looking.

She waved at her father.

Chris saw her, waved and wandered over.

"I did wonder, where you two might be hiding," he said, when he arrived.

"We're not hiding. We're sunbathing," replied Martin.

"So, I see."

"You remember, Mike?" said Caroline.

"Yes, of course"

Going over to the boy, he said, shaking his hand, "How are you doing, Mike?"

"Fine, thank you," he replied, laughing.

"This is Lucy, Dad," said Caroline.

"Hello, Lucy," said Chris, shaking her hand.

He sat down, next to them.

"Sorry to interrupt your fun, Caroline. But I did mention we'd have some tea here."

"That's alright, Dad. We were expecting you."

She started to get dressed.

"Take your time, Sweetheart. There's no rush."

"Oh, there is. I'm starving."

Martin held his hand out to her.

"I'm Martin," he said, smiling sweetly.

"*Funny!*" replied his sister, shaking it.

Caroline put her T-shirt back on.

"Mike," she said. "We're gonna get some food, over there, with my dad."

"Oh, right," he said.

"Do you want to join us, Mike?" asked Chris.

"Erm," he replied, a little shyly. "Well, maybe next time. Lucy and I were going to be going soon, anyway."

"It's up to you."

"Martin, we're going for some food," said Caroline.

"Yeah, I can see that," he replied. "Wait for me then."

Once they had packed their backpacks, everyone walked along the beach.

"See you tomorrow, Caroline," said Mike, as he reached his bike.

"Yes, hopefully"

"See you, Mike. See you, Lucy," added Martin.

"Hello," said Lucy, in Slovak.

As the Hartleys walked along the grass, Martin said, "Why did Lucy say 'hello', when she was saying 'goodbye'?"

Chris laughed.

"Because," he said. "In Slovak, hello and goodbye are the same words."

His son added, "Funny language."

The Hartley family found themselves a spare table at a beach shack, to sit at. They looked out across the lake at the mountains beyond.

Once they had ordered something to eat and drink, Chris said, "I take it, you two Herberts, had a good afternoon down here?"

"Erm, well, we had a good afternoon," replied Caroline. "But it wasn't all here."

"Oh, so where was it then?"

"Erm, there was a slight change of plan, wasn't there, Martin?"

"Yeah, we met Mike and his friend Lucy, and they took us to visit a witch's cave."

"A witch's cave?"

"It was the one Mr Slavo told us about, on the night of the thunderstorm."

"I thought that was just a story?"

"So did we," said Caroline. "But Mike took his friend Lucy and us to see it."

"That sounds interesting."

"It was. Especially as when we were in it, some people in their late teens and early twenties, came into the cave and played us some of their music."

"Did they really?"

"They did," said Martin.

"What sort of music did they play?"

"African and Australian aboriginal music."

Their father looked at them.

"Really?"

"Yeah, really," said Caroline.

"One of them had a didgeridoo," joked Martin.

"Did they now," joked his father. "Well, I must say, this all sounds incredible."

"That's what we said," added Caroline, "Especially when they played some of their music to us."

"It was awesome," added Martin.

"It sounds like, you both had an interesting afternoon."

"Yeah, we did," replied Caroline.

Once they had finished their meal, Chris said, "Well, I think it's time to head back, before it gets dark."

"Good idea," replied Martin, who didn't fancy riding home in the dark.

"Are you ready, Caroline?"

"Yes, I'm ready."

"Right, let's go then."

The three of them wandered across the grass, towards their bikes. Once Chris had unlocked them, they cycled around the lake, towards the dam. When they were on it, everyone stopped, to look out at the magnificent sunset over the mountains. The Hartleys then continued their cycle ride home to the castle, after what had been a fun but tiring day for everyone.

8

Rise and Shine

The next morning at the castle, the Hartley children had a lie in. They needed it, after their long journey and adventures the day before. The geese and ducks, nearby, still woke both of them up at dawn. But by now, they were used to it and had gone back to sleep.

When Caroline eventually surfaced, she got up, opened her shutters and was hit by the sun shining in. She walked into the conservatory and looked out of the window. The girl could see, her father sitting at a round table, in the garden, near the fountain. He was busily typing away into his laptop. After admiring the view, she walked down the steps, which led into the garden. She then walked over towards where her father sat.

"Morning, Dad," she said.

He looked up.

"Oh, good morning, Sweetheart. Did you sleep well?"

Caroline went up to him and kissed him.

"Like a log"

"Me too"

She sat down, in one of the chairs.

"Who put these here?" she asked.

"I did."

"Oh, good idea!"

"Yes, I thought so. It makes a change, from the conservatory."

"True"

"Where's your brother?"

"I think he's still in bed."

"That sounds like Martin."

Caroline was enjoying the morning sunshine.

After a few moments, she said, "Would you like me to make you a cup of tea, Dad?"

"What a marvellous idea," he replied. "That'll give me time to quickly finish this. Then we can have some breakfast."

Caroline was putting the kettle on, in the kitchen, when her brother walked in. He was still in his pyjamas.

On seeing him, she said, "I wondered when you might get up."

He replied, "Well, there's no rush. Is there?"

"Yes, I know what you mean. That's why, I didn't wake you."

"I heard you open your door."

"Oh, sorry," said Caroline. "I tried to be quiet."

"Don't worry. I was already awake."

Caroline got three mugs out from the cupboard.

"I'm making Dad and me a cup of tea. Do you want one?"

"Yes, please," he replied, sitting down.

After a moment, he said, "I see Dad's in the garden."

"Yes, he's working on his laptop, like he normally does, at this time of the morning."

"Oh, right," said Martin.

As Caroline poured some sugar into the sugar bowl, he asked, "When are we going back to 1912, to see Veronica and Manfred?"

She replied, "I thought we might visit them, either this morning or tomorrow morning."

"Really?"

"Yes," said Caroline, sitting down, opposite her brother.

She added, "I want to go back down the lake today, to see Mike and Lucy, but I also want to see Veronica and Manfred, and visit their lake."

"I want to go fishing with Manfred."

"That settles it then. We'll go this morning, after breakfast. We can see Mike and Lucy, another time."

"Great"

Caroline added, excitedly, "Actually, I can't wait to go back to 1912."

"Oh, me too. I just wasn't sure, you were."

"Are you kidding? Using the magic key is more fun than anything I've ever done in my entire life."

"It's a magic key."

"Exactly!"

"Where is it?"

"In my room," said Caroline, adding, "I just hope, it still works."

"I'll keep my fingers crossed."

"You know, if we get the date right, there's still a chance we might be able to go with Veronica and Manfred to Trieste."

"Really?"

"Of course. But only if the magic key works."

"That'll be really cool, if it does."

"Yes, I know," said Caroline.

She added, "Come on, I'll make the tea. Then after breakfast, we can get ready to go back to 1912."

"Okay," said Martin, delightedly.

Caroline carried the tea, on a tray, down the steps at the rear of the castle.

As she did so, she said, "I've just had an idea, Martin."

"Oh, what's that?"

"Let's have breakfast outside, today."

"Do you think Dad will let us?"

"It's a sunny morning. Why not?"

They walked over to their father.

"Morning, Martin," said Chris, looking up.

"Morning, Dad"

"Sleep well?"

"Not bad, thanks"

"Tea up," said Caroline, putting the tray on the table.

As she sat down, she said, "Dad…"

"Yes, Sweetheart."

"What about having breakfast out here this morning."

"Oh, that's a good idea."

"Told you!" said Caroline, smiling at her brother.

"Tell you what, Sweetheart," said Chris. "Let's enjoy our tea first. Then we can sort breakfast, after."

"Okay"

Later, as they ate breakfast on the lawn, Martin said, "What are we going to do today?"

"Up to you, Martin," replied his father.

"I don't want to do anything," said Caroline. "I'm still tired, after yesterday's journey."

"Are we going down to the lake again?" asked Martin.

"Sure, but later. We're meant to be meeting Mike at lunchtime. He's invited us for lunch, Dad," replied Caroline, as she ate her bread roll.

"Oh, that's nice of him."

"Yes, I thought so."

It was a small white lie, and Caroline and Martin knew it.

Once she had swallowed her mouthful of food, Caroline added, "I thought I might walk around the castle garden again."

"Can I come with you?" asked her brother.

"If you want to."

"Good," said Chris. "Well, I see you two have got your day planned."

Martin looked at his father.

"What are you going to do, Dad?" he asked.

Chris laughed.

"Moi?" he said. "I'm going to cut the grass."

The children laughed.

He added, "But first, I must finish this web work. I'm due to give a presentation on it, soon. So I must try to complete it, ahead of the deadline."

"Oh, right," replied Martin, who wasn't interested with what his father was doing.

The boy had other things on his mind.

Getting up, he said, "I'm going to get washed and dressed."

Caroline looked at him.

"You can give me a hand taking the plates in first, Martin," she said.

"Oh, alright then"

"That's my boy," said Chris, taking his laptop back out from its case and putting it on the table.

Once Caroline was washed and dressed, she went into the conservatory.

Martin was waiting for her.

"Took your time," he said.

"Not really," she replied.

Looking out of the window, she asked, "Where's Dad?"

"Erm, I think he's gone to get the lawn mower out, from the cellar."

"Great!"

"Have you got the magic key?"

Caroline got it out from her pocket and dangled it, in front of him.

"One key," she said. "Right, shall we go?"

As the children walked round the side of the castle, Martin said, "What about Mr Slavo?"

"What about him?"

"Isn't he still in Bratislava?"

"Yeah, as far as I know, he is. Why?"

"Didn't Dad say, he's not due back here, for the next few days?"

"Yes, he did, and what's your point, Martin?"

The boy stopped and looked at his sister, who was now looking back at him.

"If Mr Slavo isn't here, now. How are you going to get into his flat?"

Caroline momentarily thought about it.

"That's a good point, but luckily for us, in the rush to leave the castle, last week, I forgot to return the spare key I 'borrowed'."

"Oh, well, that's a bit of luck then."

"Yeah, I suppose it is."

Caroline rooted in her pocket.

"Martin, as you can see. I now have two keys. One is the magic key. The other is Mr Slavo's front door key. Problem solved."

"Yes," he said, nodding.

At Mr Slavo's front door, the children checked the coast was clear, just in case he were suddenly to appear, from nowhere. They then sneaked into his flat, using the spare key, Caroline had 'borrowed' from him, during their first visit, when they had first discovered the attic door fitted Caroline's magic key.

"Come on," she said, as they ran round to it.

After getting the magic key out from her pocket, she said to her brother, "Ready?"

"Yeah, I'm ready."

As Caroline rubbed the key for good luck, he said, "Do you remember the date we need to go back to?"

"Yes, it's five days after the garden party."

"Are you sure?"

"Yes, of course I'm sure. Veronica wrote the date down, for me."

Caroline got out the hand-written notes, Veronica had written, for her.

She added, "I've got it here. Just in case, I needed it."

"Oh, right"

After a moment, Caroline said, excitedly, "Martin, I've got the funny feeling again, in my hand."

"Really?"

"Yes!"

"Oh, that's great."

She put the key in the lock and unlocked the door.

"I feel the magic."

"Brilliant," said Martin.

After opening it, Caroline began to climb the stairs.

"Don't forget to close the door," she said.

Martin closed the door behind him and followed his sister up the stairs. The light from the rectangular window above the door at the bottom, together with the square window above the door at the top of the attic stairway, allowed the children to see where they were going.

Caroline walked slowly up the stairs, towards the upper attic door.

As she did so, her brother said, "Caroline, give me, the day of the month, the month, the year, and the time, we need."

She did.

At the top of the stairs, the girl paused and looked up at the square window that was above the door, in front of her. She put the key in the lock, turned the key and hissed, "It's happening again, Martin."

"Yes!"

The children could see the white beam forming, beyond the square window above them. They could hear the thunder. When Caroline turned the lock and undid the door, they could both, once again, see the white beam in full. Not wishing to see it disappear, they ran, holding hands, up the remaining stairs, into it.

9

Back to the Past

Caroline and Martin ran through the white magic beam, into the room in the attic. They could instantly see that they had returned, to their friend Veronica's bedroom. It was exactly where Caroline wanted them to be.

"Martin, we're back," she said, excitely looking around her.

"Yes, so I can see," replied the boy, looking around him.

Both children looked at the white beam that had brought them back in time. It shone brightly, still beaming in, through the rectangular window in the castle's roof. They watched it hover, in front of the attic door. Then after about fifteen seconds, the magic beam began to veer towards the round window that lay facing the road. It swished through it. Once outside, the beam began to disperse and disappear, into thin air.

"Wow!" said Martin, as it disappeared. "That's what I call magic."

"Yes, I know," replied Caroline.

Martin went into the train room in the attic; to double-check it was, like it had been, on previous visits. He then returned to Veronica's bedroom, where Caroline had sat down on the stool at the dressing table.

"Everything looks, like it did before," he said.

"Good," replied his sister.

"Let's hope, you got the date right."

"Of course, I have. I'm not stupid."

"Well…"

"Don't answer that," she hissed.

Caroline noticed a calendar on the side of the dressing table. Looking at it carefully, she said, "Martin, I think I've got the right date. We are back, in 1912, on the day I wanted us to be."

"Oh, that's good," he replied, sitting down on the chair by the table.

After a moment, he said, "Do you think Veronica and Manfred will come?"

"Yes, I'm sure they will. We just need to give them a few minutes."

While they waited for their friends to arrive, Caroline was looking at herself in the oval mirror. She decided to brush her hair.

As she did so, Martin said, teasingly, "Mirror, mirror, on the wall. Who is the fairest of them all? Why, this sweet sister of mine, Caroline."

"Shut up, Martin," she replied.

Looking at the mirror, she stuck her tongue out at him, and gave him 'The Look'.

"Anyway," she added. "The mirror is not on the wall. It's on the dressing table. Go and play with your toy train."

Her brother stuck his tongue out at her, then went into the other room, to play with the train set. Ten minutes or so, passed. After which, Caroline heard familiar voices, at the bottom of the attic stairs.

"They're coming, Martin," she said.

Her brother stood at the doorway into the train room, waiting for his friends to arrive.

After bounding up the stairs, Veronica and Manfred greeted them.

"Sorry, for the slight delay," said Veronica, "We were finishing our breakfast."

"No problem," replied Caroline.

"How are you both?"

"I'm okay," said Martin.

"We've had a few days, in our own time," added Caroline.

"Why not?" said Veronica. "After all, it's your summer holiday."

"Yes, but it wasn't what you might imagine."

"What do you mean?" asked Veronica.

"Long story. I'll tell you later," replied Caroline, smiling sweetly.

"Fine. I'll look forward to hearing all about it."

"I'm happy you are back, Martin," said Manfred. "It's more fun, when you are here."

Veronica added, "I am pleased, the magic still appears to be working."

"Me too," replied Caroline.

"What I like, is the fact that we are still able to talk to each other, in different languages. Yet, we can fully understand each other."

"Yes, that's true," replied Caroline.

Martin added, "My German is getting much better, because of it."

"Ja, my English too," said Manfred, smiling.

After a moment's silence, where everyone just stood there, he said, "Zo, what are we going to do, today?"

"I'd like to go fishing again at the lake, if that's possible?" asked Martin.

"Ja, it's possible," replied Manfred.

"Great! That's what I'd hope you'd say."

"Zuper," said Veronica. "I can spend the day with Caroline."

"That sounds good," she replied.

Martin's idea, suited everyone.

Once he had got changed, in the train room, into some of Manfred's clothes, the boys returned into Veronica's bedroom.

Their sisters looked at Martin.

"Yeah, I see what you mean about the shorts," said Caroline.

The boy replied, "I can live with it."

"Live with what?" asked Manfred.

"The shorts. I hate them."

"But that's what boys your age wear, Martin," said Veronica, who was a bit surprised by his comment.

"Yes, I know," he replied. "But in my time, boys wear long trousers, which I prefer. I look stupid wearing these."

Caroline looked at him.

"Well, not stupid but…"

Her brother held his hand up at her.

"I'm going, Caroline," he said, interrupting her.

Turning to his friend, he said, "Come on, Manfred. Let's go down the lake."

"Ja, gut idea"

As they went out of the door, Martin waved, and said, "See you later, girls."

"Have a nice time," replied Caroline.

"Yes, do," added Veronica, waving back.

With the boys departed for the lake, the girls could have fun together. Caroline took her time getting changed. She wanted to try on some more of Veronica's dresses and other clothes, she had in her wardrobe.

After trying on umpteen dresses and looking at what else Veronica wore, the girls played around with their hair. They took turns, to sit at the dressing table, to try out different styles.

As they did so, Veronica said, "Caroline, I need to ask you something."

"Ask me then?" she replied.

"Are you and Martin still coming with us to Trieste tomorrow?"

"Yes, if your invitation still stands."

"Of course it does."

"Great! Then we are coming," said Caroline, smiling. "However, I've got to work the time travel correctly. Otherwise, I could end up in trouble, with my dad, if we are away too long."

Veronica laughed.

"Ja, I see vhat you mean," she replied.

Caroline added, "I still worry, whether the magic will allow us to do all this. I mean, it works around the castle. But I'm not sure it will, if we travel away from it?"

"Vell, there's only one way to find out, and that is to try and see vhat happens."

"True"

Caroline added, "The other thing is, obviously, we are your guests, if you get me, Veronica?"

"Ja! Don't worry about the money side," she replied, smiling. "My father is paying for everything."

"That's very decent of him," added Caroline.

"He can afford it."

"Thank you. But there is also the issue of clothes and washing things."

"What do you mean?"

"Well," said Caroline, "Martin and I have got our own clothes. But we can't wear them in 1912, and I can't really bring our washing things, with us, if you get me?"

Veronica laughed.

"Oh, don't worry about that," she replied. "You can use some of ours. Manfred and I have got lots of clothes, we don't wear, and I can't believe soap has changed zo much, has it?"

"No, not really," said Caroline, smiling. "Mind you, I do use liquid soap, as opposed to a bar of soap."

"Liquid soap?" asked Veronica. "That's new to me."

"Yes, I thought it might be," said Caroline, grinning.

She added, "And what about a suitcase? Again, we've got travel bags. But I can't use them in 1912, as once again they are different."

Veronica got the idea.

"Caroline," she said. "We have many suitcases that we never, or hardly ever, use. There's a big cupboard next door, where some of them that aren't used often, are kept. We can choose a couple today, and start to pack vhat you vill need. Vhat do you say to that?"

"Yes," she replied. "It sounds like a good idea."

"Zuper"

"But won't the servants notice?" asked Caroline.

"Vell, seeing as they don't come up here zo often, it shouldn't matter."

"Don't they?"

"I generally don't allow it, when I am staying at the castle, as this is my area. But even if they do, who cares? Who's to say, you didn't buy your suitcase, at the same shop as I did. You know vhat I mean?"

"Yes, I'm with you."

"Anyway, with my parents away again. The castle is quiet, zo no one will know."

"Okay, that's sounds fine," said Caroline.

"Great," added Veronica. "We can start to pack our cases this afternoon."

"Fine"

Changing the subject, Caroline said, "So what are we going to do this morning?"

"Vell," said Veronica. "I thought we could go to the railway station."

"The railway station?"

"Ja! We need to find out about the trains to Trieste. What time the train departs. You know."

"That sounds like a good idea."

"Anyway, my father is expecting us, on Friday morning."

"Is he?" said a surprised Caroline.

"Ja," replied Veronica. "Zo I need to organise everything today."

"Oh, I see."

Veronica stood up.

"Vell, shall we go?" she said, keenly wanting to go, suddenly.

"Yes, we can," said a surprised Caroline.

After they had descended the attic stairs, the girls walked through the castle, towards the main entrance door.

As they approached it, Veronica said, "Oh, before we go to the railway station, I want to show you something, in my father's study."

"Are we allowed to go in there?" asked Caroline.

"Not really. But seeing as he's in Trieste, already. We can sneak in."

"Fine"

10

Let's Study and Fish

Veronica opened the huge double doors that led to her father's study and walked in. Caroline followed her. She could see that it was a big room, they were now in. Naval maps were dotted along one of the walls; a magnificent huge long bookcase on another.

"Gosh! What an amazing room," she said, looking around.

Veronica was slightly ahead of her friend.

"My father calls it the map room," she said. "As you can see, it has many naval maps on the walls; not to mention his desk."

"So, I see," said Caroline, looking at some of them on the wall.

"By the way," she added, "What are you going to show me?"

"I want to show you an atlas."

Veronica went over to a large bookshelf, searched along it, then pulled out a huge atlas. She took it over to her father's large desk, where she sat down.

Opening the atlas, she said, "Here is a large map of the Austro-Hungarian Empire."

Caroline, who was standing next to her, looked at it.

"As you can see, the Empire is quite big now," said Veronica. "Mind you, it's not as big as your British Empire."

Veronica looked up at her friend, and said, "Tell me, does the Austrian-Hungarian Empire get bigger in the future, Caroline?"

Caroline laughed: "That's the future, Veronica. I can't tell you that. Anyway, history is *not* my subject, sport is. We're doing the Middle Ages in our history lessons at school, and I know nothing about this part of the world in history, yet. You are my history lesson, Veronica."

"I see," she replied, smiling.

Caroline was studying the map. She couldn't see Slovakia. Nor for that matter, its capital, Bratislava.

"Hang on a minute," she said. "Where's Bratislava?"

"Bratislava?" replied Veronica.

"Yes, I can't see it on the map."

"Sorry, I am not with you, Caroline?" said a confused Veronica.

"Wait! I've found Vienna, and there's Budapest. I'm sure Bratislava is near Vienna. But it's not here."

She looked at the map closely, adding, "There's a place called Pressburg. No, that can't be right. When I looked on Google maps, I'm sure Bratislava is there."

"That's Pressburg, Caroline, or Pozsony in Hungarian," said Veronica, looking at where Caroline was pointing.

"I can see that," said Caroline, a bit puzzled. "But I think that's where my father lives."

"Really," said an equally puzzled Veronica.

"Yes," added Caroline. "I'm sure that's where we stayed and travelled from, to get here."

"Gosh!" said Veronica. "Zo in the future, it changes its name."

"It looks like, it does."

"Wow!"

Caroline suddenly remembered that she *did* know a little about the region, from what her father and Mr Slavo had told her. History *had* changed. The Austro-Hungarian Empire had ended after World War 1. She thought it better *not* to tell Veronica about the creation of Czechoslovakia in 1918, or for that matter Slovakia in the 90s. That, she thought, might be going 'a bit too far'.

Whilst she hadn't studied the history side of the region at school yet, Caroline did know a bit of the geography of the region, including the names of the cities, as she had studied it in her geography lessons. She also remembered the geography quiz they had had, on the last day of term…

Caroline decided to search for Zámočany on the map.

"Veronica, I know this might sound stupid, but I can't see Zámočany on the map either."

"Zámočany? I've never heard of it."

"But that's the name of this village, right?"

"Nein! This village isn't called Zámočany. It's called Straussburg."

The girls looked at each other.

"Is it?" said Caroline.

"You mean, in the future this village changes its name from Straussburg?"

"Well, in my time it's definitely called Zámočany. It's on the station sign."

"But that's impossible. It's been Straussburg for hundreds of years. Are you telling me the village changes its name?"

"It looks like it."

Caroline suddenly realised the names must have changed when Czechoslovakia was created. Not wishing to change history, she decided to 'stay mum' and act 'a bit dim' on the immediate situation she had now created for herself.

Veronica, meanwhile, was curious to pick up any future knowledge from her friend.

"Tell me, what are Google maps? Are they an atlas, like this one?"

Caroline laughed.

"Er, yes. They are, sort of," she said. "Only, I don't look at them in an atlas."

"You don't?" said Veronica, adding, "How do you look at them?"

"On a computer. My dad's laptop, actually."

Caroline realised, she was, once again, talking about the future.

"Oh, I mean, I look in my father's Google atlas."

"I see," said Veronica, not really understanding and looking at her friend oddly.

She decided to change the subject.

"Let me show you where we're going tomorrow," she said.

"Fine," replied Caroline, letting her friend lead the conversation.

"Zo, here is the castle," said Veronica, pointing. "And this is Trieste, in the Adriatic. According to my father, we vill travel first to Budapest, then go directly onto Vienna. Here, we vill change trains for Trieste. Zo we should see some of the Empire on our journey."

"Oh, that'll be really good," said Caroline, beaming.

"Ja, I think it vill be."

Veronica added, "You know, it's the gateway to the Austrian Riviera."

"Is it?"

"Ja!"

"The Austrian Riviera?" repeated Caroline, slowly. "I didn't know they had one?"

"It's more famous than the French Riviera."

"Really?" said a surprised Caroline. "Then how come I've never heard of it?"

Veronica gave Caroline one of her funny looks.

"Sometimes, Caroline, I wonder if you and I come from the same planet."

They both laughed.

"Look, here is the Austrian Riviera," said Veronica, showing its location on the map.

"Oh, right!" said Caroline. "I'm with you now, sorry."

"I think you need to practise your geography, Caroline."

"It looks like it," she replied, laughing.

Caroline realised the Austro-Hungarian Empire area, around Trieste, in her world, had been split into three; Italy, Slovenia and Croatia. With Austria losing the whole area.

Veronica added, "The Austro-Hungarian Riviera is *the* place to go in summer. Trieste is the Austro-Hungarian Empire's fourth largest city."

"Is it?" said Caroline.

"Ja"

"So, what are the other three?"

"Vienna, Budapest and Prague," said Veronica, giving her a funny look. "What do they teach you in school, Caroline?"

"Well," she replied. "I thought Trieste was in Italy?"

"Italy? No, it's Austrian. It's the Empire's largest port and belongs to the Austrian side of the Empire."

"I see," said a rather confused Caroline.

She then realised history had changed things over time. Caroline decided to let her friend continue giving her the history lesson.

Veronica continued her explanation.

"The Austrians love to go down this part of their coastline," she said. "The Austrian Riviera today is certainly more popular than the French Riviera. Venice used to be part of our Empire. But for some stupid reason, we gave it to the Italians."

"Right!" said Caroline, fascinated by it all.

"One thing, Veronica," added Caroline. "Where are we going to stay?"

"Oh, my aunt and uncle have a place, in Trieste," she replied. "My father is arranging for us to stay there."

"Has he? That's very nice of him."

"Ja, it is."

"If I remember correctly. We're going to see some of your father's battleships, right?"

"Ja, that's right."

Veronica then said, "There is going to be an inspection of the fleet taking place, and according to my father, this is something worth seeing, as it only happens every two years."

"Oh, I see," said Caroline. "Why didn't you say?"

"That's why I'm discussing it with you, now," said her frustrated friend.

"Well, it all sounds fine, Veronica."

Closing the atlas, Veronica stood up, and said, "Good, vell let's make our way down to the railway station, shall ve?"

"Good idea"

Having walked through the castle garden and the vineyards, down by the castle lake, the two boys walked round to the shed and picked up their fishing gear, from inside it. They then made their way around the lake.

As they walked, Manfred said, "Martin, let's fish on this side of the lake today."

"Fine," he replied.

"What about, over there?" said Manfred, pointing. "It's a good place to fish and it's in the shade."

The two boys walked over to a small clearing in the reeds, where they put their fishing gear down. They then set about setting their rods up. Later, when they were settled, they sat there in silence watching the water. A few birds chirped overhead. Some grasshoppers could be heard in the grass nearby.

As they sat there, Martin said, "I prefer worms as bait."

Manfred replied, "Me too."

Martin asked, "Where do you get your worms from?"

"From the garden," replied Manfred.

"Yes, I know where worms come from," said Martin, laughing. "What I mean is, do you dig them up?"

"Nein," said Manfred. "One of the gardeners collects them for me."

"Really?"

Manfred was playing with the fishing line.

"I don't like digging them up myself," he said. "Sometimes, it takes forever to find them."

"Yes, I know what you mean," replied Martin. "I go to the pet shop and buy a bucket of worms. If that's not possible, I do some fly fishing."

"Ja, but it depends what you are fishing for and where you are fishing."

"True"

Manfred reeled his rod in and cast off again.

After a while, Martin said, "My granddad was good at fly fishing."

"Was he?" replied Manfred.

"Yes, he took me fly fishing last year. Showed me how to fly fish. It was really good fun."

A few moments of silence passed.

Manfred then said, "I like to go sea fishing."

"Really?" said Martin. "I've never been sea fishing. What's it like?"

"It's good fun and is totally different to this."

"Where do you go?"

"My uncle took me sea fishing near Trieste, in the Adriatic Sea, last year."

"Did you catch anything?"

"Unfortunately, I didn't," replied Manfred. "But it was still really good fun."

Martin's rod twitched.

"Manfred," he said, excitedly. "I think I've got something."

The boy could see his friend's rod move.

"Bring it in, carefully," he said.

Martin slowly allowed the fish to swim around. Then gradually, he reeled it in and put it in his net.

"Look at that," he said. "It's huge."

"It's a carp," replied Manfred, who added, "The cook *will* be delighted."

11

Tickets, Luggage...

The sun was shining, as the girls departed the main gates of the castle. They were carrying their parasols, to shield them from the sun. Gracefully, Caroline and Veronica walked in a ladylike way, down the nearby lane towards the railway station.

"I'm looking forward to going to Trieste, Veronica," said Caroline, looking out across the fields at a group of trees that lay beyond it.

"Oh, zo am I," she replied.

As they approached the railway station, Caroline said, "Oh by the way, Veronica, my dad says this isn't an actual railway station, we are going to now."

"Zo, what is it then?"

"He calls it a railway halt. As there's no actual platform, like in a normal station."

Turning to her friend, Veronica replied, "Fine. You are probably right. But let's call it a small station, shall we?"

"Agreed"

The girls laughed in their girly way and walked on...

Nearer the main building, Veronica said, "Caroline, look at the railway sign on the wall."

She did.

On the wall was a huge sign.

'Straussburg'

"Oh, yes," she replied. "I see what you mean."

"It's *always* been Straussburg. Zo, I can't understand why it changes in your time," said Veronica.

Caroline looked at her.

"History is history, Veronica…"

The girls decided to leave it at that.

As they approached the booking office door, they saw the stationmaster sitting in his office.

"Hello, Mr Prednosta," said Veronica.

The stationmaster looked up from reading his newspaper, saw who it was and quickly stood up.

"Ah, good morning, Miss Veronica," he said. "What a pleasant surprise. Lovely day, eh?"

"Yes, isn't it," she replied.

"What can I do for you?" he asked.

The girls had walked into his back office. A mass of railway instruments was spread out all over the room, including signalling equipment, level crossing levers and point's equipment. On a desk was an old-fashioned telephone, train timetables, a kettle and a teapot. With them were some cups and saucers. A half-drunk cup of coffee sat there, next to a half-smoked cigarette. The stationmaster's cap lay upside down on the table. An open newspaper was on the desk.

Veronica asked, "I would like to find out the train times from here to Trieste."

"Trieste?" replied the stationmaster. "Oh, you're off to the Austrian Riviera, are you?"

"Ja, that's right," said Veronica, laughing.

"What a lovely place," he replied. "I was there only a month ago. That's the joy of working for the railway company. I get to travel a bit meself. See a bit of the old Empire, if you know what I mean," he added, winking at them.

He blew his nose.

"Er," he said. "When did you intend to travel, Miss Veronica?"

"Tomorrow, if possible," she replied. "We have to be in Trieste on Friday morning."

"I zee," he said.

"By the way, Mr Prednosta," added Veronica. "Let me introduce you to Miss Caroline Hartley from London."

"Pleased to meet you, Miss Caroline," said the stationmaster, shaking her hand.

"How do you do?" replied Caroline, in German.

"From London, eh?" asked the stationmaster.

"Er, yes. That's right," said Caroline, in German.

"Funny, I don't remember seeing you arrive?" he added, taking his hat off and scratching his head.

"Oh, she came by motor car," said Veronica, quickly intervening.

"Did she?" added the stationmaster, realising she must come from a rich family.

He blew his nose.

"Okay, vell, let's see what we can find, shall we?"

Sitting down, he looked through his thick railway timetable.

After studying it, the stationmaster looked up, and said, "Vell, there's a choice of three trains to Trieste. You can get the 06.58, the 13.58, or the 20.58 train."

"How long is the journey?" asked Veronica.

"Er, let me zee. The 06.58 takes seventeen hours. That gets you in at 23.58. The 13.58 takes eighteen and a half hours. This one arrives in Trieste at 08.28, and the 20.58 takes nineteen and a half hours, which let me zee, gets you in at, er, 16.28.

"Gosh! That's a long journey," added Caroline.

"Zo, the best train for you, Miss Veronica, is probably the 13.58, tomorrow afternoon. It'll get you into Trieste at 08.28, on Friday morning."

The girl replied, "That does seem rather early, but all right."

"So, is this the best train to get?" asked Caroline, double-checking.

"Vell, Miss," said the stationmaster. "If you want to be in Trieste, on Friday morning, I think this is the one you need."

"I zee," said Veronica, "Vell, thank you for the information."

"Not at all"

The stationmaster asked, "Will you be booking the tickets today?"

Veronica looked at Caroline, and said to her, "It might be an idea. Then there's no rush tomorrow."

"Fine," she replied.

"Vell," said the stationmaster, "You'll need to step into the booking office, please, ladies."

"Ja, of course," replied Veronica.

The girls walked into the booking office.

At the booking counter, Veronica said, "Zo, I would like four children's return tickets to Trieste, please."

"Certainly, Miss Veronica," replied the stationmaster. "I take it, you will be wanting overnight sleepers?"

She responded, "If we are arriving at 08.28 in Trieste and travelling overnight, then yes please."

"Sleepers?" asked a surprised Caroline.

"It's an overnight train and I'd prefer a bed to sleep in. Wouldn't you?" said Veronica, smiling at her friend.

"Yes, of course," replied Caroline.

"Just a moment," said the stationmaster. "I just need to check the prices and availability. Will it be first or second class, Miss?"

Veronica thought about it, then said, "First class."

"What about your return journey?"

The girl suddenly remembered something. She rooted in her small handbag and took a piece of paper out. Looking at it, she said, "Oh, this is when my father suggested we come back."

The stationmaster read it.

"Very vell, Miss," he said. "Give me a few minutes to sort it all, vill you? I'll need to ring Vienna, to book your overnight sleeper accommodation."

He sat down and prepared the tickets, including the cost in Krone. Caroline left Veronica to sort it all out. While she waited, she wandered around the room.

She looked at a small railway map on the wall. It showed the Austro-Hungarian railways, in 1912. Caroline was fascinated by it, knowing how the country and places would change in the future.

After several minutes, the stationmaster appeared back at the small counter.

"There you are, Miss Veronica," he said. "Everything is sorted. I've put it all in the folder."

"Thank you," she replied, taking it.

Veronica added, "Could you send the invoice to my father, like you normally do?"

"No problem"

"Thank you, Mr Prednosta"

"Not at all, Miss"

Veronica clutched the tickets in her hand

"Everything is sorted, Caroline," she said.

"Super"

As they walked outside into the hot sunshine, they waved at the stationmaster, who was now back in his office. The girls raised their parasols, to protect themselves against the hot sun.

Veronica spoke in her railway announcement voice.

"The next stop for the train, is the Austrian Riviera."

"Wonderful," said Caroline, bursting into laughter.

Back at the castle, in the attic, the girls relaxed.

Caroline crashed on the bed.

Veronica poured them a glass of fresh lemonade each.

"That was fun," she said.

"Yes, it was," replied Caroline.

"Zo, all you need now is a suitcase?"

"Give me a minute," said Caroline, resting.

Once the girls had relaxed a bit, they went into Manfred's train room, where there was a large walk-in cupboard, behind which were many suitcases.

"It's a bit dusty in here," said Veronica, climbing over a couple.

"Yes, it is," replied Caroline.

Veronica rooted amongst the many suitcases, till she found what she was looking for.

"Manfred and I can use these two suitcases, as they've got our family name and crest on them. Can you take one, please, Caroline?"

"Sure. Er, where shall I put it?"

"In my room, next to the wardrobe."

Veronica put the other suitcase on the floor in the train room. She then returned to the large walk-in cupboard, where the girl did a bit more rooting around. After moving some more suitcases, she pulled out two that didn't have the family name or crest on them.

"These should do," she said, smiling.

"Haven't you got anything smaller?" asked Caroline, who was surprised by their size.

"Vell, there's a lot to carry."

"I'm not taking the kitchen sink with me, you know."

"The kitchen sink?" asked Veronica, giving her a funny face.

"It means," said Caroline. "I am not carrying everything, including the kitchen sink."

"Why would you take a kitchen sink with you?" asked Veronica.

"Don't worry," replied Caroline. "That is the point. You wouldn't. Look, forget it."

Veronica looked at her weirdly.

"Can you take one, please?"

"Sure. Where shall I put it?"

"In my bedroom, next to the other one."

"Right"

Veronica put the case in her hand, alongside the other one, in the train room, then walked back into the walk-in cupboard again.

"Caroline," she said, from inside it. "Come here, vill you? I want to show you something."

"Oh, what's that?" she replied, walking in from Veronica's bedroom.

"Look at this, vill you?"

Veronica went to a corner of the large cupboard and moved a panel of wood.

Caroline looked closely at what her friend was showing her.

Moving the skirting board, Veronica said, "This is my secret hiding place, Caroline. I put things here, when I vant to hide them from anyone."

"I see," replied Caroline, looking on in awe.

Veronica explained. "I have several hiding places, actually."

"Oh, what a good idea"

"Ja, I thought zo," said Veronica, replacing the skirting board.

"So you could send me secret messages, in the future?" suggested Caroline.

The girls laughed.

"You never know. Maybe I might," said Veronica, smiling.

Back in Veronica's bedroom, Caroline said, "So, Veronica, what will I need to take with me to Trieste? What do you suggest?"

"Vell," she replied. "It depends on the weather and what we are going to do. Let's have a look in the wardrobe, shall we? Then we can choose together, vhat's good for you and vhat's good for me. Gut idea?"

"Good idea"

The girls had a fun time trying on various dresses, undergarments and shoes. Caroline was quite taken with some of Veronica's lace blouses. She wasn't too keen on her bloomers or swimming costume.

With their suitcases packed, they went downstairs into Manfred's bedroom.

In it, Veronica said, "The servants should really be doing this. They might get suspicious, if they see us packing both your cases upstairs."

"I see," replied Caroline, looking around the room.

Veronica was pulling some clothes out from Manfred's wardrobe.

"Have a look at these, will you?" said Veronica.

Caroline did, then said, "Veronica, Martin wouldn't be seen dead in these clothes, in our time."

"Why not? Are they really that different?"

Caroline nodded.

"Just a tad," she said.

Veronica looked at her.

"It means just a little," said Caroline explaining, by putting her thumb and finger close together.

She added, "A lot actually. Fashion changes. Most boys wear long trousers."

"Really?" said an astonished Veronica.

Once the girls had sorted out what they needed, for both Manfred and Martin, they carried it up to the attic. They then returned, to pick up the rest of the stuff they couldn't carry with them the first time.

After dumping the clothes on the bed, Caroline said, "What about everybody's wash things? You know, things like toothbrushes, face flannels and soap?"

"Don't worry," said Veronica. "I'll get the toiletries prepared tomorrow morning."

"Great!"

Once they had packed the boys' clothes into their suitcases, they closed the lids.

Caroline walked into Veronica's bedroom and flopped on her bed again.

"Veronica," she said. "Can we rest for a minute? It's very hot up here."

"Ja, gut idea," she replied, sitting on her bed.

She then lay down next to her friend and also rested.

After a short rest Veronica sat up.

"Caroline," she said. "Let's go to the drawing room? I need to get something from there."

Caroline looked at her, smiled, and said, "Alright."

As she stood up, she added, "Was it anything in particular, you wanted?"

"You'll see," replied Veronica, smiling.

Caroline was intrigued…

As they departed the bedroom, Veronica grabbed a yellow luggage label holder and followed Caroline, down the stairs…

12

Caroline

The two girls walked through the castle into the drawing room. Veronica went up to a desk, sat down at it and opened a drawer. She then got out some pink pieces of paper. Caroline sat at a chair, opposite her.

Putting the paper on the desk, Veronica said, "You'll need to write your name and address on the paper, zo we can put it on the suitcase."

"Well," said Caroline. "I can write my name. But I'm not sure about what address to use. What do you suggest?"

"The address?" said Veronica, looking across the desk at her friend.

"I can't put 55, Partridge Crescent, Welwyn Garden City, on it, can I?"

"Er, not really"

"Nor can I put my father's flat, as our address."

Veronica thought about it.

"It might be better that we use the same address. Therefore, I propose using this one. It seems the simplest solution, does it not?"

"Yes," replied Caroline. "It's a good idea."

"Can you write your name, on here?" suggested Veronica.

Caroline picked up the pen and looked at it.

"A nib pen? My, that's unusual," she said.

"Don't tell me," replied Veronica. "Pens are different in your time."

The girls laughed. Veronica knew the answer before Caroline could say anything.

"Well, yes! Some of them are, for sure," she said. "We certainly don't use nib pens. In fact, I don't think I've ever used one before."

"It's a simpler form of a fountain pen that my father uses," said Veronica.

"I see," replied Caroline.

After looking at it, she said, "Ask a silly question, but how do you use it?"

"Vell," replied Veronica. "You put the nib in the ink and you write with it – like this…"

She used another nib pen and wrote her name.

"Now you have a go," she added. "Try writing your name."

Caroline picked up the pen.

"Gosh!" she said. "It's like having your first writing lesson."

Veronica laughed.

Caroline wrote her name, '*Caroline*'.

"Now use this blotting paper," said Veronica, passing it over.

Caroline used it, like Veronica had, when she had shown her how to use the pen.

"Oh, it's really weird using this nib pen."

She added, "Wait! Let me try that again."

She rewrote her name on another piece of pink paper.

"Now try writing your name a bit bigger and add your surname," suggested Veronica. "Right, now try writing it all in capitals."

Caroline did.

"That's better," added Veronica. "Gut! Now you need to write your address."

Caroline wrote her home address underneath her name, then passed it to Veronica.

"This is no good," she said, looking at it.

"I know! I was just practising my writing using this pen."

"Oh, I zee."

"What is the address I need to write down?"

Veronica verbally gave her the address – *Strauss Castle, Straussburg, Austro-Hungary.*

As Caroline wrote it down, she said, "Is that the name of this castle?"

Veronica looked at her.

"Yes, of course it is. *Strauss Castle* is named after our relatives. It was my father who rebuilt it."

"Uh-huh," she replied, nodding.

Caroline added, "I didn't know its name, till just now."

"Really?"

"Well, I'd never really thought about it."

Veronica gave her one of her funny looks.

"I worry about you sometimes, Caroline."

She looked across the desk at her friend.

Caroline added, "I never thought to ask."

"I zee," replied Veronica.

Caroline started to write her name and the address on another piece of pink paper.

Once she had completed it, Veronica said, "You'll need to do that again. Only this time, I need it a bit bigger."

"Why do I need to write it twice?" asked Caroline.

"The first one I can use as a name tag."

Veronica took from her pocket the yellow address tag she had picked up, as she departed the attic. She showed Caroline.

"Oh, I see," she said, looking at it.

"The second one we can stick on the front of the suitcase," said Veronica, showing the size she wanted, using her hands. "It will stop the suitcase getting lost."

"Wait a minute!" said Caroline. "Now I know the sizes you want, let me do it all again neatly."

She rewrote the details.

"Is that better?" she asked.

"Ja, it's fine," said Veronica.

Now satisfied, she added, "Right, now you need to do the same for Martin."

Caroline wrote down his name and address twice, then said, "Hang on a minute, Veronica. You could have done all this?"

Her friend looked at her, smiled, and said, "Ja, of course I could. I just wanted to see your writing skills."

"Well," said Caroline. "It's *not* my normal writing style, as I have written more slowly using this nib pen."

"Your style of writing is very different to mine," responded Veronica. "Here, let me show you."

She wrote her name and address on another piece of the pink paper, and then wrote Caroline's name on another piece, next to hers.

"Yes, I see what you mean," said Caroline. "Yours is what I call Edwardian style. Mine is Marion Richardson. So, there is a bit of a difference."

"Who is Marion Richardson?" asked Veronica.

"No idea," said Caroline, laughing. "It's the style we were taught at school."

"I zee," replied Veronica.

She wrote hers and Manfred's name and address twice, in capitals, on the paper. Getting some scissors, she cut the paper up and slid the smaller one in the address tag.

"There we are. That fits," added Veronica, smiling.

For a moment or two, Caroline suddenly went very quiet. She was thinking to herself.

Veronica saw her sitting there thinking, and said, "Is everything all right, Caroline?"

After a moment, she replied slowly, "Oh, my god, Veronica. I've just realised I have written the future answer to my question."

Veronica gave her one of her funny looks.

"Sorry, I don't understand," she said. "Vhat do you mean?"

Caroline couldn't quite believe what she now realised.

"Veronica," she said. "Do you remember, I told you I received the magic key from Zurich."

Her friend looked at her with surprise.

"Ja," replied Veronica. "You did."

"Did I mention to you, it was rolled in a pink piece of paper?" said Caroline.

"No, I don't remember you telling me that."

"Well, it was. The thing is, my name was written on that piece of paper."

Veronica looked at her friend, and said, "Really?"

"Yes, really," said Caroline. "And what I found spooky, when I read it, was that *I wrote it.*"

Veronica was astounded.

"Nein! How can that be?" she asked.

Caroline replied, "Until just now, I could never work out, how I would receive a pink piece of paper from Zurich, with my name written on it that I wrote. Now, I know the answer. I just wrote it. Oh my god, Veronica. This is really spooky!"

"Nein, it is amazing, Caroline," replied Veronica. "You mean to say that one of these pieces of paper, I send you in the future."

Caroline was in shock.

After a moment, she nodded slowly.

"Yes, Veronica," she said. "You do."

"Gosh!" she replied. "No wonder you are shocked."

"You can say that again."

Veronica was keen to get back to the attic. She picked up a bottle of glue and scissors.

"Vell, Caroline," she said. "That's the future. Right now, we need to go back to the attic and stick these on the cases."

Back in the attic, once they had affixed the names and addresses on the suitcases, Veronica asked, "How do they look?"

"Fine," replied Caroline, admiring their work.

"Zuper"

Turning to Caroline, she said, "Vell, could I suggest we go into the garden? It's such a lovely day. It seems stupid to miss all the sunshine. We can have afternoon tea on the lawn."

"Why not?" replied Caroline. "It sounds like a great idea. I could do with a drink, after what I've just discovered."

13

The Decision

Outside in the garden at the back of the castle, Caroline and Veronica walked over to the fountain. As they stood there admiring the view, they saw one of the servants walking along the rear of the castle. It was Katarina the housemaid. Veronica waved to her to come over.

"Oh, good afternoon, Katarina," said Veronica, smiling.

"Good afternoon, Miss Veronica," she replied.

"Will you bring some cold refreshments for the pair of us, over to the picnic area of the garden, please?"

"Certainly, Miss," replied the housemaid. "I'll bring it out to you, shortly."

"Thank you, Katarina," added Veronica.

As she walked away, Caroline said, "The picnic area? Where's that?"

Veronica replied, "It's at the bottom of the main lawn, just to the left."

"Oh, I see," said Caroline, surprised.

Caroline found herself in the gently sloping circular area of grass, surrounded by trees, shrubs and beautiful flowerbeds. Her favourite walkway through the castle's gardens she knew lay beyond. Her friend sat down in the centre of the circular grassed area. Caroline decided to join her.

"This is the picnic area, Caroline," said Veronica, picking a daisy.

"Why do you call it 'the picnic area'?" she asked, looking around her.

"Because it's where we have picnics."

"Right"

"We used to come here a lot, when the castle was being built."

"Do you have many picnics here?"

"Not as many as we used to," replied Veronica, "Maybe three or four a year. It depends. As I got older and moved to Vienna, there seems to be fewer of them."

After a few minutes, Ivan the butler and Katarina the housemaid arrived. The butler was carrying a blanket and a small picnic basket. The housemaid was carrying another small picnic basket.

"We brought a blanket for you to sit on, Miss Veronica," said the butler.

"That's very thoughtful of you," she replied, standing up and brushing herself off.

Caroline did the same. The butler laid out the blanket and opened his picnic basket.

"I have brought you some fresh cold lemonade and glasses, Miss Veronica," he said.

"Oh, thank you, Mr Ivan," she replied.

Katarina placed her basket on the blanket, next to the other basket. She opened it and took out a freshly baked cake, some plates and a cake knife.

"Some cake, Miss Veronica?" the housemaid suggested.

"Oh, lovely," she replied. "Thank you."

"Will that be all, Miss Veronica?" asked the butler.

"Er, yes. Thank you, Mr Ivan," she replied.

As the servants made their way back to the castle, Veronica picked up the cake knife, and said, "Would you like a piece of cake, Caroline?"

She replied, "Oh, yes, please."

As Veronica cut the cake, Caroline said, "You know, that's an amazing cake. It's just like I imagine cakes might be. Pink icing covering a huge cake, with red cherries on top. This is really great, Veronica."

She replied, "The cook is good at making cakes."

"Yes, I can see that. Martin would definitely want a piece of this. Talking of whom, I wonder how he and Manfred are getting on."

"Oh, I think the boys will be enjoying their fishing," replied Veronica, pouring them both a glass of lemonade.

Passing the glass to her friend, Veronica said, "I do love homemade lemonade. It's my favourite cold drink."

After drinking some of hers, Caroline replied, "Yes, it is pretty good."

As they ate their cake, Veronica asked, "Are you looking forward to going to Trieste tomorrow?"

"Yes, of course I am," replied Caroline. "I've never been there before. Is it nice?"

"I like it, although I prefer Opatija."

"Opatija? Oh, where's that?"

"To the south of Trieste. It's one of the Austro-Hungarian Riviera's most prestigious bathing resorts."

"Is it?" said Caroline, having never heard of the place.

"Ja," replied Veronica. "We go there sometimes, when we stay with my aunt."

"I see," said Caroline, finishing her glass of lemonade.

"Would you like some more lemonade?"

"Yes please"

As Veronica poured them both another glass, she was thinking something through in her mind.

After a moment or two, she said, "Caroline, as we are going to Trieste tomorrow. Why don't you stay the night tonight?"

Caroline looked up at her friend, thought about it for a moment, then taking the refilled glass, said, "Thank you. Well, er…"

"Caroline," said Veronica, looking at her directly. "There is no real reason why you can't. You are on holiday. Surely, as a 'time traveller', it doesn't matter when you go back? I mean, you can go back today and return tomorrow. But now you know how to time travel, what is the point of that? You may as vell just stay here."

Caroline sipped her drink and thought about it.

"Erm, you have a point," she said, adding, "But I don't really know whether we should. I mean, Martin and I have got nothing with us."

"That's not true," replied Veronica. "We have just packed your suitcases for tomorrow. We can soon find some more clothes for you and Martin. I can sort some toiletries for you later. What do you say?"

Caroline was still unsure.

After a moment, she smiled, and said, "Well, er, alright. We'll stay here tonight, then go with you to Trieste tomorrow. Mind you, I don't know what Martin will say."

"I do," replied Veronica. "My guess is, he'll jump at the chance."

"You are probably right," added Caroline, taking a bite of her cake.

"Zuper," said Veronica.

She was secretly delighted that *finally*, she had persuaded Caroline to stay the night at the castle, with her.

"But what about the servants?" asked Caroline.

"Vhat about them?"

"Well, er…"

Veronica understood her point.

"I can say, you are staying the night, as part of your holiday with us. Before we all go to Trieste."

"I see."

"If anyone asks, we can tell them your father has arranged for you both to stay with us."

Caroline was thinking about Veronica's proposal. She was actually quite happy not to rush back to her own time.

"Look," said Veronica. "There's hardly anyone at the castle, since the garden party ended. My mother gave most of the servants a few days off, as a thank you for all their hard work. Zo with her now in Vienna visiting her mother, and my father already in Trieste, means the castle is relatively quiet. We've almost got the place to ourselves."

"Yes, well let's see how it all goes, shall we?" said Caroline, smiling.

She was still unsure of how this might play out.

Veronica was excited, with the sudden turn of events.

"Caroline," she said. "Why don't we go and tell Manfred and Martin the good news?"

Looking at her friend, she replied, "Later, Veronica. We've got all afternoon."

"You are right. I just thought we could take the boys some cake and get some more lemonade from the castle kitchen."

"Fine. But first I want to relax in the sun," said Caroline, lying down on her back.

Later, the girls walked up to the castle and made their way down to the kitchen. The cook was asleep in her chair. Eva the scullery maid was at the sink, washing some dishes.

"Good afternoon, Eva," said Veronica, quietly.

The scullery maid turned her head.

Surprised, she said, "Oh, hello, Miss Veronica."

The cook, on hearing voices awoke. Seeing the girls, she slowly got to her feet.

"Oh, good afternoon, Miss Veronica. I was just having my afternoon nap."

"Hello, Frau Nagy. Sorry to interrupt it," said Veronica.

"How can I help you?"

"We'd like some more lemonade, please?"

"Certainly," said the cook, a bit surprised.

She thought what she had sent down was enough.

"We want to take some fresh lemonade to Manfred and Martin," added Veronica.

"Oh, I zee," replied the cook, now understanding their request.

"We thought we'd take the boys a bit of cake, as vell," said Veronica.

"Vell, why not?" replied the cook, smiling. "Just give me a minute, will you?"

As the cook prepared some more lemonade, Veronica said to her, "By the way, Frau Nagy. I forgot to tell you, Caroline and Martin will be staying at the castle tonight. Would it be possible for you to prepare them an evening meal?"

"Ja, of course," she replied. "Why didn't you mention it before?"

"Sorry, I forgot," said Veronica, telling a bit of a white lie.

Caroline looked at her. Veronica knew what was coming.

"What are you?" said Caroline.

"Forgetful," replied Veronica, smiling.

The girls burst out laughing.

Once they had got their extra lemonade from the cook, the girls departed the large kitchen in the servants' quarters. To Caroline's surprise, Veronica led her up an outside stairway that was at the rear of the castle. As she climbed the stairs, she realised it must be what the servants used to get to and from the castle garden.

14

The Lake, the Cake and the Dinner

With their fresh supply of lemonade, Caroline and Veronica made their way through the beautifully laid out castle gardens. They walked down to the gate that led them to the vineyards. Caroline loved walking through the rows of vines towards the lake. She simply adored the scenic beauty of everything around her.

At the water's edge, the girls made their way round to the boathouse jetty.

"Oh," said Veronica. "The rowing boat is still here, Caroline."

"What does that mean?" she asked.

"It means the boys aren't on the island. They must be somewhere around the lake."

"I see."

"Let's walk round the lake a bit. We might bump into them?"

Carrying their baskets, the girls walked on around it.

Suddenly, Caroline pointed, and said, "There they are, Veronica, over there, in those reeds."

"Oh ja," she replied, looking.

"Martin, Manfred," yelled Caroline, waving.

The boys looked up.

Martin stood up.

"Oh, hello Caroline," he said. "I didn't expect to see you and Veronica down here."

"Actually," she replied. "Nor, did I. Still, life's full of surprises, Martin."

"Is it time to go back?" he asked.

"No, not yet," said Caroline. "Actually, you've plenty of time, and we've brought you boys some lemonade and cake."

"Have you?" said Martin, a bit surprised.

Manfred had now joined them.

"Manfred," said Martin. "Caroline and Veronica have brought us some lemonade and some cake."

"Really?" he replied. "That's very decent of you."

The girls sat down on the grass area next to the lake.

Manfred and Martin joined them.

"Veronica will be mum again," said Caroline.

"Ja, I will be mum," said Veronica, pouring the lemonade.

"What have you been doing?" asked Martin.

Caroline replied, "We went to the railway station."

"Did you?" he said, surprised.

"Yes," said Caroline. "At lunchtime, we booked the tickets to Trieste."

Veronica added, "And when we got back, we packed your suitcases, ready for departure, tomorrow."

"Did you?" said Martin, drinking his lemonade.

"Yes, we did," added Caroline.

"I see," said the boy.

After a moment, Veronica said, "Martin, I have asked Caroline to stay overnight at the castle."

Martin looked at his sister.

"Really?" he said, surprised. "But…"

"Don't worry, Martin," said Caroline. "It includes you, as well."

"No, you don't understand me. What I meant to say was, will the magic key let us?"

"I've no idea."

"I don't want to disappear into thin air, you know."

"Oh I don't think you're going to do that, Martin," said Veronica, reassuringly.

"How do you know that?"

"I don't. But as I said to Caroline, there's only one way to find out."

"What do you mean?" asked Manfred.

"They need to stay here the night, to see if the magic key allows them to stay."

"Oh, I zee."

"If it does, they can go with us to Trieste tomorrow."

Martin then said, "But I haven't got any clothes or washing things here. Anyway, don't we have to get back to our own time, Caroline?"

"Well, we probably do. But if you think about it, why not?" added his sister, smiling.

"Martin," said Veronica, reassuringly. "You don't need to worry about your clothes or washing things, as we have enough spares to lend you."

The boy thought about it.

Veronica added, "Anyway, if you think about it, it doesn't matter when you go back to your own time. Zo why not enjoy a bit more time here?"

Martin, like his sister, was a bit unsure.

After a moment, he said, "Well, if Caroline says it's alright, I suppose it must be."

"Wunderbar!" said Manfred.

"Vell, that's settled then," said Veronica. "You are both staying for supper and tonight, you can each sleep in one of the castle's spare bedrooms."

Martin looked at his sister.

"Caroline," he said.

"Yes," she replied.

"That means we don't need to rush back today."

"That's right," she said, smiling.

"Cool!"

Veronica had taken the cake out.

Martin's eyes, lit up.

"Wow! Look at that," he said.

"Anyone for a piece of cake?" asked Veronica.

"Yes, please," said the boys, eagerly.

The two girls spent a relaxing afternoon by the side of the lake. They left the boys to their fishing. Caroline thought it was a wonderful experience, to just lay there and do absolutely nothing. Time seemed to fly by. Before they knew it, it was early evening.

Veronica suddenly sat up. Looking at her watch, she said, "I think it's time to go back. Dinner will be served at seven, and I don't want to be late for it."

Caroline replied, "Oh right! I must admit, I am a bit hungry now."

"Me too. We skipped lunch and while the cake was nice, it was not enough."

Veronica stood up and brushed her long skirt.

"Martin, Manfred," she said. "Can you pack up your things? We need to return to the castle, in time for dinner."

"All right. Coming," said Manfred, giving Martin the nod.

Once the boys had packed up their fishing gear, the children walked round the lake, towards the small hut on the castle side of the lake. The boys put their fishing rods in it. Then carrying a bucket, with the fish they had caught, headed into the vineyards with the girls.

While in them, Caroline said, "Veronica, I am happy we are staying the night at the castle tonight. Had I thought about it more, I suppose we could have stayed before."

Veronica, who was carrying the small picnic hamper, replied, "Vell, I did ask you."

"Yes, I know you did. But let's see how this all goes, shall we?"

"Of course!"

Further up the row of vines, she said, "I do love these vines, Caroline."

She replied, "Me too. But tell me, are these red or white grapes?"

"These will be white grapes. My father says that they make very good wine."

"Oh!"

At the end of the vineyard, the children walked through the rear gate of the castle garden. They ambled through it, up towards the castle, after what had been a fun relaxing afternoon, down by the lake.

In the castle, once they had all powdered their noses, the children walked into the dining room. A long table with about 20 chairs around it was in the centre.

"This is where we're eating this evening," said Veronica.

"Gosh, it's a long table," replied Caroline. "I hope we're not sitting at opposite ends. Otherwise, we'll have to shout at each other."

The girls laughed.

"Nein, I think we're sitting at the far end, opposite each other," added Veronica, who was looking at the places set at the table.

She went and rang a bell that was situated on one of the walls.

"What are you doing?" asked Caroline.

"I'm ringing for a servant."

"Why?"

"To let them know, we're ready to eat."

"Oh, I see."

"Where shall I sit?" asked Martin.

"Over there," said Veronica, pointing.

"Opposite me," said Manfred.

"Shall we sit down?" suggested Caroline.

"Yes do," said Veronica.

Once they had sat at the table, Caroline said, "Is there only us eating?"

"I think zo," replied Veronica. "There are only four places laid."

"So I see."

"My mother is in Vienna visiting her mother, and my father is at work in Trieste. Zo that leaves just us here."

"Uh-huh"

"We normally eat here alone. Though on the odd occasion we have eaten downstairs in the servant's quarters. But don't tell my mother that."

Just then, Ivan the butler and Katarina the housemaid came into the room.

"You rang, Miss Veronica," he said.

"Good evening, Mr Ivan. Yes, I did. We are ready to eat."

"Very good, Miss. I'll inform the cook that she can serve dinner."

He motioned to the housemaid, who left the room.

The children sat there for a moment. Martin and Caroline were looking around them. It was all so different from the castle in their time.

After a few moments of silence Caroline spoke.

"Ask a silly question, but how does the cook know when to serve our meal? I mean, we just walked in."

"Vell," replied Veronica. "We normally eat at seven. I believe the grandfather clock in the hall has just struck seven. Zo I think we are on time."

"Oh, right!"

After a few minutes, Katarina returned to the room, with one of the other house servants, Martina.

They wheeled in two trolleys of different dishes.

"Wow! This looks like a feast," said Martin, as the food was unveiled on the table.

"That's because it is a feast," replied Manfred. "It's *our* feast."

"Gosh! Do you normally eat so much food?" asked Caroline.

"Vell, we don't eat everything, if that is vhat you mean," said Veronica. "Have what you want. It's up to you."

The butler and housemaids put everything on the table.

Veronica then said, "Before we eat, let me say grace."

Caroline and Martin, looked at her.

"Grace?" said a surprised Caroline.

"Yes," replied Veronica. "We always say grace before we eat. It's normal."

"I see."

Caroline decided now was not the time to argue that they never said grace in their time. In fact, she couldn't remember *ever* saying grace in her time.

Veronica put her hands together. Manfred followed. Caroline and Martin rapidly copied them.

"Lord, we thank you for putting this food on our plates. We wish our guests a healthy and enjoyable meal. May the Lord make us truly thankful. Amen."

"Amen"

After a moment, the butler said, "Shall I serve the meal now, Miss Veronica?"

"Yes, thank you, Mr Ivan"

As he served Martin his meal, the boy looked at him.

"Excuse me," he said. "What is it?"

The butler smiled, and said, "It's grouse and pheasant, Master Martin."

"Grouse. Pheasant. Oh, I don't think I've ever eaten them before."

"Haven't you?" said Manfred.

"No"

"Oh, they're my favourite."

"Would you like some carrots, Master Martin?" asked the butler.

"Er, yes please."

The boy was delighted to be waited on.

Caroline and Martin watched the housemaids help serve the meal. Eating like this, was a whole new experience for them.

"What would you like to drink, Miss Veronica?" asked the butler.

"What do you have?"

"Tonight, we have fresh blackcurrant juice or fresh lemonade."

"I'll have the blackcurrant juice please."

The butler went round the table, offering everyone whichever one they wanted.

"Please do start," said Veronica.

"I will," said Martin, who tucked in.

As they ate their meal, Caroline said, "This is really great, Veronica. It's so different to what we normally eat for dinner."

"Really?"

"Sure! There's so much more of everything. I mean, there's enough here for a week."

"Oh, I don't know about a week."

She added, "Anyway, how can dinner be different?"

"What, in the castle, or when I am at home in England?"

"Er, both"

"Well in England, my mum cooks us a pizza, or maybe sausage, egg and chips. Whilst here, it's been grilled chicken or pork, with either rice or potatoes and salad. But it varies, as we are on holiday, so it's kinda different."

"Ja, I think I understand you," said Veronica, who added, "When we go on holiday the food is also different. Mind you, I much prefer Frau Nagy's cooking, or what our cooks prepares for us in our Vienna flat, to what we are served at boarding school. Sometimes the food there is ghastly."

"Yes, school dinners are nothing special, even in our time," added Caroline.

"Do you eat meals like this every day, Manfred?" asked Martin.

"Ja, but it depends what the cook is preparing."

"You have a good cook," said Caroline. "She's much better than my mum."

"Do you not have a cook?" asked Manfred, who was sitting next to Martin.

"My mum *is* the cook," he replied, laughing.

"Really?"

Once the meal was over, Caroline said, "Veronica that was delicious."

"Yes, it was." added Martin.

"Oh, I am glad you liked it," replied Veronica.

Ivan the butler was serving the coffee.

"Is it possible to have a tea?" asked Martin.

"Certainly, Master Martin"

The butler went over and got the teapot. He returned and poured his tea.

"Thank you," said Martin.

As they sat enjoying their coffee and tea, Veronica looked at the butler.

"Mr Ivan," she said. "That was a lovely meal. Vill you thank the cook for me?"

"Certainly, Miss"

"Oh yes, do," added Caroline.

Martin then said, "What do we do after this?"

Veronica looked at him.

"We go to the drawing room."

"Oh, right!"

A short while later, Veronica stood up and placed her napkin on the table.

Looking at the butler, she said, "Mr Ivan, we will go to relax in the drawing room now."

He replied: "Very good, Miss Veronica."

15

The Piano

After their evening meal, the children retired to the drawing room. Whilst Veronica closed the double-doors behind them, Manfred led the way.

"We can sit over here on the sofas," he said, going over to sit on one of them.

Martin joined him. Caroline and Veronica sat opposite them on another sofa.

"Veronica," said Caroline. "Do you normally come in here, like this, when we are not here?"

"It depends. Normally, yes. If we have guests - definitely."

"I see."

After a moment, Caroline said, "This is where we first met your mother and father."

"It was."

Veronica added, "I must say, that was quite an entrance."

Caroline laughed.

"Yes, I suppose it was. Your parents didn't quite know what to say."

"Mamma still calls you 'The London children'."

"Does she really?"

"But we're not from London. We're from Welwyn Garden City," added her brother.

"Yes of course we are, Martin. But it's easier to say London, as everyone knows where London is."

"That's dumb."

Veronica got up and wandered over to the grand piano that was standing on one side of the room. She opened the keyboard.

"Oh, can you play?" asked Caroline, who was watching her.

"Ja, of course," she replied. "What would you like to hear?"

For once, Caroline was stumped.

"Erm," she said. "Whatever you like? I don't think I know any of your music."

"What music do you like?" asked Veronica.

"Well, erm. I'm into rap and rock music."

"Oh, what's that?"

"It's erm…"

Caroline realised her friend would be none the wiser.

"Let's just say, it's probably a bit different to whatever you know."

"I like Beethoven, Mozart and Strauss," said Veronica. "Do you know these composers?"

"Not personally"

Veronica gave her one of her funny looks.

"Only joking!" said Caroline. "Yes of course I've heard of them. They're famous – even in our time."

Martin looked at his sister.

"I've never heard of any of them. Are they rock bands?"

"What's a rock band?" asked Manfred.

"It's a band that plays rock music."

"You mean they play music with rocks?"

Caroline laughed.

"No, not exactly, Manfred," she said. "It's mostly played on keyboards and electric guitars."

"I know a guitar," said Veronica. "I've never heard of an electric guitar."

"That's because they've not been invented yet."

"Oh, right!"

"What does it sound like?" asked Manfred.

Caroline replied, "It sort of sounds like, er…"

She imagined, she was a guitarist from Status Quo…playing, '*Caroline*'…

Caroline gave them a short demo, on her imaginary electric guitar.

"You call that music?" said Veronica, interrupting her. "It's awful."

She added, "Caroline, I like music like this."

Veronica started to play.

The others watched and listened.

"Wow! That's really good," said Caroline.

She got up and went over to join Veronica at the piano.

The boys, not wishing to be left out, rapidly joined them.

"Play us a bit more," said Martin, after he had stood there watching her.

He was fascinated by her ability to play the piano.

"What would you like to hear?" asked Veronica, suddenly liking the attention.

"Anything," replied Caroline. "Let's just say, it's all a bit different to the music we know."

"Don't they play this sort of music in your time?"

"Of course they do. But it's not my cup of tea."

"I zee."

Veronica took a deep breath, and said, "Vell, let's hope this is."

She started to play another tune.

The children stood around the piano, listening.

At the end of the short piece of music everyone clapped.

"You should become a pianist, Veronica," said Caroline. "You have a talent."

"I do?"

"Sure"

She added, "Not many people can play like that in my time. Most people can't even play an instrument."

"Really?"

"You know, I watch a lot of talent contests. But most of the people in them only sing. My mum is always moaning, saying the talent contests are not like what they used to be in her day, as no one today plays any instruments."

"Surely, you need instruments to sing along with?"

"Yes, I know you do. But in my time the instruments are on a computer. So it's really more like Karaoke."

"Karaoke?" asked Veronica, not understanding her.

"Sorry, it means singing along to the instrumental music in the background."

"Oh I zee," said Veronica.

"What's a computer?" asked Manfred. "Is it like that telephone that fell in the lake?"

"Er, sort of," said Caroline, giving Martin a filthy look.

She realised she was talking about the future again.

After a moment, she said, "Imagine singing along to a record."

"What's a record?" asked Manfred.

Caroline thought about it. She knew she should stop talking about the future, otherwise her friends would continue to bombard her with questions. In the end, she kept her answer short.

"My mum once told me, a record is a short way of saying a gramophone record. Have you heard of them?"

"A gramophone record," said Veronica, "Ja, of course. Why didn't you say? My parents have got a new Berliner gramophone that plays them."

"Have they really?"

"Ja, my mother got it in Berlin last year. It's the latest model."

"Oh!"

"She's not sure which is better: the gramophone or the phonograph."

"What's a phonograph?" asked Martin.

"It's a machine you can hear music on," said Manfred. "It's really good."

"Oh, why's that?"

"Because you can listen to music and you can record yourself on it."

"Really?" said Caroline, in amazement.

"Gosh! Have we surprised you?" asked Veronica.

"Yes, you have. I didn't think recording machines were around in 1912."

"If you like, I can show you."

"Oh, that would be great."

"We've got one of each, over there, in the corner. They're my parents pride and joy when they are entertaining their guests."

"Really?" said Caroline.

Veronica got up and walked over to where they were.

"We can listen to something on it. Then we can record something onto it."

"Cor! Can we?" suggested Martin.

"What do you want to say?"

"I've no idea," said Caroline.

"Maybe we should sing something?" suggested Veronica.

"Like what?" asked Martin.

"Let me think about that," replied Veronica. "However, before we record anything. I think we need to practise a bit first."

"Oh, that's a good idea," said Caroline.

Half an hour later everything was prepared. Veronica had brought the phonograph over to the piano.

"Are you ready?" she asked.

"We're ready," replied Caroline, smiling.

"Then we'll begin."

Caroline looked at her brother, and whispered, "Gosh! This is exciting – isn't it, Martin?"

There was a moment's silence. Everyone was excited about making the recording. After starting the phonograph Veronica quickly returned to the piano stool and sat down on it. She then spoke slowly and clearly.

"Good evening," she said. "This is Veronica Strauss speaking to you from the drawing room of Strauss castle in Straussburg, in the Austro-Hungarian Empire. It is August 1912 as I am recording this. I am with my brother Manfred and our two friends Caroline and Martin, who are from London, England. Say good evening, Manfred."

"Good evening"

"I am happy to introduce you now to Caroline."

Veronica pointed to her to say something.

"Hello," she said.

"And lastly, her brother Martin"

"Yes, I'm Martin," he said, giggling.

"Tonight," said Veronica. "We are going to sing you a song."

She started to play the tune she had selected on the piano.

The four of them, who were looking closely at the music sheets, started to sing.

At the end of the short recording everyone clapped and cheered.

"That was really fun," said Caroline, excitedly.

"Ja, I enjoyed it," added Veronica, smiling.

She got up to turn the recording off.

"Would you like to hear it?" she asked.

"Yes, of course," replied Caroline.

"Give me a minute, will you?"

Veronica fiddled with the phonograph machine, after which, their recording started.

"Wow, that's really cool," said Martin, giggling, as he listened.

"That's me!" added Manfred, who was delighted with the result.

Once the recording had ended, Caroline said, "Martin, do you realise we could be making one of the first ever records."

"Really?"

"Oh everyone does this, Caroline," said Veronica.

"Do they?"

"Yes, it's the latest craze."

"You never know, Martin. Our tune might even get to number one."

"I doubt it."

"What do you mean 'it might even get to number one'?" asked Veronica.

Caroline looked at her.

"Well, in our day we have a top twenty music chart. You know, the most popular music."

"Oh, I zee," replied Veronica.

"Do they still have phonographs and gramophones in the future?" asked Manfred.

Caroline looked at him.

"Er, sort of," she said. "However, new technology has replaced all of this."

"What is technology?" he asked.

Caroline realised she had to keep her explanation simple.

"It means, machines like these that have improved or have new ideas on them."

"Gosh! How fascinating," said Veronica.

"Manfred," Caroline added, "You'll have to keep the recording as a memory for the future."

"Ja, of course"

"My dad won't believe it when I tell him I made a record in 1912."

She added, "Is it possible to get a copy?"

"Erm," said Veronica. "I don't think that's possible, is it, Manfred?"

Shaking his head, he replied, "Nein, sorry. It's not."

"Pity!" said Caroline.

Manfred added, "Tell you what, I'll keep it in a safe place. One day, I might be able to copy it for you."

"Yes, one day…" replied Caroline.

Martin was feeling a bit restless. He wanted to do something different.

"Can we go in the garden?" he suggested.

"Ja, gut idea," added Manfred. "It's too hot in here. I fancy a game of cards."

"Oh, I like that idea…"

Veronica looked at Caroline.

"What about a stroll round the garden first? We can join the boys for a game of cards later?"

"Fine," she replied.

"Is that all right, Manfred?"

"Sure"

As they were about to leave the room the double-doors opened. Katarina the housemaid walked in.

"Ah, Katarina," said Veronica. "Could you get my boxes of candles out and put them in the garden, near the fountain, please?"

"Certainly, Miss"

The housemaid curtseyed.

"Thank you very much," added Veronica.

Caroline looked at her. She was wondering what her friend was up to.

"Don't worry. You'll soon see," said the girl, smiling at her friend…

Caroline and Veronica walked down the conservatory steps into the garden. The girls then wandered around the garden for a short while to walk off their meal, as the sun was setting. The boys, meanwhile, decided to go on an exploring game in the wooded area of the garden. Later, they returned to the castle and got out a couple of packs of cards from Manfred's bedroom. The boys then returned to the garden, where they helped the girls set up Veronica's surprise.

16

The Candlelit Lawn

Later in the evening, the children were sitting on the rear lawn at the back of the castle, near the fountain. They were playing cards. Many candles and lanterns surrounded them. This was Veronica's surprise to Caroline. It was now dusk.

Manfred placed his winning hand of cards on the grass.

He said, "There you are, four Kings, five, six, seven – the winning hand."

"Lucky sod," said Martin, gnashing his teeth.

Manfred had won, yet again.

"I think we'll call it a night with the cards, boys," said Veronica.

"Oh, all right," replied Manfred.

The children sat there in silence for a few moments.

"Listen to all those grasshoppers," said Martin.

After listening to them, Caroline said, "Yeah, it's kinda weird hearing them."

The silence was shattered by the sounds of some dogs barking nearby.

"That doesn't sound like grasshoppers," said Martin. "It sounds like some dogs, and they seem to be heading this way."

Out of the darkness of the night, and, coming from the lower slopes of the castle, the children could see a man approaching. With him were dogs on leads.

Martin was scared when he saw the big dogs approaching them. They were now barking madly.

"Oh don't worry, Martin," said Veronica. "It's only the head gardener doing his rounds."

"Good evening, Miss Veronica"

"Good evening, Miroslav"

"Just doing the rounds, Miss."

"Fine," said Veronica, stroking the dogs. "Caroline, Martin, these are Falco and Kaiser."

Veronica and Caroline went and stroked the dogs.

Martin was a bit wary. He stayed sitting where he was.

Manfred got up to stroke Kaiser. The dog barked and showed its teeth, causing Martin to jump.

"Don't worry, Martin," said Manfred. "He's quite friendly."

Veronica was patting Falco, who was licking her.

Martin got up and slowly walked over to the dogs. He stroked Kaiser, who befriended him with many licks. The boy's fear was over.

"Sorry to interrupt you, Miss," said the head gardener. "We'll be on our way."

"Very good, Miroslav – goodnight," said Veronica.

"Goodnight, Miss Veronica. Goodnight, everyone."

The head gardener and the dogs then disappeared into the darkness.

When it was quiet, Caroline said, "Nice dogs."

"Ja, I like them," replied Veronica.

"What type of dogs are they?" asked Martin.

"They're Hungarian Hounds," said Manfred, proudly.

"Are they?"

"We use them as hunting dogs."

"I see," said the boy.

Manfred was looking up at the moon.

"Martin," he said. "Do you think man will ever land on the moon?"

"He already has."

"Really?" replied Manfred, enthusiastically, "When?"

"Martin!" said Caroline, sternly giving him 'The Look'.

"Sorry," he added. "That's the future, Manfred."

"I understand," he replied.

Changing the subject, Caroline quickly said, "Veronica, I do love the way you've arranged these candles around us. They look so attractive out here. Where did you get the idea from?"

Veronica replied, "My art teacher is into candle decoration. Anyway, I always use candles. Not everyone in the village has electricity. Zo it's normal here. I like to use them like this in the garden, or in my room in the attic, especially on occasions like this."

"Oh, I see," replied Caroline. "Well, I think it's a brilliant idea."

Veronica was thinking about their holiday.

She said, "Are you looking forward to going to Trieste tomorrow?"

"Yes, of course," replied Caroline. "I'm very excited about it, actually."

"Zuper! Me too"

Martin joined in the conversation.

"This afternoon, Manfred was telling me about the inspection of the fleet."

"Was he?" replied Caroline.

"Yes," said Martin. "I'm really looking forward to seeing this."

Just then, Ivan the butler approached the children.

"Sorry to disturb you, Miss Veronica. But it is ten o'clock and it is time for you to retire."

"Yes, thank you, Mr Ivan," replied Veronica. "We'll be in shortly."

"Very good, Miss Veronica"

The butler added, "I'll take your empty glasses, if I may?"

"Certainly. Thank you, Mr Ivan," said Veronica.

"Er, should I start to blow the candles out, Miss?"

"Give us a few minutes will you, Mr Ivan?"

"Very good, Miss Veronica."

Once the butler had collected their glasses and taken them inside, Caroline asked, "Does the butler always tell you it's time for bed?"

Veronica replied, "When mamma is away, he is under strict instruction from her to do zo."

"Gosh!" said Caroline surprised. "Can you imagine that in our time, Martin?"

"We haven't got any servants, like they have," he replied.

"Haven't you?" said Manfred. "How can you manage without servants?"

"Easy," said Martin. "We've got a cleaning lady and my mum does the rest."

"Really?" said Veronica. "Gosh, I can't imagine my mother doing that. She doesn't even know how to boil an egg."

"You are joking, Veronica?" replied Caroline.

"No, I'm serious. My mother is useless on anything domestic. Only servants do domestic work."

"Not in our time they don't."

"Gosh!"

"In fact, in some households it's 50/50."

"'" asked Manfred.

Caroline explained, "It means, men and women each do 50% of the housework."

"Nein, that's impossible," replied Veronica.

"It's true."

"Amazing! It sounds unbelievable. Doesn't it, Manfred?"

"Ja"

Standing up, Veronica said, "Sorry to break up the party everyone. But it's time for bed."

Caroline got the idea.

"Pity!" replied Caroline. "Still, it's been a great day, Veronica, thank you."

"Not at all. I've really enjoyed it. I'm zo happy you are here."

"Tomorrow's another day."

"Yeah," said Martin. "We're off to somewhere called Trieste tomorrow."

Manfred added, "Ja, and we're going to see my dad's battleships."

17

Good Morning 1912

Caroline woke up in her bed and realised where she was. She knew she was in the castle, but her bed was different. Coincidentally, it was the same room as the one she had in her time. However, the furniture in it was rather different, to say the least.

At first, she thought it was one big dream. Then she realised it wasn't and that she really was in 1912, in a bed with a brass headboard and tailboard. She was quite excited knowing that her situation was, putting it mildly, rather unusual.

Getting up and dressed in one of Veronica's nightdresses, she walked round her bed, picked up her potty from the corner of the room and put it under the bed. Departing her bedroom she walked along the corridor, until she got to her brother's bedroom next door. After knocking at the door she went in.

"Martin, wake up," she said.

"I am awake," he replied, sitting up.

The boy was wearing one of Manfred's sets of pyjamas, including a pointed floppy hat.

"Do you know where we are?" she asked.

He replied, "We're in the castle, Caroline."

"Do you know what year it is?"

"Yes, it's 1912, why?"

"Well, I just wanted to be sure. You know, sometimes it feels like a dream, Martin."

"Yeah, I know what you mean," he replied. "It is kinda weird."

The boy jumped out of his bed.

"I even christened the potty," he said.

"Oh, so did I!" replied his sister, giggling.

They heard footsteps behind them. Looking up, they saw Manfred coming into the room.

"Morning, Manfred," said Martin, yawning.

"Good morning, Martin, Caroline," he replied. "Did you sleep well?"

"Yes, fine thanks," said Caroline, rubbing the sleep from her eyes.

"Veronica is already up."

"Is she?" replied Caroline. "What time is it?"

"It's ten to nine," said Manfred, smiling.

"Gosh! Is it really?"

"Yes"

"We'd better get ready, Martin. We've got a train to catch."

"Oh, don't worry. We've plenty of time."

"Any chance of a cup of tea?" asked Martin.

"Cup of tea?" said his sister.

Manfred replied, "Yes of course, Martin. I'll ring for one of the servants to bring you one."

"Can you?" asked the boy. "That sounds a cool idea."

"Don't be lazy, Martin," said Caroline. "You can have one at breakfast."

Manfred went to ring a bell, but before he did, Martin said, "Hang on, Manfred. On second thoughts, I'll wait till breakfast."

"It's up to you," he replied.

"No, leave it. It's okay."

"By the way, where is breakfast?" asked Caroline.

Manfred replied, "Where it normally is, in the dining room."

"Right!"

"Talking of which," he said. "The cook asked me to inform you that breakfast is at 9.30."

"Oh, well we'd better get washed and dressed," said Caroline, still yawning.

"Fine. Vell, I'll see you both at breakfast."

In the dining room of the castle, the four children sat at the long table.

"Before we start breakfast, I think we should say grace," said Veronica.

"Grace?" replied Martin, looking at his sister.

She mouthed 'grace', back to him.

The English children followed their friend's actions, of putting their hands together and lowering their heads.

Veronica coughed, and then said, "For what we are about to receive. May the Lord make us truly thankful. Amen."

"Amen," said everyone.

Looking over at the maid, Veronica said, "Katarina, we're ready to start breakfast."

"Very good, Miss. Please help yourselves."

Turning to her friends, Veronica said, "Caroline, Martin and Manfred. Please take whatever you want, from the breakfast selection that's over there on the sideboard."

"Thank you," replied Caroline. "Erm, I think I'll follow you, Veronica."

"Fine"

The children went up and helped themselves to breakfast.

"It's another feast," said Martin, as he looked at the selection of food on offer.

He added, "They haven't got any Corn Flakes, Caroline."

"Of course, they haven't, Dumbo. They haven't been invented, yet."

He stuck his tongue out at his sister, who returned the gesture.

"That'll do, you two," said Veronica.

"Yes, Mum," replied Martin, sniggering at her in his boyish way.

Once they had sat down at the table, the maid started serving the coffee and tea.

"For your information, Martin and Caroline," said Veronica. "You might be surprised to know that Corn Flakes *have* been invented."

"Have they?" said a surprised Caroline.

"When?" asked Martin.

Veronica replied, "They were invented in 1894, by a John Harvey Kellogg, somewhere in the United States."

"Really?" said Caroline.

"How do you know that?" asked her brother.

Veronica replied, "Because I read it in a newspaper in Vienna, Martin."

"Oh!" he replied, gormlessly.

"But we don't have them in this part of the world. We eat this sort of food."

"We call this continental breakfast," said Caroline.

"Do you? Why's that?"

"Erm, dunno. Probably 'cause it's eaten on the Continent."

"Oh, I zee vhat you mean."

"Well, I think the continental breakfast is very good," said Martin, as he wolfed down some bread and ham.

"I like it," replied Manfred.

"Your tea, Master Martin," said Katarina, to the boy, in German.

"Oh, thank you," he replied, also in German.

Caroline added, "It's a bit different to our breakfasts, Martin, eh?"

"I'll say," he replied, as he ate his sandwich.

"How can breakfast be different?" asked Manfred.

"Well," said Caroline. "In our time, the choice is a bit less and we don't eat it in this room."

"Oh, what room do you eat it in?" asked Veronica.

"In the kitchen," said Martin.

"Do you really?"

"Yes," said Caroline. "But not the kitchen you know. It's another smaller kitchen that's in our flat."

"In your flat? What do you mean?" asked Manfred.

"In our time, the castle is split into flats."

"Gosh!" replied Veronica. "How can that be zo?"

"I don't know, but it is."

"Zo, what is in this room?"

Caroline looked around it.

"Er, nothing"

"Nothing?" said Veronica. "How can that be?"

"Well, many of the rooms are all empty."

"Empty?"

"Yes"

"Zo, no one lives there?"

"Not that I know of. But to be honest, I don't really know. Mr Slavo lives in one flat. But as for the others, it's hard to say. We are on holiday, Veronica. How it really is, unfortunately I have no idea, sorry."

"No, it's fine, Caroline. I was just curious."

"Me too. That's why I love this castle."

Changing the subject, Veronica asked, "Are you looking forward to Trieste later, Martin?"

"Yes, I am," he replied. "It sounds a really cool place this Austrian Riviera."

"It is," said Manfred. "We go there every year."

"Do you?"

"Ja, we do. Don't we, Veronica?"

"Ja," she replied. "We normally stay with my aunt and uncle. But father sent a message saying, they are themselves on holiday in Paris this week. Zo he's trying to find us some alternative accommodation."

"Oh, I didn't know that," said Caroline, a bit alarmed.

"Don't worry. I only just found out myself. Ivan the butler got a telegram this morning about it."

"A telegram," said a fascinated Caroline. "Did he really?"

"Ja, I've got it here."

"Oh, can I see it?"

"Ja, of course," replied Veronica, getting it out.

"I've never seen a telegram before."

"Really?" said Veronica, giving her one of her funny looks. "But it's the fastest way to send a message."

Caroline laughed.

"Not in our time it isn't."

"Don't tell me," said Veronica, smiling. "It's on that machine that fell in the lake."

"Yes, that's right. We send instant messages on it."

"Do you really?" said Manfred, eagerly listening.

"Yes, we do," said Martin, smiling sweetly.

"Gosh! The future sounds interesting."

"Well," replied Caroline. "That's one way of looking at it."

Martin then asked, "Excuse me, is it possible to have some more tea, please?"

Katarina the housemaid, looked over and replied, "Certainly, Master Martin. Just a minute."

She walked round to him and poured the boy some more tea, before going round and giving everyone else some more coffee.

Martin was stirring his tea, when he looked up, and said, "Caroline, what time's the train we're getting later. I forgot?"

"It's at 13.58, Martin, and what are you?" said his sister, sounding like her mother.

"Forgetful," he replied, smiling.

They both laughed.

Manfred then asked, "Do we have time for a bit of fishing, Veronica?"

"Vell, not really. As you need to be back here before one."

"Why don't you go and play a game of football, Martin?" suggested his sister.

"Yeah, that sounds like a good idea. Can we do that, Manfred?"

"Fine," he replied.

"We need to be ready to leave at one thirty, Manfred," said Veronica. "Got that?"

"Ja, I've got that," he said, nodding.

"Gut," added Veronica, a bit more assured he had got it.

Turning to his friend, Manfred said, "Come on, Martin. Let's leave the girls to it."

"Okay," he replied.

As the boys got up, Veronica wiped her mouth with her napkin.

"Caroline," she said. "Let's go for a walk around the garden, shall we?"

"Yes, let's."

18

Leisure and Pleasure

After leaving the dining room, the boys went to Manfred's bedroom. It was a small room, with a metal bed on one side of it. On the other wall was a large wardrobe. Next to it was an old wooden chest of drawers. Manfred walked over to it and took out a hat.

"I've decided, I am going to take this with me to Trieste," he said.

"Are you?" replied Martin. "Why?"

"Because it's my favourite hat."

"I see."

"Do you like it?"

"It's alright."

The boy wasn't that particular. He just wanted to go into the garden for a kick about.

Manfred's hat was actually typical of what men and boys wore at folk festivals.

He said, "As you can see, it's got a nice long feather on it. That's why I got it."

"Oh!" said Martin, who was none the wiser.

Manfred located a football. Picking it up, he said, "Here, catch this, Martin."

He did, adding, "Come on then. Let's go."

Outside the front of the castle, Martin said, "We can play football here, Manfred?"

He replied, "We can do. But it might be better to go down to the meadow."

"Alright, but I normally play football here."

"Lucky, old you. Mamma doesn't like me playing here."

"Why not?"

"Because she thinks I might damage the flowers in the flowerbeds."

"Oh, I see," said Martin, laughing.

He added, "We haven't got that problem in our time, as there aren't any flowerbeds."

"Oh!" replied Manfred.

The boys dribbled the ball between each other, down towards the Eastern Terrace.

"We need to find a couple of logs, Manfred," suggested Martin, as he passed him the ball.

"What for?"

"To use as goalposts."

"Oh, that's a gut idea."

When the boys got to a table and chairs that were made from tree trunks, they sat down for a moment.

"I like it here," said Manfred.

"So do I," replied Martin.

"We sometimes have a picnic on this table, or afternoon tea with mamma."

Manfred decided to remove his hat. He placed it on the wooden table.

"We could have a picnic here," suggested Martin.

"Gut idea. Vell not today. We're going to Trieste later, remember."

"Yes, I'm looking forward to it."

"Me too"

Standing up, Manfred said, "Come on, Martin. Pass me the ball."

The boys resumed their game of kick about on the Eastern Terrace.

A short while later, the head gardener walked past the boys.

"Morning, Mr Miroslav," said Manfred.

"Morning, Master Manfred. Morning, Master Martin"

"Mornin'," replied the boy, waving at him.

During their game of football, a couple of the maids carrying baskets walked past the boys. They waved at each other.

"Where are they going?" asked Martin.

"It looks like they're going fruit picking in the Eastern Orchard."

"Oh, I see. Er, is that far from here?"

"No, it's next to the meadow."

The boys dribbled the ball towards the presentation field. This was where the folk dancing evening had taken place the previous weekend, during the 1912 Strauss annual summer garden party that the emperor himself had personally attended.

"We can play football here?" suggested Martin.

"Fine," said Manfred. "But the logs we need, are in the wood further down."

"Oh, this'll do for now. We can go there later."

"Suit yourself"

Once the girls had powdered their noses, they returned to Veronica's bedroom in the attic, where they picked up a couple of parasols from her large round white ceramic umbrella pot. Descending the attic stairs, once again, the girls made their way outside into the garden.

As they walked along the side of the castle, Veronica opened her parasol.

"It's a lovely day," she said.

"Yes, it is," replied Caroline, who opened hers.

"Just right for going to Trieste"

"Let's hope the train journey later, isn't too hot and stuffy."

"Oh, I am sure everything vill be just fine, Caroline. After all, we are traveling first class."

"Yes, that's true."

She added, "I don't think I've ever travelled first class, before."

"Haven't you?"

"No," replied Caroline, shaking her head.

"Come on," said Veronica, taking Caroline's hand. "I want to walk along my favourite walkways."

When the girls reached the fountain, in the rear garden of the castle, they looked out at the garden and vineyards in front of them.

"It's a wonderful view from here," said Veronica.

"Yes, it is."

The girls listened to the birds sing in the nearby trees.

"What sort of birdsong do you think that is?" asked Veronica.

"Oh, I've no idea," replied Caroline. "Martin is better at that sort of thing than me."

After a moment of silence, Veronica said, "I wonder where the boys are."

"Didn't they say they're playing football?"

"Oh, ja. You are right, they did. Maybe, we might bump into them on our walk."

Veronica started to walk to her right.

"Let's start over here, Caroline."

"If you like."

As the girls entered the walkway, Veronica closed her parasol.

"I don't think we'll need these, whilst we're under cover."

"No, probably not," replied Caroline, closing hers.

The girls walked slowly along the walkway that had some large green shrubs on one side of it and semi-dense forest on the other.

"It's much cooler here," said Veronica, sitting down on one of the many benches that were dotted around the castle gardens.

Caroline replied, "Yes, that's true."

After a moment, Veronica said, "Are these walkways here in your time?"

"Yes, as far as I know they are, why?"

"Vell, it's such a lovely garden. It would such a shame if they were destroyed."

"To be honest, Veronica, this bit of the garden is actually very overgrown."

"It's hard to imagine."

"Yes, I take your point," said Caroline, looking around her. "Martin and I call it 'thick jungle', as when we first got here, we fought our way through it."

"It's hardly jungle, Caroline."

"You haven't seen how thick it gets, in the future."

"You'll be telling me next, you saw lions and tigers in this jungle."

"Oh, I see great minds think alike."

"Don't tell me it's true. Is it?"

Caroline laughed.

"No, but that's what we imagined. My dad told us we might see a deer or a fox."

"Yes, you might or indeed a rabbit or two."

She stood up and brushed her long dress.

"Come on. Let's go down to the lower patio."

"Alright"

After leaving the presentation field, the boys dribbled their ball down a couple of garden paths to the meadow.

"Here we are," said Manfred, taking off his hat. "Oh, dam! I've lost my feather."

"Does it matter?" said Martin, looking at his friend's hat.

"Ja, of course it matters. It's the most important part of the hat."

"You're kidding."

Manfred looked at him, with his, 'I don't understand you' look.

Martin explained: "It means, you are joking."

"Nein, I'm not. I must find it. You can't wear this hat without its feather."

"Why not?"

"Because it doesn't look right without it."

"Manfred, it's only a feather. I'm sure we can find you another one."

"Nein, I must find *this* one. It goes with the hat."

The boy started to walk back towards the castle.

"Where are you going, Manfred?" asked Martin.

"To find the feather."

Martin followed his friend, in his quest to find his feather.

The boys retraced their steps along a walkway.

"It could be anywhere," said Martin, looking in front of him.

"Ja, it could," replied Manfred, who was determined to find his lost feather.

They searched the presentation field.

"It's not here," said Martin.

"Ja, I can see that," replied Manfred, who was annoyed with himself for losing it.

He walked on towards the Eastern Terrace, with Martin following on behind.

Manfred headed for the tree-trunked table, where they had been earlier.

"Found it," he said, delightedly.

"Where was it?" asked Martin.

"Under the table," said Manfred, picking up his beloved feather from under it. "It must have fallen off when we left here."

"It looks like it."

"Come on," said Manfred, holding his hat and feather tightly. "Race you to the meadow."

Martin picked up the ball.

"Here! That's not fair," he said, running after his friend. "You've got a head start."

When the girls reached the lower patio in the garden, they stood looking back towards the castle.

"You know, Veronica," said Caroline, "This walkway in front of us, is in the centre. Yet in my time it's all so overgrown. You don't know it's actually here."

"Really?"

"I didn't know the design of the garden was, like it is, till I saw it with you, during our first visit here."

"Gosh, how amazing!"

"No, magic actually!"

The girls laughed.

"Come on," said Caroline. "Let's go and find the boys."

"Ja, all right"

When the boys arrived at the meadow, they quickly located a couple of logs that Manfred knew were nearby in the forest. He went in goal. Martin began practising his shooting. He had just scored again; when he saw the girls emerge from the nearby garden walkway.

"Look Manfred! There's Caroline and Veronica," he said, after kicking the ball over to him.

Waving, he said, "Over here, Caroline."

The girls saw them and walked over.

"I thought I might find both of you down here," said Caroline.

Manfred replied, "It's a good place to play football, as it's away from preying eyes and interruption."

"Yes, I take your point."

She added, "Are you going to pass me the ball, Manfred?"

He did. Caroline passed it to Veronica, who kicked it to Martin.

"I thought you didn't like football, Veronica," said the boy.

"I don't. But this isn't really football, is it?"

"What is it then?" said Martin, kicking the ball back to Veronica.

"Vell, you can hardly have a game with just two players."

"Why not? I do, and there are four of us now."

Veronica decided she had had enough of this game she hated.

"I think I'll leave you three to it," she said, going to sit down on a nearby bench.

She opened her parasol.

"Oh come on, Veronica," pleaded Caroline, looking at her. "Come and join us."

"No, no, it's not my cup of tea. I don't like running in these shoes or dress."

"Yes, I must admit, it is not so simple."

Caroline kicked the ball towards Manfred, who was in goal. She scored.

"Goal!" yelled her brother.

Just then, some maids emerged from the nearby orchard. They were each carrying a basket that had covers over them. Veronica spotted them and waved. The maids waved back.

"Katarina, Martina," said Veronica, beckoning them over.

The game of football stopped, as the children gathered around the maids.

"What have you got in there, Katarina?" asked Veronica.

"Cherries, Miss. We just picked them in the orchard."

"May I have a couple?"

"Yes, Miss. Help yourself"

"Thank you"

"Can I have some?" asked Manfred.

"Have as many as you like, Master Manfred."

The maids offered them around. Everyone took a handful each.

"Thank you," said Caroline, as she popped a couple in her mouth.

"Not at all, Miss," replied the housemaid, smiling.

"Umgh…these are really nice, Veronica."

She replied, "Yes, they are."

"Maybe we could take some with us to eat on the train journey?"

"Oh, that's a gut idea."

Once the boys had taken some more cherries, the maids said, "We'd best be going back to the castle, Miss Veronica. We've got other jobs to do."

"Ja all right, Katarina. Thank you for the cherries."

"Our pleasure, Miss"

As the maids departed, the three children resumed their game of football.

Sometime later, Veronica decided she wanted to continue her walk.

"Caroline," she said, getting up. "I think we should leave the boys to it."

"Oh, must we?"

Caroline was quite enjoying herself, even though she was terribly hot running around in her long dress.

"I would like to walk on, up this walkway," said Veronica, pointing with her parasol.

Caroline didn't wish to offend her friend. She decided to go with her.

"Martin, I'm leaving."

"Yeah, alright"

"See you later, boys," she said, giving them a girlie wave.

"And don't be late back, Manfred," said his sister.

"We've got till one, right?"

"Ja"

The girls walked back towards the castle, along another covered walkway that ran along the outer edges of the castle's garden.

"This is a real English country garden," said Veronica.

Caroline replied, "Yes, I must admit, it does look rather English in its style."

She wasn't particularly into gardens. But she knew this one was special.

A little further up the walkway, she said, "Are there many English gardens in the Austro-Hungarian Empire?"

"Erm, I've no idea. I don't think there are. I do know that my father brought in a top landscape gardener from England, especially to design the castle gardens, like you zee."

"Really?"

"Ja, as he wanted an English-style garden."

"It looks like the landscape gardener did a good job."

"Ja, I think zo."

Ahead of them, on the tree-lined covered walkway, the girls could see the head gardener, two of his assistants and a ladder.

"What are you doing, Mr Miroslav?" asked Veronica.

"We're repairing the fence, Miss."

"Oh, I zee."

"Need to keep the castle secure from thieves."

"Indeed! Vell, carry on the good work."

"Ve vill, Miss."

The girls waved, as they walked on.

"Pity they don't do that in our time," said Caroline.

"Don't they?" said Veronica.

"Veronica, the place is falling down. The garden isn't managed, like it is now. It's totally overgrown. No one manages things, like repairing fences or maintaining the garden, like your gardeners do now. You'd be absolutely shocked."

"Ja, I probably would be. Still, let's not think about that now. Come on…"

On reaching the Eastern Terrace, Caroline said to her friend, "Let's go over here."

"We can sit at that table," suggested Veronica.

"That sounds like a good idea, as I need to chill a while."

Veronica looked at her, in her strange way: "Chill?"

"It means relax."

"Oh, right! Vell, I do too."

The girls sat down at the small round tree-trunked table and chairs.

After a moment of silence and of listening to the birds in the trees, Veronica said, "It is clever how they made these tables and chairs, don't you think, Caroline?"

"Yeah, I suppose it is."

"I like to relax here and talk to my mother. She likes it here."

"How is she?"

"Mamma? Oh, she's the same as ever."

The girls sat under the trees relaxing for a while. They were enjoying the moment together. Veronica then glanced at her watch.

"Gosh! Look at the time," she said, surprised.

"What time is it?" asked Caroline.

"It's nearly noon. I suppose, we'd better go back to the castle. I need to powder my nose and double-check we have everything for the journey ahead."

"Yes that seems like a good idea."

The girls got up from their viewpoint at the wooden table and chairs that were near the stone wall, which surrounded the edge of the Eastern Terrace. Both had been admiring 'the presentation and entertainment area' of the garden. In reality, this was just a large sloping rectangular piece of lawn, which occasionally had functions held on it.

A bird chirped in a tree nearby, as the girls walked gracefully under the shade of the tall old oak trees on the Eastern Terrace, towards the rear of the castle garden and the conservatory.

19

Your Train Miss

Veronica glanced at her watch, as the four children departed her bedroom in the attic. They walked down the left wing of the castle towards the front entrance. They were luggage free, as Ivan the butler had already taken their luggage and put it next to the large old grandfather clock in the hall.

As they walked in, the grandfather clock struck one thirty. Three of the servants had assembled nearby; Ivan the butler, Katarina the housemaid and Frau Nagy the cook.

"Have you got everything, Miss Veronica?" asked the housemaid.

The girl replied, "Ja, I think zo."

"I hope you have a pleasant journey to Trieste, Miss," said the butler.

"Thank you, Mr Ivan"

The housemaid then said, "Try to behave, Master Manfred, and don't get into any trouble on your holiday. Is that clear?"

He replied, "Don't worry, Katarina. I vill be on my best behaviour."

The maid smiled.

Veronica looked at her friends and then at the clock.

"Gut," she said. "Vell, we'd better go now, if we want to get that train."

The cook stepped forward.

"Miss Veronica," she said. "Here are your food packs for the journey that you asked for."

She replied, "Oh, thank you, Frau Nagy."

"Not at all, Miss"

Caroline added, "You've got it all organised, Veronica."

"Of course! We don't want to starve, do we?"

"Er, no," she replied, feeling rather stupid.

Signalling their departure to Mr Ivan, the butler went to open the front door for them.

He said, "I took the trouble to ask Miroslav to prepare one of the horses and carriages for you, Miss."

Veronica replied, "Oh, that's very thoughtful of you, Mr Ivan. Thank you."

"Not at all, Miss," he added, smiling.

The butler hailed the horses and carriage that was waiting nearby, in front of the castle. The head gardener drove it up towards the covered entrance area.

"Wow! Are we going to the station in that?" said Martin, as it drew up alongside the front door.

"Yes, we are, Martin," said Veronica, smiling at him.

"That's really cool."

"Yes, it is rather," said Caroline, a tad surprised.

The horses and carriage pulled up outside the main front door of the castle.

The driver jumped off the vehicle, and said, "Good afternoon, Miss Veronica."

She replied, "Good afternoon, Mr Miroslav."

"May I take the luggage from you all?"

"Certainly"

The butler helped him sort the luggage. While they did, the children climbed into the carriage. Its leather seats the English children simply adored.

"Gosh! This is very posh," said Caroline to Martin.

"Yes, it is. We must do this again, Caroline," he replied, thoroughly enjoying the moment.

With everything loaded, the driver took his position on the carriage. Cracking his whip, they departed. As the horse and carriage went around the fountain and headed out of the castle, the children all waved to the servants, who waved back.

The cook whilst waving, said quietly to Katarina the housemaid, "You know, there's something funny about those children. It's almost as if they're not from this time."

The housemaid replied, winking, "Ja, I know vhat you mean. I hear them say things I've never heard of. I think it's the magic of this castle once again."

At the station, the horse and carriage pulled up. The children got off the carriage, while Miroslav unloaded their luggage and carried it onto the platform. Nearby, other people were waiting for the train.

Caroline was wearing one of Veronica's old dresses. Martin was in another of Manfred's pair of shorts. The girl felt like they all looked like brothers and sisters, dressed like they were, as she looked at them standing there.

In the distance a whistle blew. The train came into view, as it rounded the bend. The steam engine looked magnificent, as it approached the halt. Its line of smoke from its chimney, clearly visible, as it trailed above the train.

"Wow! Look at that," said Martin.

"Yeah, it is rather cool," replied Caroline.

"Are we going all the way to Trieste, on this train?" asked Martin to Veronica.

"Nein," she replied. "We will change trains in Vienna."

"Oh, I see," he said, watching the steam engine slowly pass him.

The train stopped just in front of them. Its smoke and steam going everywhere, including covering the children. Caroline and Martin found the moment very exciting.

"Come on, Caroline. Let's get on?" suggested Veronica.

"Allow me, Miss," said Miroslav.

He lifted the luggage aboard, putting it on the overhead racks for them.

"Thank you," said Caroline, in German.

When everyone was seated and after Miroslav had jumped off, Veronica closed the door. She opened the window and sat down opposite Caroline. The boys were sitting by the window.

The stationmaster blew his whistle and waved his flag at the train driver. With steam gushing out around its wheels, the steam train little by little, began edging its way out of the station halt, blowing its whistle in the process.

As it gradually speeded up, the children waved madly at Miroslav. He was now standing by the horse and carriage waving back at them. The train then disappeared round the bend and into the forest.

Sometime later in the train carriage, Veronica looked over at her best friend.

She said, "You did remember to bring the magic key with you, Caroline?"

"Er," she replied, while thinking about it for a moment.

The girl suddenly went rather red and looked shocked.

"Oh my god," she said, slowly. "I think I've left it on the top of your dressing table, Veronica."

"Did you?" she replied, suddenly looking equally worried.

She then said, "What are we going to do?"

"Is there a problem?" asked Manfred.

"Well, there could be," said Caroline. "The thing is, we're not sure whether the magic key will let us go to Trieste, or not."

"It's a bit late now. We're halfway there."

"Vell, we're not halfway," said Veronica. "But I know vhat you mean."

"So what are we going to do?" asked Caroline.

Veronica was thinking.

"Are we going back for it?" asked Manfred.

"Hardly," said Veronica. "I suppose, we could get off at the next stop and go back. But I am not sure what time the next train is. Anyway, I don't think Papa will be too happy if we fail to turn up in Trieste on time. Do you?"

"You've got a point."

Veronica had a thought.

"Maybe, Caroline and Martin are going to disappear in front of us and return to their own time?"

The three of them laughed.

Martin was listening. He hadn't said a word throughout their banter.

Veronica had noticed.

"Is everything all right, Martin?" she asked.

The boy smiled.

Everyone was now looking at him.

He put his hand in his pocket and produced the magic key.

Dangling it in front of his sister, he said, "What are you, Caroline?"

"Forgetful," she replied.

They all burst into laughter, including Martin, who had burst into his wicked laugh.

"You are naughty, Martin," said Veronica, teasing him.

He replied, "I know. But it's fun. Mind you, had I *not* picked it up, we could have been in trouble."

"Ja, you are right," added Veronica. "Vell, let's hope this magic key lets us enjoy this journey, eh?"

"Anything could happen, Martin," said Caroline, mightily relieved her brother had rescued the situation.

"Yes, I know," he said, smiling at her.

"Why don't you keep it in your handbag, Caroline?" suggested Veronica.

"Good idea," she said. "May I, Martin?"

"Sure," he replied, handing the key to her. "But don't lose it this time."

The train journey took them via Budapest and onwards again towards Vienna. During this part of the journey, Veronica decided to root in her small handbag. She got out a pink notebook and a pencil. She started to write.

"What are you doing?" asked Caroline, who had been looking out of the window.

Veronica replied, "Let me finish writing this down. Then I'll explain."

"Oh, right"

Once she had finished, Veronica said, "As we've got a bit of time to spare, I thought it a gut idea to jot down some dates. Zo you will know when to visit us in the future."

"Oh, that's a good idea," said Martin.

"For example, Christmas and Easter"

"Well," said Caroline. "I know when they are."

"Ja," replied Veronica. "But there are some other dates that might interest you."

"Like what?"

"Like my birthday"

"Which is?"

"The twentieth of September"

"Let me see," said Manfred, leaning over to look at what his sister had written. "Why have you written the first of November?"

"Because I think it's an interesting date."

"Is it?"

"Ja"

Manfred thought about it.

"Isn't that when we visit the cemetery?"

"Ja, that's right," replied Veronica.

"But it's boring visiting all those graves."

"Vell, I thought it might interest Caroline."

She was looking at them both, wondering what an earth they were talking about.

"Well go on then, Veronica," she said. "Explain to me, whatever you're going to tell me."

"Ja, all right," she replied, clearing her throat. "The first of November is known as *the Day of the Dead.*"

"Is it?"

"Ja. It's the day we visit our dead relatives in the graveyard."

"Do you?"

Veronica looked at her friend.

"Don't you visit your relative's graves on this day, in your country?"

Caroline laughed.

"No, you're joking, right?"

"Nein"

"I don't think I've visited any of my dead relatives."

"Why ever not?"

"Er, dunno?"

After a moment, she said, "I think one of my grans is buried in Birmingham and one granddad was cremated in Southampton. Neither of which is close to where I live. So I guess that's why we don't go there. You know I've never really thought about it, till now."

"Oh, I zee."

She added, "We always visit our relative's graves."

"Why?"

"It's our tradition."

"Funny tradition," said Martin.

"May I see the list?" asked Caroline.

"Sure! You can have it," said Veronica, tearing it out from her notebook and giving it to her.

She added, "Caroline, I made it especially for you."

"Thanks," she replied, looking at it. "What's this 'Name day'?"

"It's the day when you celebrate your name."

"You mean, like your birthday?"

Veronica replied, "Ja, that's right. It's actually the day your name is on the calendar. We celebrate both our birthday and our name day."

"Do you?"

"Ja"

"So, when is your name day?"

"It's on the twelfth of July."

"What about yours, Manfred?"

"Mine is on the twenty-eighth of January."

"How do you celebrate it?" asked Caroline.

"We have a party."

"Do you?" said Martin.

He added, "We should do that, Caroline?"

"Yeah we should, as I wouldn't mind two parties."

Looking at the list a bit more, she looked up, and said, "Wait a minute, Veronica. This is all very well you giving me this list of dates.

But you have to remember that the chances of Martin and I visiting you again, are, to say the least, pretty slim. What we are doing is not normal. It's…"

"Magic," said Martin, smiling through his teeth.

"Exactly!"

"Fine," added Veronica. "I was just trying to be helpful."

She was a bit peeved by her best friend's comments.

"Look," said Caroline, smiling. "I'll put it in my handbag, just in case."

The steam train continued its journey west. Its steam rising above the train in an elegant manner, as it chuffed its way across the lowlands near the river Danube, towards its end destination of Vienna.

20

The Waiting Room

In the early evening, the steam train arrived in the Austro-Hungarian capital of Vienna. It pulled into Vienna South railway station, letting out huge amounts of steam and smoke, as it arrived at the platform. The children could see the imperial grandeur of the station terminus, as they got off the train.

Some porters advanced towards them.

"May we be of service, Miss?" one asked, in German.

"Yes, you could," replied Veronica. "We are going to Trieste. But we've got about two hours to wait for our train. Could you take our luggage to the waiting room, please?"

"Certainly, Miss," replied the taller one.

"Thank you"

"Not at all, Miss"

He signalled to the other porter, to assist him load up their luggage. Once this was done, the children walked on down the platform with their luggage, following the many other arriving passengers.

"It's a bit different to our time," said Martin, as he walked alongside the luggage.

"What do you mean?" asked Manfred.

Martin replied, "I have to carry my own luggage."

"Do you?" asked Manfred.

"Yes"

132

"Don't you have porters in England?" asked Veronica.

Caroline laughed. "You mean, like this? Cor, you're joking!"

"Gosh!" said Veronica. "And I thought things would have improved, over time."

In the busy, huge, waiting room, with chandeliers that seemed to hang down forever, the children found themselves a spare coffee table to sit at. Smoke filled the air all around them, as passengers sat drinking their beers or coffees. Travel and news of what was happening in the Austro-Hungarian Empire, could be heard all around the room.

With everyone seated, Veronica signalled the porters to leave the luggage next to them. She then gave the porters a coin each.

"Thank you, Miss," they said, in gratitude.

The room was packed with people from all over the empire; all going here, there and everywhere. Yet for a moment, each seeming to have a brief encounter with someone, in the railway stations waiting room.

A smoke-filled bar area was on one side of the vast room, where tea, coffee and cakes were being served, as well as alcoholic drinks. Waiters rushed round taking orders and delivering drinks to customers. One such waiter arrived at the children's table.

"Can I take your order, Miss?" he asked.

"Oh, yes," replied Veronica. "Would anyone like a drink?"

"I'd like an orange juice, please," said Caroline.

"Could I have a cup of tea?" asked Martin.

"Manfred?"

"A lemonade, please"

Veronica turned to the waiter.

"Could we have two lemonades, one orange juice and a tea with milk, please?"

"Certainly, Miss"

While the waiter went to get the drinks, Caroline and Martin looked around them. They were fascinated by how everything looked. It was like being in another world.

Martin then said, "Caroline, I need the toilet."

"Oh I think it's over there, Martin," replied Veronica, pointing. The boy got up and walked towards it.

"I need to go as vell," said Manfred, following him.

The girls started to chat, whilst enjoying the atmosphere.

"Have you been to Vienna before?" asked Veronica.

"No, it's my first time," replied Caroline.

"Really?"

She added, "Vell, there's a lot more to see than just this railway station."

"Yes, I gather that," added Caroline, smiling.

Veronica was thinking.

"Perhaps, next time you come to visit me, I can show you around Vienna?"

"Oh, that would be nice."

"We could go shopping or to the park."

"Yes, that's a good idea. But we can only do that, if the magic key will allow it."

"Vell, it got you here. Zo why not?"

"Yes, that's true."

"Had I thought about it more, Caroline, we could have stopped off here, en route to Trieste."

"Never mind. There's always next time."

"Ja, indeed"

After a moment, Caroline said, "Veronica, didn't you say you lived here in Vienna, as well?"

"Ja, I do. I go to school here. My father has a large flat in the centre of Vienna that I also live at."

"Oh, right! Is it near this station?"

"Er, quite near. It's a short tram ride or horse cab ride away, why?"

"Well, I just wondered, seeing as we met at the castle. That's all."

Veronica thought about it.

"Ja, I understand you. Vell, when I am at school, I live here in Vienna. I use the train to go to the castle at weekends and during school holidays."

"Oh, I see."

Caroline added, "So I take it you know this station quite well?"

"Ja, quite vell. I come here a lot, actually. I like to wait in here, especially if I just miss a train. Sometimes, I have to wait an hour or more for another."

"I'm surprised your mother allows you to travel to the castle on your own."

Veronica laughed.

"Vell," she said. "I usually travel with Manfred. We used to travel with one of the servants. Manfred still does, as mama says he is far too young to travel on his own. Now I am older, she lets me travel alone."

"Aren't you afraid of travelling on your own?"

Veronica shook her head: "Nein. I normally travel in a first class compartment that is full of people, just to be sure."

"Oh, right!"

The girls watched a family sit down near them. An old couple got up and departed the table opposite them.

"We must come here again, Caroline," said Veronica. "Then I can show you exactly where I live in Vienna."

"Oh, yes. I'd like that."

"We could also go to the famous Vienna Riding School, or even see a show together."

"That would be excellent."

Veronica was thinking fast.

"If you come in February, we could go and watch the Vienna Ball. Come to think about it, if you decide to visit me at Christmas time, we could go to the New Year's Eve Ball together."

"Oh, what's that?" asked Caroline.

Veronica looked at her in her funny way, then explained.

"It's where high society, especially young ladies and gentlemen, come together to dance the Vienna Waltz. The young ladies wear ball gowns, the young men wear evening suits. It's very glamorous."

"Really?" replied Caroline.

Veronica looked at her.

"You must have heard of them," she said. "They're the talk of the Empire. The Balls are *the* high society events of the year, in Vienna."

Caroline shook her head.

"No," she replied. "I can't say that I have. Have you been to them?"

"My father took me to see the Vienna Ball last year. We sat in one of the boxes at the Royal Opera House. It was really good. I can't wait to go there again."

"Well," said Caroline smiling. "Maybe we should go?"

"Ja that would be great. Can you dance?"

"Er, yes, I can. But not that type of dancing."

Veronica looked at her.

"What type of dancing can you do?"

Caroline had to think about that. She suddenly realised, she could only jig and bop around at the local disco.

"Erm," she said. "In my time, I don't really dance like you do The Waltz. I do my own thing."

"What do you mean?" asked Veronica.

"Well, I dance on my own."

"But you need a partner?"

"Not in my time," replied Caroline, smiling. "Like I say, I just do my own thing."

"How do you mean?" asked Veronica.

Caroline got up.

"Like this," she said.

She did a brief demonstration of her dancing skills. As she danced, she imagined she was listening to her new iPod. Afterwards, she sat down again.

Veronica looked at her, giving her one of her funny looks.

She said, "I worry about you sometimes, Caroline. It's as if we are from two different worlds."

"Well," replied Caroline. "I suppose we are."

The girls laughed.

The waiter arrived with the drinks. Veronica paid him for them. As the girls started to sip their drinks, the boys returned and sat down again at the coffee table.

"Where've you been, Manfred?" asked Veronica.

"Sorry," he said. "Martin and I had a quick look round."

"Your drinks are here."

"Thanks," replied Manfred, taking his and gulping it down.

"It's a big room," said Martin, sipping his tea.

"It's a big station."

"This is Vienna South railway station, Martin," said Veronica.

"So I see," he said.

Having finished their drinks, Caroline leaned across to her friend.

"Veronica," she said quietly. "I need to powder my nose."

"Oh, zo do I."

Veronica stood up.

"Manfred, Martin," she said. "Caroline and I are just going to powder our noses. Wait here and look after the luggage. Don't let it run off. Got that?"

"Got it," said Manfred, groaning and getting the point.

Once the girls had powered their noses, Veronica took Caroline into the main entrance of Vienna South railway station.

"Wow, look at this. It's spectacular," said Caroline, looking around in awe.

"I thought you might like it," replied Veronica.

She walked over to a huge map that was high up on a wall.

"This is what I wanted to show you," she said. "It is a map of the Austro-Hungarian Empire. I think it's got every railway station in the Empire, on it."

"It's a pretty cool map," replied Caroline, looking up at it.

"As you can zee," said Veronica, "Trains depart from here to the furthest corners of the Empire. From here they go to Prague, Lemberg, Cracow and Budapest. It's also a big departure point for the Austrian Riviera, including Trieste. If you look, the railway map stretches right across to Nový Sad and Braşov."

"So I see," said Caroline.

She added, "I've heard of Cracow. But I have to admit, I've never heard of Lemberg, Nový Sad, or Braşov."

"Vell, Lemberg is the Austro-Hungarian's fifth biggest city."

"Is it?"

"Yes! And as for Nový Sad, I'm sorry, I don't know much about it, other than a lot of Hungarians and Serbs live there."

"And Brașov?"

"It's in Transylvania."

"Transylvania? That's where Dracula comes from, isn't it?" Veronica laughed.

"Ja, that's right."

Caroline was still looking up at the large map on the wall.

"So, from what I can see, yours is actually quite a big Empire?"

"It is," replied Veronica, adding, "But not as big as your British Empire. Let's just say, it's different."

Veronica looked oddly at her friend.

"Don't they teach you any of this in school, Caroline?"

"You might find this funny, but no. We're not even taught about the British Empire."

"You are joking?" replied Veronica.

"It's true. We're not," said Caroline, laughing.

"Gosh! It sounds unbelievable."

"Veronica," replied Caroline. "Honestly, I haven't a clue about any of this. You are my history and geography teacher here."

"I zee."

Caroline was now looking at another large map that was next to the one she had been looking at on the wall. On it was a map of Europe in 1912. The Europe she knew, was, to say the least, different.

"That's a country map of Europe, showing all the major railway destinations, like Berlin, Moscow, Vienna and Paris," said Veronica, explaining it.

"Fascinating," replied Caroline.

Veronica looked over at the huge clock that sat on one wall.

"Caroline," she said. "We have a few minutes. Let's visit the tourist information office. They might have some information on Trieste."

"Oh, that's a good idea," replied Caroline.

Veronica and Caroline soon located the Vienna Tourist Information Office. Lacing its windows and walls were posters of the Austrian Riviera. Going in, they went up to the counter. Some men in railway uniforms were serving some passengers. At one counter, a man smiled at them.

"Can I help you, Miss?" he asked.

"Oh, ja. Gut evening," replied Veronica. "Do you have any information about Trieste, on the Austrian Riviera, please?"

"Ah, the Austrian Riviera," he replied, with a light in his eye.

He added, smiling, "Ja, ve do."

Veronica added, "Ve're on our way there, in about half an hour."

"Are you?" the man replied. "Vell, in that case, I won't keep you a moment."

He went into another room and returned carrying some pamphlets.

"Is this what you might be looking for, Miss?" he asked, putting them on the counter.

Veronica and Caroline quickly flicked though them.

"Ja, this looks fine," said Veronica. "May I take them?"

"Of course," the man replied. "Vill there be anything else, Miss requires?"

"No, that will be all, thank you," replied Veronica.

The salesman smiled, and added, "Vell, have a lovely trip to Trieste."

"Don't worry. Ve will."

"Bye," said Caroline, in German, waving in her girlie way, as she departed with Veronica.

Back at the suitcases, Martin said, "We thought you two had got lost."

"Not lost," replied Veronica. "We just went to the tourist information office."

"What for?" asked Manfred.

"To get some information on Trieste. I thought it might be interesting, to look at the pamphlets we got, on the train."

"Oh I zee," replied the boy, who wasn't particularly interested in her reply.

Changing the subject, Martin said, "Have you still got the magic key, Caroline?"

She replied, "Yes, hopefully I have, why?"

"Well, you forgot it earlier and I'm just checking you've still got it."

The girl decided to get it out. Reaching into her small handbag, which she had borrowed from Veronica, she took it out.

"Look, Veronica," said Manfred. "It's turned green."

"Oh, ja! Zo it has."

"Wunderbar!"

"Why's it turned green, Caroline?" asked her brother.

"No idea. But probably because we're a distance away from the castle."

"Really?"

"Honestly – I've no idea. The key has a mind of its own."

As she popped the magic key back in her handbag, Veronica looked at her watch.

She said, "I think it's time we departed."

Getting up, Veronica added, "Boys, wait here a moment. Caroline and I will go to find a porter or two, to help us with this luggage."

Outside on the main station platform, a mass of people rushed around them. Various steam trains sat at the platforms. Steam and smoke filled the air. Caroline and Martin found it all tremendously exciting.

A station announcement said over the tannoy system, "The 21.30, Riviera Express train to Trieste, departs from platform 12."

"That's our train," said Manfred.

"Ja, it is," added Veronica.

The four children followed the porters onto the platform, where Martin stopped to look around him. He found it exciting to see so many steam trains together in one place.

"Hurry up, Martin," said Caroline. "I don't want to miss the train."

"Don't worry. I'm here," he said, running after her.

Once they had located their wagon, everyone got on. Veronica got the porters to put the luggage in the overnight cabin, she had thoughtfully pre-booked.

With everything sorted, the children looked out of the window in the corridor. Their eyes were glued to the stationmaster outside. The man was looking at his large watch that was attached to its gold chain. He walked up and down the platform, near them.

After a few minutes, the stationmaster blew his whistle and waved his coloured flag at the driver. The steam engine released a huge amount of steam and smoke that spread all around the roof of Vienna South railway station. The giant wheels on the engine roared into action. Smoke bellowed from the steam train's chimney, before its whistle blew. It then slowly edged its way along the platform and headed out of the station.

21

The Riviera Express

During the night, the Riviera Express steam train meandered its way south westwards along the Austrian Southern Railway, through the mountains, valleys and plains, stopping at various stations en route.

Caroline woke up, to see the train crossing death-defying valleys and passing through unlit tunnels. The smoke filling the tunnels, meant that the windows had needed to be kept shut or the compartment would fill with smoke and soot.

She looked across at Veronica, who was in the top bunk opposite. She was wide-awake and was looking over at Caroline.

"Gut morning," she said, quietly.

"Morning, Veronica," Caroline replied, in a whisper.

"Did you sleep vell?"

"Yes, thanks"

With the boys still sleeping, as the train journeyed onwards, towards Trieste, the girls just laid in their beds, watching the spectacular mountain scenery pass by. Later, with Manfred and Martin awake, the children worked out how to fold the beds away and how to reassemble the seats. Once this was done, as they sat there looking out of the train window, there was a knocking at the compartment door.

A man's voice said, "Tea, coffee, breakfast?"

Veronica got up and opened the door.

A train guard greeted her.

"Gut morning, Miss," he said.

"Oh, gut morning," she replied.

"Could I offer you, tea, coffee, cappuccino, or croissants?"

"Oh, that seems like a good idea," said Veronica, smiling at him.

Turning to the others, she said, "Caroline, what would you like?"

"Could I have a croissant and a cappuccino, please?"

"Martin?"

He replied, "A cup of tea and a croissant, thanks."

"Manfred, what do you want?" asked Veronica.

He replied, eagerly, "I'll have a coffee and a croissant."

Veronica ordered the breakfast and paid the train guard.

In the compartment the children ate their breakfast.

Later, as the steam train passed through the first of several small tunnels, the driver blew its whistle. Smoke filled the outside of the tunnel. The compartment, once again, became pitch black. Caroline's imagination began to wander…

She imagined they were playing the game 'Whodunit?'

The girl could visualise the train guard, who had served them breakfast earlier, knocking at the door again. After Veronica had opened the door, he entered the compartment to collect the breakfast plates that were on the table. As he walked in the door, the train had entered another tunnel. The train compartment, once again, turned pitch black.

One minute, the children were all sitting together in the compartment, minding their own business. The next minute, after they had passed through the tunnel, they found the train guard lying dead on his front in the compartment, with a knife in his back; his white shirt covered in blood from the wound.

On seeing the situation in front of them, the children had all started screaming… Caroline's mind continued wandering… she could hear Veronica screaming at the train guard, who lay dead on the floor in front of her…

In those few moments that passed, the question of 'who did it?' and 'how?' crossed Caroline's mind. It could have been a scene straight out of 'Murder on the Orient Express', only this was the 'Riviera Express', and their next stop was Trieste.

Caroline asked herself: Who stuck the knife in him? Was the train guard knifed, before he entered the compartment? Why did he choose to enter the children's compartment to collapse and die there? Perhaps someone had stuck the knife in his back, in the compartment, as the train entered the tunnel?

Was it someone in the corridor who had knifed him? Perhaps it was the girl opposite her in the nice cream dress? Could it have been the small boy in the blue shirt looking out of the window? Was it the boy wearing the green shorts and green shirt dozing next to her?

Veronica was still screaming loudly…

Caroline was brought back into the real world, when the steam train sped out of the tunnel into the countryside, its whistle blowing, as it did so.

Her brother had been glancing out of the window.

Looking over at his sister, he said, "I take it you've still got the magic key, Caroline?"

She looked at him.

"Yes, of course I have," she replied. "However, I will double-check, Martin. Okay?"

"Fine," he said, smiling sweetly.

Caroline reached up to her handbag, pulled it down, opened it and pulled out the magic key.

"Oh, my god, Martin. Look!" she said, inspecting it.

"It's turned orange," he said, in disbelief. "Er, can I look at it?"

She passed him the magic key. After inspecting it, he handed it onto Veronica.

Surprised, she said, while looking at it, "Gosh! How amazing."

"Maybe, it's trying to tell us something?" suggested Martin.

"Like what?" asked Manfred, who had just taken the magic key from his sister.

Caroline thought about it: "Maybe, it's because we are too far from the castle?"

"I told you it wouldn't like it," added Martin.

"What are we going to do?" asked Veronica.

"Nothing," said Caroline.

She took the key from Manfred and looked at it again, closely.

Veronica replied, "Nothing?"

"Look," said Caroline. "There's not a lot we can do. Let's hope, it doesn't send us back to our own time."

"You have a point," replied Veronica.

Caroline put the magic key back in her handbag.

"You haven't had any funny feelings again, have you, Caroline?" asked Martin.

"Not so far."

"Oh, that's okay then."

"What do you mean?" asked Manfred.

Martin explained: "Well, if Caroline gets a funny feeling, we're in trouble, as it generally involves the magic key."

"Oh I zee," said Manfred, nodding.

The steam train entered another tunnel. It was another black moment for the children, before it came out of the tunnel into the bright summer sunshine.

Suddenly, Martin said, "Look, Manfred. I can see the sea."

Sure enough, to their right was the Adriatic Sea.

"Wow," said Martin. "That looks pretty cool."

"It looks like we're nearly there," said Veronica to Caroline.

The countryside soon turned into buildings. They were now on the outskirts of Trieste, the Austro-Hungarians' fourth largest city. The steam train started to slow down. It blew its whistle once again.

The children could now, just see, to the right of the steam train, bits of the sea, in between the buildings. Soon, the sea was replaced by the city's municipal buildings and large tall cranes that stood in the nearby dock area.

As the steam train pulled into the platform, Caroline got up, and said, "Shall we get the luggage down?"

"Ja, we can try," replied Veronica, smiling.

The four of them lifted the cases down. A fun event, if ever there was one, with a lot of laughing and cursing in the process.

The engine driver had edged the Riviera Express steam train into Trieste Central railway station, with ease. On arrival, the passengers alighted. Porters ran around, looking for holiday passengers needing assistance. This included the children. Veronica waved one down, asked for another, and then got everything organised, as she usually did.

As they walked down the busy platform, Veronica said to Caroline, "I hope my father is here."

She replied, "So do I."

At the end of the platform Veronica recognised someone. A man stood in a line of people, all with placards in their hands. His said 'STRAUSS' on it. He was waving at them.

"Look, Manfred. There's Josef," said Veronica, waving back.

After looking, he replied, "Oh, ja. Zo it is."

Martin too, saw the sign the man was holding.

Recognising who it was, he said to Manfred, "Didn't I meet that man at the castle?"

Manfred replied, "Ja, that's right. You did."

Veronica walked over to the man with the placard.

"Good morning, Miss Veronica," he said. "Did you have a good journey?"

"Good morning, Josef," she replied, adding, "Ja, we did, thank you."

Veronica was looking around.

"Where's Papa?" she asked.

Josef replied, "Oh, your father sent me down to pick you up. He apologises for not being able to personally meet you all. But unfortunately, he's rather busy preparing this afternoon's events."

"I zee," said Veronica, a little peeved her father couldn't be bothered to pick his own children up.

Turning to her right, she said, "Josef, allow me to introduce my friends, Miss Caroline Hartley and her brother Master Martin Hartley."

"Pleased to meet you," said Josef, shaking hands with everyone.

Looking closely at Martin, he said, "I believe I met Master Martin at the castle."

"Did you?" said Veronica, surprised.

"Ja," replied Josef. "We met during the garden party, when he and young Master Manfred were looking at your father's motor car."

Caroline and Veronica looked at each other.

Turning to Manfred, the chauffeur said, "Hello, Manfred. How are you?"

"I am fine, thank you."

Josef then said, "This way, Miss Veronica. I've left the motor car outside the railway station, in the parking area."

"Very good, Josef"

The children and porters followed.

Caroline and Martin were wondering just what lay ahead. Veronica hadn't told them much. Caroline did think that it might be because she didn't know herself.

The chauffeur walked round to the cream-coloured motor car that was parked next to a black one. He tied some of the suitcases onto the back of it. With the aid of the porters, he loaded some of the luggage onto its roof, and then tied it on securely.

As they stood there watching, Martin said, "It's a lovely car, isn't it, Caroline?"

"Yes, it is," she replied, while looking at it.

Caroline wasn't 'into' motor cars. However, she was excited about the thought of riding in it.

"This is Sophie," said Manfred, smiling and patting her.

"Is it?" replied Caroline, walking around her.

"Hello, Sophie," said Martin.

The chauffeur turned to Veronica, and said, "We might need to put some of this luggage in the back seating area, Miss."

"Jolly good, Josef," she replied. "I'll leave it up to you to manage."

"Very good, Miss"

Caroline was looking at the inside of the car.

"What do you think about her?" asked Martin.

"Erm, yeah. She's pretty cool," she replied.

"Get in, will you?" said Veronica.

After everyone was in, she tipped the porters and got in herself.

The chauffeur closed the passenger doors, picked up a crank handle and walked round to the front of the motor car, where he cranked started the engine. After getting in his seat, he drove out of the railway station.

As the motor car drove along the streets of Trieste, Martin said, "Where are we going, Veronica?"

She replied, "This might sound stupid, but I really don't know."

Turning to the chauffeur, she said, "Josef, where *are* we going?"

He replied, "To the harbour, Miss."

"The harbour? Why are we going there?"

"I am taking you to your accommodation, Miss."

"Are you?"

Turning to Martin, Veronica said, "It looks like my father is putting us up in one of the hotels on the seafront."

The boy replied, "Oh!"

There were few motor cars on the road, as Josef drove the cream-coloured motor car along the streets of Trieste. There were however, plenty of horses and carriages going here, there and everywhere. It was still early morning.

As they drove along, Caroline looked out of the window. She noticed that many people had hung a flag outside their houses. The girl saw that lots of flags had been strung together in a line and many had been draped across the streets. Caroline realised they were all the same flag and that it was the Austro-Hungarian flag that she had first seen at the castle. She wondered if it might be because of the inspection of the fleet that was taking place, later in the day.

The English girl felt Trieste had a distinct Mediterranean feel to it. This she liked. Perhaps it was because they were now by the sea? The weather here was so hot.

Caroline was now in holiday mode. The city of Trieste, she thought, suddenly felt like an exciting place for them to be in. She felt like going swimming in the sea.

The motor car that Caroline sat in, drove on, with the children none-the-wiser where the chauffeur was actually taking them…

22

Hello Sailor!

As the cream-coloured motor car approached the harbour in Trieste, it suddenly pulled into a naval dockyard entrance, stopping by a security gate. After speaking with the guards on the gate, they lifted it. The motor car drove through, into the naval dockyard.

Sailors in Austro-Hungarian uniforms were running around everywhere. Some battleships were moored nearby, alongside the dock.

Inside the car, the children were looking out, eagerly.

"This doesn't look like a hotel to me, Veronica," said Caroline.

She replied, "No, it doesn't. Does it."

"Maybe, we are visiting your father?" suggested Martin.

More sailors were wandering around the vicinity.

The cream-coloured motor car pulled up, outside an office building.

The chauffeur got out, opened the rear passenger door and let the children out.

Closing the door, he said, "This way, Miss Veronica."

As they followed the chauffeur into the building, Veronica said to Caroline, "This isn't where we normally go. I can't understand what's going on."

The children walked up some stairs. They were led into an office, full of many Austro-Hungarian naval officers.

"Please sit here, will you," said the chauffeur, in German, to the children.

They sat down.

He walked up to a naval officer, who was manning a desk.

Speaking to the officer, the chauffeur said, "Gut morning. I've picked up the Commander's children and guests, as requested, sir."

"Oh, zo I see. Jolly good," said the naval man, looking at them down his long-rimmed glasses.

The chauffeur added, "Could you inform Commander Strauss they are here?"

"Ja, of course," replied the naval man. "Please take a seat for a moment, vill you, Josef?"

"Very good, sir," he replied.

The naval man picked up a telephone, dialled a number and spoke into the telephone.

"Look at the phone," said Martin, whispering to his sister.

"Gosh!" said Caroline. "It's a bit different to my old mobile."

The naval officer, having replaced the telephone signalled to the chauffeur, who was now sitting down, and said, "You can take the children around to jetty No. 4, Josef. A handover will be done there."

"Very good, sir," said the chauffeur, saluting.

Turning to the children, he said, "This way, please."

As they walked down the stairs, Caroline said, "I thought we were meeting your father?"

"Zo did I," replied Veronica.

She added, "You know, this is most unusual. I have never known anything like it. I mean, we normally just go to my Aunt's house. I can't understand what's going on."

"No doubt we'll find out, soon enough," said Caroline, who was fascinated with all the sailors around her.

Outside, the chauffeur led the children back to the cream-coloured motor car.

"Sorry about all this, Miss Veronica," he said. "We'll soon be there."

"I hope zo, Josef," she replied. "This is not at all normal."

The chauffeur added, "Just following orders, Miss Veronica."

She replied, "I zee."

The cream-coloured motor car drove through the naval dockyard that seemed to be buzzing with sailors. It continued past several more military buildings, warehouses and cranes, which were loading supplies onto several battleships and a couple of supply ships that were lined up alongside the docks.

As they drove along, the children were looking out in awe.

"Wow! Look at that battleship, Martin," said Manfred. "It's huge."

He replied, "This is really cool."

The motor car drove around to jetty No. 4.

Next to it, the chauffeur got out and, after opening the passenger doors, he started to unload the luggage.

"Not quite sure, how we're going to manage these," he said.

Four sailors began to approach the car.

"Gut morning," said one.

"Oh, gut morning," replied the chauffeur.

"We're the pick-up party," added the sailor, smiling.

"Oh, jolly good," said Josef, rather relieved.

As the chauffeur finished unloading the luggage, Veronica asked, "Where exactly are we going, Josef, or is it top secret!"

"Oh no, Miss," he replied, laughing. "It's not top secret. I am just following orders."

"But that doesn't answer my question," she said, a bit peeved.

"No, it doesn't, Miss," he replied, whilst closing a passenger door.

He added, "Vell, due to your father having to rearrange your accommodation, and one or two other things, there had to be a slight change of plan, and…"

"And?" said Veronica, still wondering where they might end up.

"Your accommodation is over there, Miss," he said, pointing.

The children looked over, in the direction in which he was pointing.

"Josef," said Veronica, "All I can see, over there, is the harbour. Do you mean, we are staying on the other side of it?"

"No, Miss," he replied, "You are staying over there, in it."

Veronica gave him one of her funny looks.

"You mean, on one of those boats over there?"

The chauffeur replied, "Yes, that's right. And by the way, Miss. *Those* boats are ships – battleships. The middle one is *SMS Tegetthoff*. It's actually one of the Austro-Hungarians newest dreadnought battleships. It's your father's General Headquarters and battleship."

Veronica was a bit taken aback.

She said, "You mean, we're staying on my father's battleship *SMS Tegetthoff?*"

"Yes, Miss," said the chauffeur, smiling. "That's right."

"I zee," said the girl, who rather shocked added, "Now it all makes sense."

"It's certainly a bit different to what I expected," said Caroline.

Martin and Manfred couldn't quite believe the news.

"Manfred," said Martin, excitedly. "We're going to stay on a battleship. That's really cool."

"Ja, it is," he replied.

The boys were looking out at it.

Manfred added, "You know, Martin. Every boy of our age plays 'Battleships'. Now we are going to go on one."

The chauffeur turned to Veronica, and said, "This is where I say goodbye, Miss Veronica."

"Oh, vell, thank you, Josef," she said.

He replied, "Not at all, Miss. Enjoy your holiday."

"Thank you"

The sailors picked up their luggage.

One of them said, "Would you all follow me, please?"

"Oh, ja, of course," replied Veronica.

"See you later, Josef," said Manfred, waving.

The children walked away from the chauffeur and the cream-coloured motor car. They followed the sailors, who walked towards a harbour stone wall. Disappearing down a gap in its wall, they were closely followed by the children, who found themselves walking down a wooden gangway, towards a small-motorised boat that was moored alongside a small jetty. Once everyone was aboard it, the sailors cast off. The motor boat set off towards *SMS Tegetthoff,* with the children wondering, what a dreadnought battleship was really like…

23

The Dreadnought Battleship

The harbour in Trieste seemed to be abuzz with naval activity. None of the children had seen anything quite like it. Battleships were arriving from other ports, including the Austro-Hungarian Empire's second port of Pola, which was located further along the Adriatic coast, as well as from other destinations outside the Empire.

The dreadnought battleship *SMS Tegetthoff* was moored in the centre of the harbour. Anchored, either side, of the *Tegetthoff-class* battleship, were her sister ships *SMS Prinz Eugen* and *SMS Viribus Unitis.* Other naval battleships stood docked nearby.

As their small motor boat got closer to *SMS Tegetthoff,* the children could see sailors on its decks doing various chores. The children thought the dreadnought battleship looked ginormous, as they sailed around the side of it, looking up at its vast structure.

After pulling up alongside, a small lift was lowered that the children got in. They were hoisted upwards, towards an open door, halfway up the side of the battleship. Caroline was excited. She looked out across the harbour one last time, then stepped aboard *SMS Tegetthoff.*

Inside the dreadnought battleship, one of the sailors, who was escorting the children, said, "This way, Miss Veronica."

He took them to a couple of cabins in the lower decks.

Outside one door, he said, "This is your accommodation for the next few days. One cabin is for you, ladies. The other is for the boys. It's the best the navy can offer you, right now."

"Thank you," said Veronica, "But I still do not understand, why we are staying here, rather than in a hotel?"

The sailor replied, "Perhaps you might like to discuss that with your father, Miss?"

"I would like to. But zo far that's proved impossible."

"Your father is a busy man, especially today, Miss Veronica. However, now I have shown you to your quarters, I can take you to him."

"Oh he's on board, is he? Vell that will be nice." said Veronica, who was a bit exasperated about the whole situation.

Some other sailors arrived, lugging the children's luggage.

"In there, Lyshka, me old mate," said the sailor, to his counterpart.

"Righty-Ho," replied the sailor.

Once the luggage had been deposited, the children followed the first sailor along many corridors and levels.

"Well, I must say, this is fun, Veronica," said Caroline, enthusiastically.

"Is that what you call it?" she replied, rather unenthusiastically.

"All these sailors and us!"

Her friend rolled her eyes upwards. The whole experience was *not* what she was prepared for.

The sailor knocked on a door.

"Enter," was the reply.

Opening the door, he went in and said, saluting, "Commander Strauss, your children and guests are outside, sir."

He replied, "Thank you, Brano. Show them in, vill you?"

"Yes sir."

Turning to the children, he said to them, "This way, please." They entered.

Veronica saw her father, who was sitting at his desk.

"Papa," she said, delightedly.

"Veronica, Manfred. How are you?" asked the Commander, standing up and giving them both a big hug and kiss each, as they ran round to greet him.

"Fine, Papa. And how are you?" asked Veronica.

"Vell," he replied. "As you can see, I am rather busy."

"Zo I see. But I thought you were coming to meet us at the railway station?"

The Commander replied, "I was. But unfortunately, events here overtook me. Zo I sent Josef down. I must apologise for disappointing you, yet again, Veronica. But regretfully, this is the nature of this job."

"Ja, I understand," said his daughter, disappointedly.

"And how is Manfred today?"

"I am fine, Papa."

"Gut," replied his father, adding, "Are you going to introduce me, once again, to your friends?"

"Ja, of course, Papa," said Veronica, "This is Miss Caroline Hartley and Master Martin Hartley."

"Welcome. How are you both?" asked the Commander, shaking hands with both of them.

"Very well, thank you," said Caroline, smiling.

"And you, Martin?"

"Yes, I am okay, thanks."

Looking around him, he added, "It's a super battleship, Commander."

He replied, "Ja, I thought you might like it. It's one of our best and newest dreadnought battleships. I am sure you and Manfred will thoroughly enjoy exploring it."

"Papa," asked Veronica. "I thought we were staying in a hotel, or with one of your friends?"

He replied, "That was the original idea, Veronica. But what with events happening later today. I thought it might be better to have you here."

"I zee," she added, now understanding.

Caroline then said, "May I ask, *what* events, Commander?"

"Vell, Caroline," he replied, sitting back down at his desk. "I'm glad you asked the question. Let me explain what's happening. Today, is a special day for the Austro-Hungarian navy. This afternoon, there will be an inspection of the fleet at 15.00 hours, by the Emperor Franz W. Joseph."

"Oh, that sounds interesting."

"I had hoped you might say that. That's why I invited you all aboard *SMS Tegetthoff.* Normally, it's *not* naval policy to allow children on board its ships, *except* in exceptional circumstances. As Commander of the Fleet, I think we can bend the rules once in a while, eh?" he said, winking at her.

"Yes sir, I mean, Commander."

Caroline added, "Er, do I have to salute you, Commander?"

He laughed.

"No, I don't think we need to go that far."

The Commander added, "My First Officer will take care of you. Zo if you need anything, please ask him. As I mentioned, the Emperor, will be inspecting the fleet later. Zo I am extremely busy organising it all. Last minute preparations and all that, what!"

"Where will the Emperor be inspecting the fleet?" asked Manfred.

"On this battleship. This is why I was unable to come and collect you. The Emperor is arriving at 14.30 hours, and will be ready to inspect the fleet at 15.00 hours. You'll be able to watch events this afternoon on deck, as my VIP guests. Does that sound all right, Manfred?"

"It all sounds brilliant, Papa."

Veronica then said, "Brano mentioned, we will be on board for a couple of days, Papa? Is that right?"

"Ja, that is correct. The thing is, that once the inspection is over, and all the guests have departed, we'll be departing on a short naval patrol, en route to Pola."

The Commander lit his pipe.

"Tomorrow morning we'll dock in Pola harbour. The crew will then have a short rest period, ahead of our returning to Trieste, in time for next week's naval exercises with the German navy."

He added, smiling, "Is that all right?"

"It sounds really great, Commander," said Caroline.

"Ja, I suppose it does," added Veronica, reluctantly.

"I think it sounds brilliant," said Martin.

The Commander then said, "Oh and I forgot to mention that in between, we'll be doing one or two naval exercises, as part of the crew's training."

He looked at the boys.

"Zo, Manfred and Martin. Rather than just play 'Battleships', you'll be able to see them, in action."

"Zuper," said Manfred, amazed.

"Wow! That will be really cool," added Martin.

All the children were excited, now that they knew where they were going and what was going to happen.

The Commander added, "Ja, I thought you children might like it."

He re-lit his pipe.

"As you can see, there are more than one or two battleships in the harbour today. Zo it makes sense to return some of them to our other naval fortress in Pola. That'll give you children time to step ashore and have a look round. The thing is, I thought it might be a bit of an adventure for you all."

"I'll say," said Manfred, beaming.

"Thank you, Commander," said Caroline, in her best German. "I am already looking forward to it."

"Gut," he replied. "Vell, I hope to see you all later. In the meantime, you'll have to excuse me, as I have many activities to manage. I hope you will all have lots of fun. But obviously, be careful, and try not to fall overboard. Veronica, I'll try to spare you a few moments, later on today."

"Thank you, Papa," she replied.

The sailor opened the door and the children started to depart.

As they did, Martin turned around, stood to attention, saluted, smiled at the Commander, and said, "Thank you Commander."

"Thank you, Martin," replied the Commander, returning the salute to the boy.

He added, "We'll make a sailor of you yet, young man."

The boy ran after the others, feeling mighty happy with himself, for not only saluting a ship's Commander, but also the top man in the Austro-Hungarian navy.

24

The Inspection of the Fleet

During the rest of the morning, the children explored the battleship *SMS Tegetthoff*. They ran along its deck and up and down the stairways. The children looked carefully at its guns. They went to the captain's room, the galley and the ship's mess. Martin and Manfred were fascinated by the engine room and the guns.

SMS Tegetthoff was full of sailors, whom Caroline adored. Veronica too, changed her tune. Word got about that the Commander's daughter was on board.

All around them, the children could see last minute preparations being done, ahead of the Emperor coming aboard at 14.30 hours. Decks were being scrubbed; sailors were pressing their uniforms, and were brushing their canvas deck shoes. In the galley, a buffet was being prepared.

A bit further up the corridor, in one of the cabins, some sailors took the children's clothes measurements. An Austro-Hungarian naval uniform was then quickly made, for each of them to wear. It was an exciting moment for the children, being kitted out, as they each began to feel like sailors.

Later, on deck, the children stood watching, as a red carpet was laid out in front of a seating area. Caroline found out it had been prepared for the Emperor, his granddaughter, the Archduchess of

Austria, Elisabeth W. Marie, and many VIP guests, to sit at, so they could enjoy the afternoon's events.

Caroline, like the others, was thoroughly enjoying her visit to *SMS Tegetthoff*. As she stood on deck, looking out to sea, she said, "You know, Veronica, I think you look really cool dressed in that sailor's uniform."

She replied, "Zo do you. I can't believe how quickly those sailors created them for us."

"No. Nor, can I."

Just then, a man dressed in a white uniform walked along the deck towards the children. He stopped to give some orders to a couple of sailors. On seeing the children standing there watching him, he decided to walk over to speak to them.

"Ah, good afternoon," he said. "You must be the Commander's children and guests."

"Yes, that's right, we are," replied Veronica.

"Allow me to introduce myself. I'm Captain Daniel von Trapp. I'm the Captain of this battleship."

Veronica's eyes lit up with surprise.

She replied, "Delighted to meet you, Captain. I am Veronica. The daughter of Commander Strauss."

"Glad to meet you," he said, shaking her hand. "I've heard zo much about you from your father. I thought it only polite to come over and introduce myself."

"That's jolly decent of you."

Turning towards the others, she said, "This is my brother, Manfred. And these are my two English friends from London, Caroline and Martin Hartley, who are visiting us."

"I zee. London eh, what! Vell, I do hope all of you are enjoying your stay on *my* battleship?"

"Er, yes, Captain," said Caroline. "We are."

"Gut, gut. Vell, I do hope that my officers and sailors are looking after you?"

"Yes, I believe they are, thanks."

"What about you boys? Is everything shipshape and Trieste fashion?"

"Er, ja, it is, Captain," said Manfred.

"Is the battleship what you imagined, before you came on board, boys?"

"Definitely," said Martin.

"Gut, I am pleased to hear that, young man."

He turned towards Manfred.

"Perhaps you might follow in your father's footsteps and be Captain of your own battleship, one day. Would you like that, young man?"

"Er, as a matter of fact, Captain. I would."

"Gut, gut, vell do come and see me in the bridge and I'll run through how it all works, if you like?"

"Zuper. I'm already looking forward to it."

"Jolly good, young man," said the Captain, patting the boy on the head.

Turning to the girls, he said, "I hear you're with us for a few days, Veronica."

"Ja, it is true."

"Vell, if you get any trouble or hanky panky from the sailors. Just let me know and I'll sort them out."

"Oh, I don't think that'll be necessary, Captain."

"Veronica," he said, laughing. "You obviously don't know the Austro-Hungarian navy."

"Er, no, Captain"

"But she'd like to!" added Caroline, jokingly.

"Caroline," said Veronica, going red.

The Captain could see now was a good time to depart.

"Vell, I must be going. I'll catch up with you all later. Do have fun."

"Don't worry. We will," said Martin, cheekily.

As the man walked off, Veronica said, "Martin that was the Captain you were speaking to."

"I know it was. But he's still the same as us."

"Whatever do you mean?"

"Well, he's human, right?"

"Ja, I zee vhat you mean."

In the early afternoon, several VIP guests had come aboard *SMS Tegetthoff*. Some of them were milling about the VIP area on the battleship. The Commander of the Fleet was here, there and everywhere, issuing orders to the fleet. There was a general air of excitement on board the dreadnought battleship.

Just before 14.30 hours, the children were looking out from the deck, waiting for the Emperor to arrive. They looked smart in their new Austro-Hungarian naval uniforms that the ship's crew had specially prepared for them. Martin and Manfred thought they looked pretty cool in their new uniforms. Even the girls were thrilled to be dressed, like they were, for an afternoon.

As they looked out at the harbour, Veronica said, "Gosh! Look at all those people, who are gathered around the harbour. There must be thousands of them."

Caroline, who was rather surprised, replied, "Yes, I'm amazed by just how many people there are watching this display this afternoon."

"Vell," added Veronica. "I did say this was an important naval event."

"Yes, you did," said Caroline. "But until you actually see it, it's hard to appreciate just how big this occasion really is."

Suddenly, Martin said, "Look! Over there, Manfred."

He was pointing at the shore, where a motor vessel had just set off from jetty No. 4. It was heading towards their dreadnought battleship *SMS Tegetthoff*.

They watched, as it gradually came nearer.

Manfred suddenly yelled, "The Emperor. He's on board."

Martin replied, "Oh yes. So he is."

On deck, the sailors had lined up, facing the approaching Emperor, all wearing their smart new Austro-Hungarian naval uniforms. The children took their seats at the back of the VIP area, where they watched and waited, as the afternoon's events began.

A band was in position on the deck of *SMS Tegetthoff*.

The military bandleader tapped his music stand and the band started to play. It was typical Austro-Hungarian naval military music of the era.

The small boat, carrying the Emperor and Archduchess of Austria Elisabeth W. Marie, arrived alongside the battleship. As they stepped into the lift, a band on deck played the national anthem. The Emperor and Archduchess were winched upwards, in the same way the children had been earlier in the day.

Inside the battleship, the welcoming party of the Commander, Captain and First Officer, lined up with other senior members of the crew behind them, to greet the Emperor Franz W. Joseph and Archduchess of Austria, Elisabeth W. Marie, once they stepped aboard *SMS Tegetthoff.*

As they did so, a small whistle blasted that a sailor blew.

In German, he yelled, 'Emperor on board'.

The Austro-Hungarian's most senior naval personnel welcomed them. Some photographers took pictures of the moment. The Emperor and the Archduchess were then escorted up to the VIP seating area.

As they stepped onto the battleship's deck, the ship's crew stood to attention. The band played a military tune, as the Emperor did an inspection of the ship's crew. Following him along the line was Commander Strauss.

Returning to the central area on the dreadnought battleship, the Commander stood behind a microphone, and said, "Please stand for the national anthem."

Everyone stood up and the anthem was played again.

At the end of it, the Commander yelled, "Three cheers for the Emperor. Hip, hip,"

"Hurray," was the response, from the crew and it was repeated, twice more.

In the corner of *SMS Tegetthoff,* stood some photographers and members of the world's press. One man was using a new device called a movie camera, to film the occasion in black and white, for a movie company called Pathé news, a British news organisation.

As Veronica sat in her chair, she whispered to Caroline, "I think he's filming the event for the cinema news."

"Really?" she replied, fascinated by it all.

The press were allowed to line up in front of the Emperor and VIP guests, to take their photographs. This included a long minute shot of the group of everyone.

Various photographs were taken. This time of the guests and senior VIP guests, who stood next to and behind the Emperor. The children did as they were told and lined up either side of the Emperor.

Once these photographs had been taken, everyone lined up, so that the Emperor could be introduced to them by the Commander.

When the Emperor got to the children, he paused and turned to the Commander.

"Oh, I see we've got some new recruits, Gustov," he said, jokingly.

Commanded Strauss replied, "Your Imperial and Royal Apostolic Majesty. May I introduce my children, Veronica and Manfred Strauss."

They both shook the Emperor's hand.

"Hello, Veronica, Manfred," said the Emperor, to them. "I do hope you enjoy yourselves this afternoon."

"Thank you, Your Imperial and Royal Apostolic Majesty," responded Veronica, curtseying.

Manfred stood to attention and saluted.

The Emperor looked at him, and said, "Haven't we met before, young man?"

He nodded, and replied, "Ja, we have, Your Imperial and Royal Apostolic Majesty. We met at the garden party my parents held at Strauss Castle."

"Oh ja, that's right," said the Emperor, now remembering and looking again at his sister. "Fancy meeting an Emperor, twice," he added, roaring with laughter.

Turning to the Commander, the Emperor said, "Gustov, you should have told me your children were coming today. I could have brought them some Emperor's Cookies."

"Apologies, Your Imperial and Royal Apostolic Majesty. Another time, eh?" the Commander replied, smiling.

Looking at Manfred, the Emperor said, "Vell, I must say, you do look very smart in that naval uniform, young man. We'll make a naval officer of you yet. What!"

"Thank you," said Manfred, not having a clue what to say to an Emperor.

As the Commander introduced Caroline and Martin, some photographers took their photograph with the Emperor. The movie cameraman also filmed the moment.

The Commander said, "Your Imperial and Royal Apostolic Majesty, these are my children's best friends from London. This is Miss Caroline Hartley and her brother Master Martin Hartley. I invited them here today, to witness such a marvellous occasion."

The Emperor replied, "Oh, good idea, Gustav."

After shaking their hands, the Emperor looked at them.

"You were also at the castle?" he said, in German, to the Hartley children.

"Yes, Your Imperial Majesty, we were," replied Caroline, in German.

"Vell, Miss Caroline, Martin," said the Emperor, "Enjoy yourselves!"

He added, "This is a fine fleet. As good as your British Empire naval fleet, eh? What!"

He winked at them.

"Yes sir," said Martin, also saluting the Emperor.

"A pleasure, Your Imperial Majesty," said Caroline, curtseying in her naval uniform.

The Emperor moved on to greet more of the VIP guests. Once they had all been introduced, everyone sat down. The Commander and the Emperor then stood on a small platform that was located in front of the guests.

Using a microphone, the Commander said, "Good afternoon everyone. I would like to welcome you all here today, to *SMS Tegetthoff*, to witness the bi-annual inspection of the great Austro-Hungarian naval Fleet by his Imperial and Royal Apostolic Majesty, the Emperor of Austria and King of Hungary, Franz W. Joseph. I would also like to welcome his granddaughter, Archduchess of Austria, Elisabeth W. Marie. I hope you will both enjoy this afternoon's naval display."

The Commander stood back, so the Emperor could speak.

"Commander, Archduchess of Austria, Elisabeth W. Marie, naval personnel, ladies and gentlemen," he said. "I have been welcomed on board *SMS Tegetthoff*, today, by Commander Strauss. I would like to thank him for organising this special occasion this afternoon. It is highly important for the Austro-Hungarian navy, as I hope it sends out the right message to our Allies and foes that the Austro–Hungarian navy is building itself into a great modern navy. We have new battleships. The new dreadnought battleships, like *SMS Tegetthoff*, are a great asset to the navy, as indeed are the new submarines that can creep behind enemy lines. Zo I say to you all today, 'with united forces', the defence and expansion of the great Austro-Hungarian Empire is vital, in order to quash our enemies."

The Emperor paused, as the audience politely applauded him.

After a moment, he said, "Commander, let the inspection begin."

The Commander signalled to a sailor to fire the giant 305mm guns that would inform the fleet the inspection had begun and for the ships to pass by one-by-one, in front of the Emperor. Morse code and flashlights were also used in the communications between the ships.

The children shielded their ears, as the guns blasted from one of the battleship's guns. Martin and Manfred found the whole thing terribly exciting.

One by one the fleet of the Austro-Hungarian navy began to pass the dreadnought battleship *SMS Tegetthoff*. The crews of every ship lining the decks of every vessel. The sailors were standing to attention, when the order was given by their captain, as their vessels approached the Emperor's battleship. All eyes were in front, heads held high and every sailor saluted their Emperor, as their battleships passed by. The Emperor stood there and returned the salute to every ship and sailor on it that passed.

The first ships to pass by were *SMS Tegetthoff's* sister battleships, *SMS Prinz Eugen and SMS Viribus Unitis.* In the morning, they had been anchored either side of her, but had now manoeuvred into position, ready to pass the Emperor for inspection.

A sailor gave a running commentary to the VIP guests, who could hear it on the loudspeaker tannoy system that had been rigged up.

The sailor explained, "*SMS Prinz Eugen and SMS Viribus Unitis* form part of the *Tegetthoff-class* battleships range. And as you can see, their crew look extremely smart in their new naval uniforms."

He added, "Next ladies and gentlemen, we see steaming towards us, the *Habsburg class* battleships *SMS Habsburg, SMS Árpád and SMS Bebenberg.* These are what we call semi-dreadnought battleships."

After a small break, the sailor continued: "Coming towards us now, from the seaward side of the harbour, are the *Erzherzog Karl class* battleships. These are another class of pre-dreadnought battleships. You can now see *SMS Erzherzog Karl, SMS Erzherzog Friedrich* and *SMS Erzherzog Ferdinand Max."*

During the inspection, the band played many military tunes, which seemed to keep the Emperor happy. A short break followed, while the battleships positioned themselves.

The sailor, who was giving the commentary, then recommenced.

"Ladies and gentlemen, you can now see the *Radetzky class* of battleship approaching. These semi-dreadnought battleships passing us, have been waiting patiently for this moment of celebration, just outside of Trieste harbour. In this class, you can see firstly, *SMS Erzherzog Franz Ferdinand,* then *SMS Radetzky and* lastly, *SMS Zrínyi."*

"Moving on, we can now see some coastal defence ships, namely, *SMS Monarch, SMS Budapest and SMS Vienna.* These are *Monarch class* battleships and they form the oldest of the current Austro-Hungarian fleet of battleships."

The harbour was a buzz of ships that appeared to be going everywhere. Yet, were fully coordinated for the afternoon's inspection.

The sailor added, "Following on next are some light cruisers. These are slightly smaller ships. You can now see *SMS Zenta, SMS*

Aspern and SMS Szigetvar, together with *SMS Admiral Spaun.* These are in fact part of the *Zenta class* of cruisers."

After a minute or two the commentary continued.

"Next in line for inspection, you will see a line of destroyers. These *Blitz class* destroyers include this afternoon *SMS Tural, SMS Streiter and SMS Wildfang.*"

"Approaching us now is the *Tatra class* of destroyers," said the commentator. "Again, we have a selection of these vessels. You can see now *SMS Balaton, SMS Tatra* and *SMS Triglav.*"

"Lastly, ladies and gentlemen are the navy's newest *submarines.* The first is the U1 *class* submarine, followed by the *U3 class.* As you can see, their crews are lining the top of the two submarines. These sailors need a strong sense of balance, wouldn't you say? Now watch them quickly disappear below decks, once they have sailed past."

At the end of the inspection, the commentator said, "And that concludes this afternoon's inspection of the Austro-Hungarian naval fleet. Thank you very much everybody. I do hope that you enjoyed it. Thank you, Emperor Franz W. Joseph."

There was a round of applause by everyone.

The children had sat quietly throughout the afternoon's performance. They found the experience a wonderful thing to witness. Manfred and Martin thought it was like playing a game of real life *Battleships.* They imagined they would attack their opponent's positions, ultimately sinking their battleships. Both boys felt they had won all of their games.

Finally, when it was over, the Emperor and the Archduchess of Austria, Elisabeth W. Marie, stood up and waved to everyone. The national anthem was once again played. The Emperor waved again, before the Commander led him and the Archduchess over to a small marquee area, where they had a cup of tea in private.

Later, the Emperor and the Commander made their way down a set of stairs onto the lower deck, followed by the Archduchess and the Captain.

After a few minutes, the Emperor and the Archduchess stepped into the lift. They were then gently lowered down the side of *SMS Tegetthoff,* before they stepped aboard the small-motorised boat that, shortly afterwards, set off towards the shore.

As it did so, the crew on *SMS Tegetthoff* cheered the Emperor one last time, before he slowly disappeared from view.

The VIP guests were watching him depart from the side of the battleship. Once the Emperor and the Archduchess had departed, the band finished playing its tune, and then it was all over. The inspection of the fleet had been completed.

25

On-board a Dreadnought Battleship

Following the departure of the Emperor, the battleships crew on *SMS Tegetthoff,* could relax a bit. The sailors stood down, after being dismissed by the captain. The VIP guests could also relax. This included the four children, who were the special guests of the Commander. They now stood on the deck of the dreadnought battleship, looking out towards jetty No. 4. The children watched, as the Emperor arrived at the jetty. They could just about see the events taking place on dry land.

"There he goes," said Martin.

"Looks like he's getting into his motor car," added Manfred.

They watched, as it drove away.

Their sister's hair blew in the slight breeze that now drifted across the dreadnought battleships deck.

"That was tremendous fun," said Veronica.

"Yes, I have to say it was," replied Caroline. "But the inspection of the fleet was a bit long and boring in places."

"Do you think zo?"

"Yes! But overall, I think it was alright."

"Was it worth coming?"

"Definitely!"

"Gut, I am pleased."

"What are we gonna do now?" asked Martin.

"It's up to you."

"I'm hungry," said Manfred. "Can we get something to eat, Veronica?"

"That's a gut idea. I must admit I too am a bit peckish."

"I'm starving," added Martin.

His sister held her hand out.

As they shook hands, she said, "I'm Caroline. Nice to meet you starving."

"Ha, ha!"

Veronica started to walk down the deck.

"Where are you going?" asked Manfred.

"To look for some food and to stretch my legs. Is that all right?"

"Ja, it's gut."

As they walked down the deck, they could see some sailors grouping themselves around two of the big guns.

"Look Veronica," said Manfred. "There's a photographer taking some photos of those sailors."

"Oh, ja. Zo, there is."

"Let's go and have a look," said Martin.

The children walked over to where the action was taking place.

Some sailors were following the instructions of the photographer.

"Maybe, you could line up in front of the guns," he suggested, motioning them into position. "Ja, that's gut. Thank you."

He placed his head under the cloth of the camera.

"Give me a smile and don't move, till I say."

He took the photo then reappearing, added, "Could ve do another. This time, maybe a few of you could sit on the guns?"

It was a comical moment, as some of the sailors assisted each other to sit astride the huge guns.

"Wunderbar!" said the photographer. "Now, if you could keep that position, I vill take the photo." Putting his head under the cloth, he said, "Don't move, till I say, and, smile. And, three, two, one, cheese." After a moment, he said, "Action complete. Thank you."

The children stood close by, watching.

The photographer spotted them standing there. It gave him an idea…

He beckoned them over.

Caroline looked at Veronica.

"I think he's calling us over."

"Ja, it appears zo. Come on…"

Excited, the four children went over to join the group of sailors.

The photographer walked over to them, and said, "Hello, I'm Pavol. I'm taking some photographs for the Vienna Times. Would you like to be in a photo with the sailors?"

"Oh, yes please," said Manfred.

"Is that all right, Miss?"

Veronica replied, "Ja, it vill be fine."

"Gut, gut. Vell if you children could stand in between, or in front of the sailors. That would be great."

They did what they were asked to do. The photographer experimented with the layout of everyone. He then positioned himself under his cloth and looked through the camera lens at them all.

"Ja, that looks gut. Now everyone, please stay absolutely still. And, three, two, one, cheese."

Just as the photograph was being taken, the Commander and Captain walked down the deck. They stopped to watch the shot. Veronica, while posing, spotted the two men. Once the photograph was taken she waved at her father.

"Papa," she shouted.

The Commander waved back, with his pipe in his hand.

It gave the photographer another idea.

He walked over to the Commander and Captain.

"Good evening," he said. "I'm a photographer from the Vienna Times. Would you mind awfully if I asked you gentlemen to pose for a photograph with the children."

"Yes, do come and join us, Papa," said Veronica, running over to him.

"Vell, er,"

The Commander looked at the Captain: "What about it, Daniel. Shall we?"

After a short pause, he replied, "Umgh, vell umgh. Yes, all right."

The two men went over to where the children stood.

"Where do you want us?" asked the Commander.

The photographer replied, "Just there, vill be fine."

When the photographer was fully satisfied with his work, he said, "Gut, gut, thank you everyone. Have a nice day."

"Right!" said the Commander. "We must continue our duties. Veronica, I'll catch up with you all, later."

"Fine, Papa"

The Commander, Captain and sailors then went their separate ways.

"That was fun," said Martin.

"Ja, it was," replied Veronica.

Manfred's stomach was now rumbling.

"Veronica," he said. "Can we get some food now? I'm really hungry."

"Sure"

The children walked towards a small marquee tent that had been erected on deck.

Some VIP guests stood inside it drinking.

The girls stood outside it hovering.

"Shall we get a drink?" suggested Veronica.

Caroline looked into the marquee. It wasn't for her.

"Er," she said. "Can we not go down to the mess hall for something to eat first?"

"As you wish. But I thought we could get a drink here, as I am rather thirsty."

Caroline pulled her to one side of the marquee.

"There are too many VIP people in there, talking to the top brass of the navy."

"Zo?"

"It's a bit awfully awfully, and I feel out of place in such a small space, with all those important people talking to the ship's senior crew."

Veronica looked at her and laughed.

"Don't worry! They won't bite you," she said.

"No, no. That's not the point," said Caroline. "It doesn't feel right, as we are the only children here."

"Oh, I zee. Zo, what do you suggest?"

"I'd rather be in the mess hall, with the sailors."

After getting her drift, Veronica smiled.

"Come on," she said. "Let's go and find you a sailor."

Just then, the ship's First Officer walked up to them.

"Good evening, Miss Veronica"

"Good evening, Brano"

"I expect you children are feeling a bit peckish?"

"That's one way to put it," said Manfred.

Veronica was a little more diplomatic than her brother.

She replied, "I think we are all beginning to feel a little hungry."

"Gut," said the First Officer. "Vell, if you would like to follow me. I'll take you down to the officers' mess for something to eat."

"Yes, all right"

As they began to walk, Brano said, "You'll be pleased to know that the chefs have prepared a buffet for all the VIP guests."

"Oh that sounds nice. Does that include us?" asked Veronica.

"Yes, of course, Miss"

The First Officer led them along a long corridor, into the officers' mess hall.

Just inside the door of it, he said, "Here we are, Miss Veronica."

"Oh, thank you, Brano"

"Do help yourself to whatever you want. Hopefully, I'll catch up with you later."

"Jolly good"

The officers' mess hall was already packed with many of the VIP guests, who stood chatting to each other. The children felt a bit isolated and out of place. So they stuck together, in a corner. Along one side of the room a buffet had been prepared and laid out on some of the tables that had been joined together.

"It looks like most of the VIPs beat us to it," said Martin.

Manfred looked at him: "I thought we were VIPs."

"We are, aren't we, Caroline?"

"Erm…"

Veronica interrupted her: "Yes, boys. We are."

Manfred went to look at the food.

"Where are you going, Manfred?" asked his sister.

"To get a plate."

"Oh, gut idea."

Caroline was looking at all the food.

She said, "I must say, Veronica. It all looks exceedingly good."

"Ja, you are right. It does."

She wandered along the table.

"Come on, let's get ourselves a plate each and tuck in."

Once the children had taken whatever they wanted to eat, they sat down at one of the nearby tables.

"Can we start, Veronica? Or do we need to say grace?" asked Manfred.

"No, I think we can skip grace, while we are on board this battleship."

The English children looked at each other strangely, but decided to say nothing.

"Guten appetite," said Veronica, to them all.

Caroline replied, "Yes, enjoy your meal."

As she ate, Veronica said, "That was really great, us getting our photo taken with Papa and the Captain. Don't you think, Caroline?"

"Yes, it was pretty cool. But I prefer the photo we did with the sailors. It was more fun."

"This food's alright," said Martin, as he tucked in.

"Ja, it is gut," added Manfred.

"Can we get a drink, Veronica?"

"Ja, I think zo."

Pointing, she said, "I think you get it over there, Martin."

As the boys went to get themselves a drink, Veronica shouted after them, "Perhaps you could get us one too, please boys?"

"Yeah alright," replied Martin.

It gave the girls time to chat.

"Which sailor do you fancy?" asked Caroline.

"Gosh, Caroline," replied Veronica. "I hadn't really thought about it."

"I have. I like that Italian looking sailor we met, who sat on the gun."

"Ja, he was pretty good looking. His friend wasn't bad."

After a moment, she said, "But I can't go chatting up sailors."

"Why ever not?"

"I am the Commander's daughter. I should be talking to officers."

"I take your point," said Caroline, nodding slowly. "But you can still talk to the sailors, surely?"

Veronica thought about it: "Ja, I suppose I can."

"Do I detect a bit of snobbery coming on?"

"No, not snobbery, Caroline. But it's simply *not* done. It might be in your time, but not here."

"Uh-huh"

After a moment, she said, "To be honest, I'm not sure."

Caroline had finished what was on her plate.

"Veronica, I'm going to help myself to some dessert."

"Ja, gut idea. Er, moment."

At the end of their meal, Martin sat there looking around the room. He was thinking. Looking at his sister, he said, "Caroline, it's a bit boring listening to these VIPs rabbiting on all around us."

"Yeah, I know what you mean."

"Do ya mind if Manfred and I go on deck?"

"No, be my guest. Er, can they, Veronica?"

"Ja, I think zo."

"Good," said the boy, standing up. "Come on, Manfred?"

As he began to walk away, his sister added, "Just behave yourself, Martin."

The boy looked at her, and with his arms on his hips, said, "Yes, Mum," before giving her one of his wicked laughs.

"Boys!" said Caroline, as they walked away.

Later, when the girls stepped on deck, they walked gracefully along it. Both were enjoying the moment. Several sailors leered at them. A couple wolf-whistled. The girls waved at a few of them.

"What about a walk round the deck, Veronica?" suggested Caroline.

"Ja, gut idea. I feel I need to walk off my meal."

"Oh, so do I. In fact, I think I need to stretch my legs, after sitting on that chair most of the afternoon."

"Ja, I know vhat you mean."

"I got a numb bum, just sitting there."

"A numb bum?" said Veronica, looking at her in her funny way.

"It means, my bottom went to sleep."

"Oh, I zee."

She added, "Zo did mine."

A girly laugh followed.

The boys were enjoying their walk round the deck. They checked out the flags, the shoreline and the other battleships around them. As they did so, Martin spotted a group of sailors sitting on the deck.

"Look Manfred," he said. "It looks as if those sailors are playing dominos."

"Ja, it looks like it."

"Maybe, we can join in?"

The boys went over to watch the game.

One of the sailors looked up and saw them standing there.

"Wanna join us, son?" he said.

"Can we?" replied Manfred, enthusiastically.

"Sure! Take a pew."

The boys sat down cross-legged with the sailors.

"Smart uniform you're wearin'," said another sailor.

Manfred replied, "Ja, it's just like yours."

"It is indeed."

After the boys introduced themselves, another sailor said to them, "Do you boys know how to play dominos?"

"Of course!" replied Manfred.

"Only asking, me old son."

The boys thoroughly enjoyed their games of dominos with the sailors.

At the end of one particular game, some loud bells rang out across the ship.

"What were those bells for?" asked Manfred.

A sailor replied, "That's the 19.00 leaving bell."

"What do you mean?"

"It's when the VIP guests have to start departing the battleship. They have till 20.00 to depart the vessel."

"Oh, I zee."

"Does that mean we have to leave?" asked Martin.

"Er, I don't think zo. We've got our own cabin. Zo, I think not."

"Oh," replied Martin, in his gormless way.

A couple of small motor boats began ferrying the VIP guests back to shore. There were several shuttle runs that took place, as there were many guests to take back to shore.

On deck, the four children watched, as some of the guests were lowered down the side of the dreadnought battleship. They were helped by some of the ship's crew, as they carefully stepped onto the waiting motor boat.

When everyone was aboard, the shuttle craft departed. The dreadnought battleship appeared to tower over the small motor vessel, as it headed past some other navy battleships that were docked in the harbour, on its way towards jetty No. 4.

26

Decking Out

The sun was beginning to set, as the children looked out across the harbour from the deck of the dreadnought battleship. They had a unique magnificent panoramic view of all the battleships that were now moored up in the harbour.

As they chatted, Commander Strauss appeared on deck. On seeing them, he walked over towards where they now stood.

"Papa," said Veronica, kissing her father.

"Hello, Veronica," he replied. "Sorry for not being about zo much. It's been a bit of a busy day."

"Don't worry. We've had a fabulous time exploring the ship. Haven't we, Caroline?"

"Oh, yes," she replied. "It's been really great, Commander."

"Gut! Vell, I thought you might like it," he said, smiling.

"Did the Emperor like his visit?" asked Manfred.

The Commander replied, "Yes, he did actually."

"What did he say?" asked Martin.

The Commander laughed.

"What do you expect an emperor to say, young man?"

"I don't know?" said the boy. "Maybe, he likes inspecting ships?"

"Vell, it's all part of an emperor's job, Martin."

"It must be an interesting job, Commander."

"Ja, that's one way to put it."

Changing the subject, Caroline said, "It's a beautiful evening."

"Ja, it is," replied the Commander, smiling.

He got out his pipe.

"Just right for a sail along the Austrian Riviera, wouldn't you say?"

"Definitely!" said Caroline.

"When do we set sail?" asked Manfred.

The Commander replied, "We shall depart for Pola at 22.00 hours."

"Oh, right," said Caroline.

The Commander lit his pipe.

"There will actually be a small convoy of battleships and other navy ships travelling with us."

"Really?" said Manfred, excitedly.

The Commander relit his pipe.

"Be aware also, that when we're *en route,* we'll be undertaking some night-time procedures and testing out some military hardware."

"What does that mean?" asked Martin.

The Commander replied, "It means, we're going to be firing a few guns during the night, young man."

"Wow!" said Martin, who was quite excited at the thought.

"It'll give the ships' crews some much needed training. And, following the inspection this afternoon, it will be an additional morale booster."

"I see," said Caroline.

The Commander relit his pipe, then said, "What you saw today, Caroline, is the highlight of our naval calendar year."

He added, "Did you enjoy it, Martin?"

"Yes, Commander, it was super, thanks."

"Gut! Vell, stick around on deck around 22.00 hours and you'll see the convoy set sail."

"What time will we get to Pola, Commander?" asked Caroline.

He replied, "Estimated time of arrival is 03.30 hours."

"Oh, quite early then"

"Yes, it's not that far."

"What's it like there?"

The Commander laughed.

"Vell," he said. "You'll find out tomorrow."

"Vill we be able to look round?" asked Manfred.

"Ja of course. You'll be granted some shore leave, just like the other sailors. Zo don't worry. You'll have plenty of fun, I'm sure."

The Commander looked at his watch.

"Now, if you'll excuse me," he said. "I have a dinner appointment in the officers' mess to go to. The Captain is expecting me. Will you be all right?"

"Yes, thank you, Commander," said Caroline.

"Gut," he replied. "Vell, see you all later, or if not, tomorrow morning."

"Bye, Papa," said Veronica, waving.

The Commander walked on down the deck, disappearing from view.

"What are we gonna do now?" asked Martin.

Manfred replied, "Erm, vell I have got one idea…"

"Oh, vhat is that?" asked his sister.

"Vell, if you follow me. You'll find out…"

Manfred led the other three children down a long corridor.

"Where are we going?" asked Caroline.

"No idea," replied her brother. "Manfred, where are we going?"

He replied, "You'll soon zee."

Martin turned to his sister: "I think we're going on a wild goose chase."

She replied, "Yeah, it looks like it."

Manfred led his friends into a room that was full of sailors, who were drinking, smoking, laughing and relaxing.

"Here we are," he said. "This is where I thought we could come."

Veronica was looking at the sign on the door.

"Manfred, this is the sailors' mess, *not* the officers' mess."

"And?" said her brother.

"This is for common sailors, Manfred. We should be mixing with the officers, not the sailors."

Caroline laughed.

"Now you *are* sounding like a snob, Veronica."

"No, I'm not."

"Come on, Manfred," said Caroline, walking off towards a group of sailors.

"Where are you going, Caroline?" asked Veronica.

Her friend paused, returned to where she stood, grabbed her hand, and said, "I thought *we'd* both enjoy a game of chess with these sailors, Veronica. You told me you played it, right?"

"Ja, but…"

Caroline had led them over to the group of sailors.

"Hello, I'm Caroline and this is my friend Veronica. Can we join you for a game of chess?"

"Ja, we'd be delighted, Miss," replied one of the sailors, who was playing a game.

The other sailors quickly abandoned their game, in order to accommodate the girls.

"Here! What about us?" asked Martin.

Caroline looked over at her brother: "I'm sure the sailors will find you another chess set, Martin."

"Oh, well that's alright then."

The children quickly got to know the sailors. Before they knew it, they were enjoying a few laughs and jokes with them, as they played their different games of chess. Veronica rapidly discovered that she was thoroughly enjoying herself. Though, she didn't like to admit it to Caroline. A great time was had by all.

Later at 22.00 hours, the children went back on deck. By now, it was dark. They stood, looking out across the harbour.

Further up the deck, Manfred spotted some action.

"Look, Martin. Down there," he said, pointing.

Caroline then said, "It looks like they're pulling the anchor chain up."

"Does that mean we're leaving?" asked Martin.

"I think zo," added Manfred.

Some whistles blew, an instruction or two yelled. Then, following a blast of the dreadnought battleship's horn, the ship's engines suddenly came into their own. They had been powered up, ready for the moment.

SMS Tegetthoff edged its way forward, turning a little, before it set sail out of Trieste harbour. Behind it, was its sister ship *SMS Prinz Eugen*. A small flotilla of other naval ships followed, either side of the ships.

The children stood on the deck of *SMS Tegetthoff*. Their faces blasted by the night wind. They ran to the stern of the battleship. Caroline and Veronica left the boys and went to look out on the starboard side, before walking down to the aft of the battleship. Here, they looked at its sister ship *SMS Prinz Eugen* that was now sailing behind them. The girls crossed to the port side, so they could look out on the coastal side. However, they preferred the aft of the battleship, as they could see Trieste. The port slowly disappeared from view, as the dreadnought battleships cruised southwards, down the Adriatic, past some small coves and inlets that all formed the heart of the Austrian Riviera.

The moon and the stars were shining, as the girls stood on deck. The moon seemed to light up *SMS Prinz Eugen*.

"This is really nice," said Caroline, who was looking out at the shore.

Jokingly, she added, "All we need now is a sailor or two each, Veronica."

She replied, "We are too young. Anyway, Papa said that's strictly off limits for us young ladies."

"Yes, I know. But when I'm older, it'll be 'hello sailor!'"

The girls laughed, then wandered further along the deck.

Veronica was getting a bit bored with looking out on the coastline.

"What are we going to do now, Caroline?"

"Well," she replied. "I don't know about you. But I'm ready for bed. I am feeling really tired."

"Actually, I am too. I just wasn't sure if you were."

"It's been a great day. But I am lacking sleep after our long journey. In fact, I think I'll sleep like a log."

Veronica looked at her oddly. Giving her one of her funny faces.

Caroline explained. "It means I will sleep well."

"Ja, I am with you now."

After a moment, Caroline said, "Umgh, if I understand it correctly. Didn't your father mention something, earlier, about some night time training activities?"

Veronica replied, "Oh, ja. Come to think about it, he did."

"Well, I definitely need to get some sleep, before they start."

"Zo do I. Come on, let's go to our cabin?"

"Good idea"

The girls looked out from the back of the battleship one last time, then walked down the deck. Martin and Manfred, who were walking around another part of the deck, saw the girls and ran over to them.

"Where are you going?" asked Martin.

"To bed," said Caroline, "Which is where you need to go."

"But I'm not tired," he replied.

"The Commander told us it could be noisy during the night, as they're going to be firing the guns. So it is best we all try to get some sleep now, as we're bound to get woken up later."

The boy groaned, and said, "Oh alright, Caroline. I suppose you're right."

He turned to Manfred.

"Come on, Manfred. Mother has spoken," said the boy, adding one of his wicked laughs.

27

Battleships

In what seemed like the middle of the night, Caroline was woken suddenly in her bunk, by the deafening sound of several guns being fired from the deck of the dreadnought battleship. The noise and vibration of the guns caused the entire cabin to shake violently.

"Gosh! What was that?" she said, sitting up.

"It sounded like a couple of the guns on deck going off," replied Veronica, who had also been woken up by the massive noise.

Caroline jumped down from her bunk and turned the light on.

More guns began firing from the dreadnought battleship.

"Come on," she said, excitedly. "I want to see what's going on?"

"Should we?" asked Veronica, nervously.

"Well, you can stay here. But I'm going on deck."

Not wishing to miss out, Veronica sat up.

"Wait a minute," she said, getting up. "I'm coming with you."

Just then, there was a knocking at the door.

"Caroline, open up," said Martin, who was on the other side.

She opened the door.

Her brother rushed in, with Manfred behind him. They were dressed in their pyjamas.

"Did you hear the firing?" asked Martin.

His sister replied, "I could hardly miss it."

At that moment, another couple of guns fired, shaking the entire cabin again.

"Come on, Martin," said Manfred. "Let's quickly get changed. Then we can go on deck and see the guns firing."

"Good idea"

"Martin, Manfred," said Veronica. "We must be careful not to get in anyone's way. Let's all go together, shall we?"

"Yes alright," said Martin, who added, "Hurry up, Caroline. I don't want to miss it."

"Okay, Martin. We'll be ready in a jiffy."

The children quickly dressed.

As they made their way along a corridor, towards the main deck, guns continued to fire; shaking the entire battleship.

Veronica was unsure they should be going on deck to watch.

"Are you sure we're allowed to do this?" she asked Caroline, as they walked down the corridor.

She replied, "I'm not sure. But I want to have look, don't you?"

"Er, yes"

As the children approached the door to the deck, Caroline bumped into the battleships First Officer.

Surprised to see them, he said, "Where are you children going?"

Veronica replied, "To have a look at the guns being fired."

"Oh, I am not sure you're authorised."

"Vell, my father didn't say we weren't allowed to watch them."

The First Officer quickly thought about it: "Oh, vell you'd better follow me then. But stick together and *don't* disappear from my view. Is that clear?"

"Yes sir," replied Veronica.

The children got the idea.

They arrived on deck, in time to see one of the gun crews preparing to fire one of the dreadnought battleships huge guns. The Commander, who was walking down the deck towards them, saw the First Officer and the children. He walked over to where they stood.

"Commander," said the First Officer. "I discovered your guests wandering around the battleship."

"We weren't wandering, Papa," said Manfred, a bit annoyed.

"No, we came up here to see the action," added Martin.

"I zee," replied the Commander.

He was suddenly wondering, quite how much he should allow the children to see.

"Look," he added. "You are not really meant to be here. But now you are, just stand over there and stay with my First Officer. These guns are really very dangerous right now. Zo do exactly what he says. Is that clear, Manfred?"

He replied, "Ja, it's clear."

Veronica watched the Commander disappear inside the battleship. It was the first time she had seen her father, like this.

Just then, a crew member nearby yelled, "Ten seconds."

"Cover your ears," shouted the First Officer.

Two of the guns fired out to sea. Their noise, deafening to the ear. Yet, massively exciting for the children to witness, as they stood there watching events unfold.

"Wow! Look at that," yelled Martin.

One of the launched shells hit a small boat that was further out to sea. The other landed in the sea, next to it.

"Gosh! One of them hit that boat," yelled Manfred.

The explosion lit up the night sky.

"Cor! That was really cool," yelled Martin.

Turning to the Commander's First Officer, he asked, "Was that meant to happen?"

"Ja, don't worry. It was," he replied. "We're actually using a couple of old fishing boats we brought down with us, as target practice."

"Oh, I see," said Martin.

At that moment, the sound of more guns firing nearby could be heard. Their shells landing in the sea.

"Wow! Where did those guns fire from?" asked Manfred.

The children were looking out, eagerly, in the direction of the firing.

The First Officer replied, "They're being fired from our sister dreadnought battleship *SMS Prinz Eugen.*"

"Ja, I see now," said Manfred, who could just see the battleship, in the darkness of the night.

"But they're not firing at the fishing boat, are they?" asked Martin.

"Nein," replied the First Officer. "They're firing at a second fishing boat."

"Oh, right," said Martin, surprised.

He added, "Where's that?"

"Over there," said the First Officer, pointing into the darkness.

"What happened to the Captains and crew of the fishing boats?" yelled Caroline to the First Officer.

Realising she was concerned about their safety, he said, "Oh, don't worry. They're all - all right. They transferred earlier to *SMS Prinz Eugen.*"

"Uh-huh"

Just then, everyone heard, "Ten seconds," yelled again.

"Cover your ears again," shouted the First Officer, to the children.

Two of the guns, that were further up the battleship, fired more shells. They raced over the sea towards the fishing boat. This time, both hit the target. The fishing boat exploded in massive balls of fire. The explosions lit up the sea and sky around.

"Wunderbar! They both got it," yelled Manfred, excitedly.

"This is really great," said Martin.

"Ja, it is," added Manfred.

He added, "This is real target practice, Martin."

"Look!" said Caroline, who was watching the fishing vessel. "It's sinking."

Sure enough, it was. Within moments, it had disappeared before their eyes.

"Crikey! It's sunk," said Veronica.

The children looked out at where the fishing vessel had been. Only fragments of fire now lit up the immediate area around where it had been positioned.

Some whistles blew.

"Look, Manfred," said Martin. "I can see the second fishing boat."

Another round of shells roared from the guns of the sister battleship. This time, both guns hit their target. A second explosion lit up the night sky.

The children cheered.

"They got it," yelled Martin, excitedly.

"Great shots," shouted Manfred.

The fishing boat was totally engulfed in flames. Some minor explosions came from within, before it slowly sank into the sea.

More whistles blew. Some flashing lights flashed between the ships. Hooters from the other battleship could be heard in the wind.

"Look, they're sending a signal," said Manfred.

"Are they?" asked Martin.

"Yes, it's in Morse Code. But I can't make out what message was sent."

The First Officer turned to the children.

"Vell, I can tell you the signal sent indicated the night time target practice has been successfully completed."

"I zee," said Manfred.

"That was amazing," said Veronica to Caroline.

"Better than a game of battleships," added Manfred.

The First Officer looked down the deck.

"Right," he said. "Let's get you children safely back to your cabins and back to bed, shall we?"

"Yes sir," said Martin, cheekily saluting him.

Caroline led her brother and friends back along the narrow, dimly lit, dreadnought battleship's corridors to their cabins. The children had thoroughly enjoyed venturing on deck and seeing the action take place. It had woken them up. However, once everyone was back in their bed, sleep caught up with them. Only the sounds of the sailors walking down the corridors could be heard and then it was dreamtime.

28

Good Morning Battleship

The next morning, Caroline was woken by the noise of sailors noisily moving along the corridor. She had been dreaming of guns firing on battleships and sailors. Turning her light on, she looked down at Veronica, who was laying there still asleep.

Suddenly, there was a knock at the door.

"Wake-up call," said a sailor, moving on to the next door.

Veronica stirred from her sleep and opened her eyes.

Caroline then said, "Good morning, Veronica. Sleep well?"

She replied, "Zo, zo!"

"Yeah, I know what you mean."

After a moment, she added, "I believe that was the alarm call."

"Zo I gather," said Veronica.

She added, "I could do with a bit more sleep, following last night's gun firing."

"Me too," said Caroline, who yawned.

Lying there, she said, "We don't appear to be moving."

"That's because we should be in Pola, by now," replied Veronica.

Caroline jumped down from her bunk and looked out of the port hole.

"Yes, it looks like we're here," she said.

"What time is it?" asked Veronica.

Looking at Veronica's watch that lay next to the basin, Caroline said, "Crickey! It's gone eight thirty."

"Is it?" said Veronica, also yawning. "Gosh, I'd better get up."

Caroline added, "Oh, take your time, Veronica. We've got plenty of time. We're on holiday, remember."

Once they were dressed in their 1912 normal clothes, the girls departed their cabin.

In the corridor, Caroline knocked on the boys' cabin door.

"Martin," she said. "Wake up."

Hearing no response, she knocked at the cabin door again.

"Alright, I'm awake," he said.

"Open the door," said Caroline.

After a moment, the boy slowly unlocked the door and opened it.

"Didn't you or Manfred hear the wake-up call?" asked his sister.

"Sort of," he replied. "I must have gone back to sleep."

"Wake up, Manfred," said Veronica.

"I am awake!" he said, looking at the girls, as he lay in his bed.

Caroline added, "Veronica and I are going on deck. Then we're going for some breakfast."

"Oh, wait for us," said Martin.

"No, you'll be forever. Look, see you in the sailors' mess hall in ten minutes."

"Oh, alright," he replied, moaning.

Outside on deck, the girls could see *SMS Tegetthoff* was lined up next to its sister dreadnought battleship *SMS Prinz Eugen.* Beyond it, laid another.

"Gosh! There're a lot of battleships here," said Caroline, looking out at them.

"That's because it's the Austro-Hungarians' most important naval port and shipbuilding port."

"I thought that was Trieste."

"No, that's the biggest port in the Empire, which includes the naval facilities."

"Oh, I see," said Caroline, who was always fascinated by Veronica's alternative history lessons.

The girls walked slowly along the deck of the battleship. They were looking at the magnificent view of the harbour.

"It's a lovely morning," said Caroline.

"Ja, it is," replied Veronica, "Just right for looking around Pola."

"I'm looking forward to seeing what's there."

"Oh, zo am I."

"Have you been here before, Veronica?"

"Nein, it's my first time, and you?"

"Mine too. But I never thought I'd see it in 1912!"

Caroline suddenly felt hungry.

"Gosh," she said. "My stomach's rumbling. I think I need to get some breakfast."

"That sounds like a good idea," replied Veronica.

Turning around, she said, "Come on. Let's go down to the ship's mess."

The girls walked back down the deck of the battleship, before going inside one of the doorways. Walking down some stairs and along some corridors, the girls made their way to the sailors' ship's mess. At the entrance they joined some sailors, who were in a queue waiting to get their breakfast. Once the girls had been served, they carried their trays over to a spare table, sat down and started to eat their breakfast.

As the girls sipped their coffee, Martin and Manfred arrived in the mess hall. The girls waved at them, as they queued up and got their breakfast.

Once the boys had joined them at the table, Caroline said, "Took your time."

Her brother replied, "We don't have to rush. We've got all day."

"Yes, I know that."

"Manfred and I just went on deck."

"Oh, zo did ve," said Veronica. "It looks like it's going to be a nice day."

The boy started to eat a bread roll.

He said, "I'm really looking forward to exploring Pola."

"Me too," added Manfred.

"Last night, we were talking to some sailors, who were telling us all about it. It sounds like a really cool place."

"What are we going to see first?"

"Let's wait and see, shall we?" replied Veronica, smiling.

Changing the subject, she said, "I need another coffee."

"Oh, so do I," added Caroline.

As the girls got up to get themselves another drink, Martin looked up.

"Could you get me another tea, please, Caroline?"

"Sure. Manfred, would you like another one?"

"Oh, ja, please"

Having got the drinks, the children sat at their table quietly drinking them.

"There are a lot of sailors everywhere," said Martin, looking around the room.

"Of course there are!" said Veronica, laughing. "It's a battleship."

Once he had supped the last of his tea, Martin burped.

"Pardon, Martin," said Veronica.

"Sorry, pardon"

"Boys!" added Caroline, looking at her friend.

Manfred countered, with another loud burp.

"Pardon me," he said, smiling sweetly at the girls.

Standing up and stretching, Martin said, "I'm ready to go. Are you ready, Manfred?"

"Almost," he replied, as he quickly finished eating his bread and jam.

"Wait a minute, you two," said Veronica. "We've plenty of time. Anyway, before we go anywhere, I need to go back to the cabin to powder my nose."

"Oh right," said Manfred, looking at Martin.

"What about, if we rendezvous in say, twenty minutes, outside our cabin? Is that all right?"

"Ja, it's good."

Back in their cabin, Caroline sat on her bunk watching Veronica brush her teeth in the small basin.

"Is there a beach near here, Veronica?"

"Probably," she replied, rinsing her teeth. "After all, we are by the sea."

"We've definitely got to find a beach."

"Why?"

Caroline looked at her, giving her, her 'odd look'.

"We can't come all the way to the sea and not go on a beach."

"True"

After a moment of just sitting there doing nothing, Caroline jumped down from her bunk.

"I've just had an idea," she said.

"Oh, what's that?" mumbled Veronica, as she dried her face with a towel.

"Let's look at the magic key?"

"Gut idea"

Caroline picked up her small handbag that was on the nearby chair. Rummaging around it, she pulled it out.

"Oh, my goodness, Veronica," she said, surprised. "Look!"

"Gosh! It's turned red."

She took the key from Caroline's hand, looked at it, and said, "That's *not* a good sign, surely?"

"I think you're right."

"What are you going to do?" asked Veronica.

"Nothing! Like I said before, I think it's trying to tell us, we're a bit too far from the castle."

"You're probably right, we are."

Caroline was thinking.

"Red is a sign of danger, is it not?"

"Vell, it could be," replied Veronica, unsure.

She handed the key back, adding, "I just hope everything will be fine."

"Let's hope so."

Caroline put it back in her handbag, which she then put on the bed.

"Anyway," she added, "I am sure it only works in the attic."

"You may have a point. But then again, as it's a magic key, maybe it might work elsewhere?"

"Maybe? Look, I've no idea."

At that moment, there was a knock at the cabin door. Veronica went to open it.

Martin and Manfred were standing there.

"Are you ready?" asked Martin.

"Almost," replied Veronica.

"Coming," said Caroline, picking up her small handbag.

The girls departed their cabin. After locking its door, Veronica led the way up the corridor.

"Let's go up to my father's cabin," she suggested.

"I thought we were going ashore?" said Martin.

"We are. But first, we need to go there. Zo we can go ashore."

"Oh, I see," said the boy, in his gormless way.

After Veronica knocked at the Commander's door, his First Officer, Brano, opened it.

"Good morning everyone," he said.

"Good morning," replied the children.

"Did you all manage to get some sleep?"

"Ja, thanks," replied Veronica.

"Gut," said the Commander's First Officer.

He added, "How can I help you?"

"We'd like to go ashore," said Manfred.

"Would you?" replied the navy man, grinning.

"Yes!" added the boy, with a cheeky grin on his face.

"Vell," said the Commander's First Officer. "I think we can arrange that. Are you ready to leave?"

"Yes, that's why we're here," said Martin, cheekily.

"Is my father in his cabin?" asked Veronica.

"Ja, he is. But he's still asleep, Miss," said the Commander's First Officer.

"I zee," said Veronica. "Er, well, will you tell him that we've gone ashore."

"Ja, of course!"

As the First Officer closed the cabin door, he suddenly remembered something.

"Oh, just a minute," he said, going back into the room.

Picking up an envelope from the Commanders desk, he departed the room.

Walking down the corridor, he said, "Could you follow me, please? Let's see if the ship to shore landing craft is close by, eh?"

"Super," replied Veronica.

"Oh, this is for you," said the First Officer, handing her the envelope.

"What is it?" she said, rather surprised.

"It's some money and an address of a small restaurant, your father frequents, when he's in town. He has reserved you a table at the restaurant this evening at 18.00."

"Oh, that's jolly decent of him."

"Your father is a decent man, Miss Veronica."

"Ja, I believe he is."

The First Officer added, jokingly, "And I don't think he wanted you to starve, Miss."

Veronica knew from previous experience, why her father had really done this. It would allow the children somewhere to eat in town; without having the need to have an adult with them.

At the dreadnought battleship's open entrance door, the First Officer looked downwards. He could see a small motor boat alongside SMS *Tegetthoff.*

"It looks like you're in luck," he said, to the children.

Just then, another sailor appeared.

"Ah, Lyshka," he said.

"Yes sir"

"Would you take Commander Strauss's children and their guests ashore, please?"

"Certainly, sir," he said, saluting him.

"You'll need to take them into town and arrange a rendezvous point, with them, this evening."

"Yes sir"

"What time do we need to be back?" asked Veronica.

The Commanders First Officer looked at his watch.

"You need to be back here by 20.00 hours."

"That sounds fine," replied Veronica, looking at her watch.

"Why do we need to be back so early?" asked a surprised Caroline.

The Commander's First Officer explained. "Because this is a big naval port and with various ships' crews on shore leave, it is best you are all back early."

He added, "It is for your own safety."

"Is Pola dangerous?"

"No, it's not dangerous, Caroline. But let's just say, there will be a lot of drunken sailors about later, who might want to take advantage of any female they can get their hands on. Do you understand what I am saying ladies?"

Veronica blushed.

"Er, yes, I do," said Caroline, smiling.

"Right!" said Lyshka. "Let's be having you children ashore."

"Vell, have a safe and fun day," added the First Officer. "Lyshka will be waiting for you. I suggest a rendezvous point, somewhere in the town at 19.30. Got that, Lyshka?"

"Yes sir. 19.30, sir," he said, saluting.

The children followed the sailor into the lift, which then lowered them down to the landing craft. After jumping on board, they set off on the short journey towards the shore.

29

Shore Leave

The landing craft made its way around the two other dreadnought battleships that *SMS Tegetthoff* was moored next to. The children looked out, in awe, at their vast structures that towered above the small craft they were in. A light wind blew the girls hair.

"Lyshka, which battleship is this?" asked Caroline.

The sailor looked up at the vessel.

"This one is *SMS Prinz Eugen.*"

"And that one?" asked Martin, pointing at the other dreadnought battleship.

"That's *SMS Viribus Unitis.*"

"Oh, right!"

They moored up alongside a small wooden jetty. A sailor tossed a line to another sailor, who was on the jetty. Once the motor boat was secure, everyone got off it and walked along the jetty towards the shore. The children realised they were in the middle of a vast Austro-Hungarian naval dockyard.

"This place is massive," said Martin.

"Ja, it is," replied Manfred.

"I didn't realise there would be so many battleships here," said Caroline to Veronica, as she looked around her.

"Me, neither"

Veronica added, "Maybe, it's because of the inspection of the fleet yesterday."

"But that was in Trieste."

"True! But this is the main naval base. Zo many ships are based here."

"Uh-huh"

Once they were on dry land, Lyshka stopped, to let the children lookout across the harbour. In the middle, several naval boats were manoeuvring, as were some smaller fishing boats.

"It's a wonderful harbour," said Veronica.

The sailor replied, "Ja, it is, Miss."

The naval port was alive with activity. Sailors were everywhere.

"What are they putting on those battleships, Lyshka?" asked Martin.

He replied, "It looks like they're being resupplied, ready for their next assignment."

"Which is, where?"

The sailor laughed.

"It could be anywhere along the Adriatic coast or Mediterranean Sea. It depends on their orders."

"Oh, I see."

As they stood there looking out at the battleships, something else had caught Caroline's eye.

"Look, Veronica," she said, pointing.

She did.

The children could see a man standing with a tripod, on some wooden crates.

"What's he doing?" asked Martin.

Manfred, who was looking, replied, "It looks like he's taking a photograph."

Caroline was curious.

"Lyshka, let's go and have a look?"

"Sure," said the sailor, nodding.

They wandered over to investigate.

"Good morning," said Veronica, as she looked up at the man and his tripod.

"Oh good morning, Miss," he replied, looking down at her. "Lovely day!"

"Yes, it is."

"Could you tell us what you are taking a photograph of, sir?" asked Martin.

The photographer laughed.

"Vell," he said. "Seeing as you're asking, young man, I am happy to tell you."

He walked round the camera, to make an adjustment on the camera lens, and then said, "Why don't you all come up and have a look?"

They did.

Once they were by the camera, Veronica said, "You didn't answer my brother's question."

"Oh, sorry, Miss," replied the photographer. "I am taking a photograph of these battleships, here."

Manfred butted in. "They're not battleships. They're dreadnought battleships."

"Exactly!" replied the photographer.

"Why are you taking a photograph of them?" asked Martin.

The photographer replied, "For the newspaper."

"Really? Oh, which one?" asked Veronica.

"The Budapest Echo, Miss. They're running a story on the navy, next week."

"I zee."

"Thought it might be a good idea, to get a photo or two."

Manfred pointed at the dreadnought battleships.

"My father's the Commander of all of them."

"Is he now?"

"Ja, he is!" replied the boy, grinning proudly.

"Zo, will we be able to see your photo?" asked Veronica.

"Hopefully," said the photographer. "But first, I need to take it, Miss."

He walked round to the camera lens.

Manfred was standing the closest to the tripod.

"If you'd like to look through here, young man. You can see the shot, I'm about to take."

"Can I?" asked the boy.

Manfred stood on a box and looked through the viewfinder.

"It looks a good shot," he said, stepping back from the camera.

"We'll see," said the photographer.

"Oh, let me zee," asked Veronica.

After everyone had looked into the viewfinder, the photographer put his head under the curtain and took the shot.

"There, it's done," he said.

"Thanks for showing us," said Manfred.

"Not at all, enjoy your day," replied the photographer, raising his cap.

At the exit barrier of the naval base, Lyshka showed his pass to the guard, who then raised the barrier, so they could walk through.

Outside in the street, Martin asked Lyshka, "Is it far to the centre of town?"

"Nein, it's about a fifteen minute walk," replied the sailor, grinning.

As they walked along, Lyshka gave the children some tips about where to go in Pola. Caroline thought it was a perfect day for sightseeing.

On reaching an old archway, the sailor said, "This will be our rendezvous point."

He added, "This is the entranceway to Pola's Old Town."

"Oh, right," said Caroline.

"It's an old arch," added Martin, looking up at it.

"Ja, it's an old Roman arch," replied the sailor. "It's where people meet in this city."

"Really?"

Veronica was looking at a sign on a wall.

"It says it's called 'Pola's Triumph Arch of Sergius'. It was built in 27BC to commemorate the Sergius family, who were a powerful clan at the time."

Caroline added, "It also says it's called 'The Golden Gate'."

Martin was looking up at it.

"It doesn't look very golden to me," he said. "It looks like it's made of stone."

"That's because it is," said Manfred.

Lyshka had lit himself a cigarette.

"Vell," he said. "That's my task completed. I'll leave you children to enjoy your day. I'll meet you here at 19.30, Veronica."

"Fine"

"Zee you later."

As the sailor walked off, he turned, waved, and said, "Ciao."

"Ciao," replied Martin, copying him.

The children set off on their adventure tour. They started by looking around the Old Town, including a visit to the local church. At the local flea market Caroline and Veronica bought themselves a parasol each, so they could shelter from the sun.

In the park, the children treated themselves to an ice cream, eating it on a park bench. The girls relaxed and chatted under their parasols, while Manfred and Martin burnt some energy, running around the park gardens.

Later that morning, the children found themselves in front of the famous Roman amphitheatre.

"Cor! It looks massive," said Martin, as he looked up at it.

"Come on," said Manfred, "Let's go inside."

They did.

In the centre of the amphitheatre, Caroline was looking around her.

"Wow!" she said. "This is really amazing."

"It's huge," said Manfred.

Veronica was reading a small pamphlet.

"It says, 'the amphitheatre was started during the reign of Emperor Augustus (31BC-14AD)'. Apparently, it's the sixth largest amphitheatre in the world."

"Gosh!" replied Caroline. "I wonder what the biggest one looks like?"

"Probably like this one," added Veronica, grinning.

"Come on, let's go over here," said Martin, running off ahead of them all.

The children spent a while looking around the amphitheatre. They explored its subterranean caverns.

"This is where the Romans kept their wild animals," said Veronica, who was reading her booklet.

She added, "Apparently, the Christians that the animals were about to tear apart, were also locked up here."

"Nice!" replied Caroline.

Having thoroughly enjoyed their visit to the amphitheatre, the children made their way to the exit.

Outside it, Martin said, "What are we going to do now?"

"We're going to the beach," replied Veronica.

"Are we?" asked Manfred.

"Caroline wanted to go there."

"Oh, so do I," added Martin.

Veronica hailed an open-topped horse and carriage. The driver pulled up.

"We'd like to go to the beach," she said, to the driver.

"Hop in then, Miss," he replied.

The four children got in the carriage.

"Is it far?" asked Veronica, to the driver.

"About ten minutes, Miss," he replied.

"Very good. Vell, drive on, will you?"

The driver cracked his whip. The horse and carriage set off.

As they went down the road, Martin said to his sister, "This is really cool, Caroline."

"Yes, I must admit, it is," she replied, as she looked out from the carriage.

D. J. Robinson

"What are we going to do when we get there?" asked Manfred.

"Let's wait and zee," replied Veronica.

The horse and carriage drove on, down the tree lined road that sheltered them from the hot summer sun, towards the beach. The children were enjoying the ride. They were on holiday.

30

The Peninsula

After driving the horse and carriage round to a nearby peninsula, the driver pulled up on an area of grass, near a beach. The children hopped off the open topped carriage and looked around them, as Veronica paid the driver.

Once she had done so, Caroline asked him, "Where's the beach?"

"Over there, Miss," he replied, pointing.

He added, "Once you start walking round the peninsula, you'll find plenty of other beaches, as well."

"Oh, right. Thank you"

The children crossed the grassy area they were on and headed over to the beach. When they got there, they looked around.

"You call this a beach?" said Caroline.

"Yes, this is the beach," replied Veronica.

"You're kidding?"

Veronica gave her friend, one of her famous 'I don't understand you' looks.

"Kidding?" she asked.

Caroline explained: "It means you are joking."

"Why would I be joking?"

"Look, it doesn't matter," said Caroline. "What I mean is, where's the sand? It looks like rock."

"That's because it is."

"You mean to say, I've come all this way to lay on a bit of rock?"

"It is normal around this part of the Adriatic Sea."

"Gosh! How disappointing. I wanted to sit on some sand."

"Yeah, me too," said Martin.

"Maybe, there's a sandy beach round the corner?" suggested Manfred.

Caroline started to walk away.

"Well," she said. "I don't want to sunbathe here. Let's go and have a look, shall we?"

As the children walked across the peninsula, they discovered some grassy areas; within the forest they were now in, where people were relaxing. Some families were eating picnics.

"Caroline, I'm feeling rather hungry," said Veronica. "Let's sit over there, under the trees and eat our lunch."

"Yes, good idea. I must admit, I'm starving."

The girls set off, towards the trees.

"We're sitting over there, boys," shouted Veronica, pointing at a shady area under some trees.

Once they were all seated, Veronica said, "I vill be mum."

Caroline laughed.

"Yes, you can be mum," she replied.

Veronica handed out the picnic lunch; they had bought earlier, in town.

As they sat there eating it, Caroline said to her, "I can now understand why you suggested sitting in the shade under these trees, rather than in the sun. It is uncomfortably hot wearing these clothes."

"Ja, it is. But you get used to it."

"Yes, I suppose so."

After lunch, Caroline said, "Veronica, I know it's not my business. But I'm dying to know what's inside the envelope that sailor gave you this morning, when we were departing."

"Yeah, what did he give you?" asked Martin, curiously.

"Vell," said Veronica. "Let's have a look, shall we?"

She got the envelope out and undid it.

"It looks like there's some money here, a business card and a piece of paper."

"What's on the paper?" asked Caroline.

After reading it, Veronica said, "It says, 'Reserved you a table for four at Mario's at 18.00, Papa'. He signed and stamped it Commander Strauss."

"Oh!"

"And the business card?" asked Martin.

Veronica looked at it.

"It's a business card and address for Mario's."

"Oh, what's that?"

"It's the name of the restaurant, we are going to be going to."

"Is it?"

"Veronica just told you, Dumbo!" said Caroline.

They both stuck their tongues out at each other.

"But I didn't know there were tongue sandwiches for us to eat, as vell," joked Veronica.

They both gave her a filthy look.

"What about the money?" asked Manfred.

His sister replied, "I guess it's for the meal this evening."

Veronica popped everything back in the envelope, which she then put in her small handbag.

"Right," she said. "Shall we go and explore this peninsula?"

Martin replied, "Yeah, good idea."

As they walked down a lane in the forest, Manfred suddenly said, "Look, Martin. There's a fort ahead."

"Oh, yes!"

"It looks like there are some sailors guarding it."

"Come on, Caroline. Let's go and have a look."

They walked up to the guard house, where two men in navy uniform were standing.

"Can we go in?" asked Manfred, to one of them.

"Sorry, son. Navy personnel only," replied the guard, pointing at a sign.

Veronica was reading it.

"It says, '*Private Keep Out. Navy Personnel Only*'."

"So I see," replied Caroline, who was also looking at the sign.

"Do you know what's inside, Manfred?" asked Martin.

"Erm, nein. Sorry, I don't."

Veronica answered his question.

"Martin, I think this is where the sailors live, when they are not working on the battleships."

"Oh, I see."

"You mean barracks?" asked Caroline.

"Ja that's right," replied Veronica.

After a moment, Martin said, "But don't the sailors go home, when they come off the battleships?"

Veronica thought about it.

"Vell," she said. "They probably do. But maybe they live here, when they are training."

She wasn't sure.

"Oh, right," said Martin.

Caroline had spotted a path.

"Maybe, we can walk round the fort, if we use that path over there?" she suggested, pointing at it.

"Ja, gut idea," replied Manfred.

The children followed the forest path around the naval fortress. Naval guards were patrolling around the outside of it.

As they walked around it, Caroline said to Veronica, "Why are the forts round?"

She replied, "That's an interesting question."

After thinking about it for a moment, she added, "If I remember correctly, my father once told me, it helps repel any cannon balls that might be fired from enemy ships."

"Really?"

"Yes, because when a fort is round, the cannonballs rebound off the curved fortress wall, causing the fort less damage."

"I see," said Caroline, adding, "That's a pretty clever idea."

"Ja, I thought zo as vell."

"Come on. Let's see what's down here?" suggested Martin.

He and Manfred were walking ahead of the girls.

The path led the children down onto another rocky beach. Craggy rocks jutted out in the sea beyond.

"We can stop here for a while," suggested Veronica, looking around. "I wish to rest my feet."

"Oh, me too," added Caroline. "In fact, I want to dip my feet in the sea, seeing as we forgot to bring our swimming costumes."

"I'm going to explore the rocks," said Martin. "Coming, Manfred?"

"Ja"

As the girls sat there under their parasols, they dipped their feet in the sea.

"Veronica," said Caroline. "I am rather glad I did forget my swimming costume."

"Oh, why's that?"

"Well, I didn't fancy wearing it."

She burst out laughing.

"Because," she said, giggling, "If I looked like that fat lady over there, in it. I'd die of embarrassment. Actually, I wouldn't want to be seen dead wearing it."

Veronica gave her another of her funny looks.

"Sorry," she said. "I am not with you, Caroline."

"What I want to say, is, I wouldn't want to wear a swimming costume, like that."

"But that's what I wear, when I go swimming."

Caroline laughed again. She tried to be polite.

"Well, maybe I might wear it."

She added, "I think I would only wear it, if you were also wearing the same styled swimsuit."

Caroline could visualise the two of them wearing it, on a modern fashion parade.

"What sort of swimming costume do you wear?" asked Veronica.

"Me?" replied Caroline. "I wear a bikini."

"A bikini? Oh, what's that?"

"It's, er, a two piece swimming costume, you wear here and here," she replied, demonstrating how she wore it.

"Gosh! I couldn't wear that. It's obscene," replied Veronica, rolling her eyes upwards.

"No, it's not," said Caroline. "I mean, when you go to the beach, you strip off to get a good tan. Well, that's what I do. We're hardly doing that, sitting here under these parasols. Maybe, I should strip off and go swimming?"

"Nein, definitely not!" replied Veronica, shocked. "It's *not* the done thing. We young ladies can't to do things like that, in public. Anyway, you'd get arrested."

"Well," said Caroline, looking around her. "I hardly think there are any policemen around here."

She added, "Anyway, we stripped off in the castle lake."

"Ja! But that was different. That's our secret lake, Caroline."

"Uh-huh. Yes, I take your point."

Caroline was waving her parasol about. In the clothes she was wearing, she found it uncomfortably hot. She was touching the rocks they sat on.

"You know, Veronica, these rocks are very hot."

She replied, "Ja, they are. But it is normal when it is hot weather."

"I think I could fry an egg on them."

Her friend looked at her, and said, "Why would you want to fry an egg on them?"

"Because as they're so hot to sit on, you literally could."

"But *why* would I want to fry an egg on them? I would get a servant to fry me an egg, if I wanted one cooked."

Caroline laughed.

"It's a saying, Veronica."

Giving her a funny look, Veronica replied, "What a funny saying."

The children were enjoying their afternoon on the peninsula in Pola. Whilst the girls relaxed dipping their feet in the sea, Manfred and Martin were on the rocks, throwing a few stones into it.

"This is really cool being here, Manfred," said Martin.

"Ja, I like it."

"How many times can you get your stone to bounce?"

"That depends on how flat the water is."

"True!"

Martin walked on ahead.

"Come on," he said. "Let's explore those rocks over there."

The boys continued their rock climbing by the water's edge, jumping between the rocks. Further round the peninsular, they discovered a long sea defensive wall that stretched a long way into the sea.

"Look, Manfred," said Martin. "We must go on that."

"Ja, why not?"

The boys were looking at it.

Manfred said, "It looks like people are walking on it."

"So they are," replied Martin, adding, "Come on. Let's go and tell the girls about it."

"Gut idea!"

The boys turned around and started to retrace their steps along the cragged rocks that were all along the peninsular coastline. They jumped over the many rock pools the sea had left behind, as it retreated, due to the tide going out. The boys leapt across some bigger rocks, as there was no path on the route they had taken. They were thoroughly enjoying their day out by the sea.

31

A Pleasant Time in Pola

Manfred and Martin returned to where the girls sat relaxing, dipping their feet in a large rock pool they had found. The boys explained to them what they had discovered. Caroline and Veronica were ready to explore some more of the peninsula, so once they had dried their feet and put their shoes back on, the four of them set off for the sea wall…

On reaching it, the children stood there looking out along the narrow rugged wall that jutted right out to sea. It had a walkway along one side of it; for people to walk and fish on.

"It looks quite long," said Caroline, who was admiring the view.

"Ja, it does," replied Veronica.

"Come on, Manfred," said Martin, running off along the wall.

"See you later, Caroline," he said, waving.

She returned the wave.

"Come on, Veronica," said Caroline, holding her arm. "Let's gracefully walk along the wall, like these other ladies."

"What a lovely idea"

The girls laughed, then started their walk. Many holidaymakers were walking along it, as it was one of the big attractions on the peninsula.

Veronica and Caroline, like many of the ladies, who they walked past, sheltered from the sun under their parasols, as they strolled gracefully along the sea wall.

"My mother likes to walk along sea walls," said Veronica.

"Does she?" replied Caroline.

"She says the sea air is good for you."

"I suppose it is."

"If you live in a big industrial city, like Vienna, there is a lot of pollution and smog from the factories. The dirt gets everywhere, especially on your lungs."

"I see."

Caroline had never lived in a big city with pollution, so she could only imagine the difference. She knew that Welwyn Garden City didn't suffer from pollution, like Veronica was describing.

Changing the subject, Caroline said, "I must say, this is a very enjoyable experience. It's a bit different to what I normally do."

Veronica looked at her.

"Don't tell me, in your time you don't walk on sea walls."

Caroline laughed.

"Oh, we do! What I meant was, I don't carry a parasol and I wear different clothes."

Veronica looked at her.

"What do you mean?" she said.

Caroline replied, "I wear shorts and a T-shirt. Like what I wear sometimes when we arrive back in your time."

"Oh, I zee," replied Veronica, who was now thinking about Caroline's clothes.

She added, "To be honest, what you wear is what I call vulgar. I mean, you show your legs. Ladies don't do that."

Caroline laughed.

"Yes, they do. You know where I come from, you dress as you feel."

"We do too!"

Caroline decided it was probably better to drop the subject.

Further up the sea wall, Caroline pointed, and said, "Look, Veronica. There are some fishermen over there. Let's go and see if they have caught anything?"

"Gut idea"

The girls wandered over to where two fishermen were sitting watching over their rods.

"Good afternoon, Miss," said one of the fishermen.

"Good afternoon," replied Veronica.

"Lovely day, Miss"

"Ja, it is. Tell me, sir, have you caught anything?"

"Not much, Miss. Just a couple of small ones."

He showed the girls his catch.

"But my friend here's caught a couple worth cooking for supper."

He looked at the other fisherman.

"Alfred," he said. "Can you show the ladies your catch?"

The man removed a cloth that was covering a bucket. The girls could see some medium-sized fish swimming about in it.

"Ja, they look all right," said Veronica.

"Gosh! It makes me feel hungry," added Caroline.

Veronica then said to the fishermen, "Thank you for showing us."

"Not at all, Miss," replied the first one.

The girls walked up to the end of the sea wall, where Manfred and Martin were standing looking out.

"Caroline, do you know what's over there?" asked Martin, pointing.

"No, what?"

"Italy"

"Is it? Oh right," she replied, laughing.

The girls were looking around them.

"It's a lovely view," said Veronica.

"Yes, it is," replied Caroline.

After a few minutes of enjoying the view, Veronica said, "Caroline, I think it's time to go back."

"Yes, I think you are right."

Back on the peninsula, the children found themselves a grassy area under some trees to sit down. The girls sat under their parasols relaxing. Martin was restless. He got his new football out from his bag.

"Come on, Manfred," he said. "I fancy a game of football."

"Ja, gut idea"

"Caroline, Veronica, we can play against you."

"Alright," replied Caroline, putting her parasol down and getting up.

Veronica sat there, looking up at her.

"Are you not going to join us?" asked Caroline.

"If you don't mind, I think I'll watch," she replied.

"Up to you"

"It's zo unladylike to play football."

"I play it all the time."

Veronica rolled her eyes upwards.

Caroline ran over to the boys.

"Come on, Martin. Pass me the ball."

He did.

Manfred, Martin and Caroline then played a short game of kick about football.

After a while, Caroline stopped, and said, "Boys, I think I'll leave you two to play on your own. I need to take a break. I am rather hot."

"Okay," replied Martin.

She wandered over to where Veronica was sitting.

"I can see why you don't like running about much," said Caroline. "It's hard work wearing these clothes."

"Ja, I know," replied Veronica, smiling. "That's why I prefer to watch. Anyway, young ladies don't play football."

"Well, I do."

"Ja, vell…"

"Anyway, it gives me an appetite. Talking of which, I am looking forward to our evening meal."

"Oh, me too. I thought I might try some fish, after seeing those fishermen earlier."

"Now that's a good idea."

Later, the children took a horse and carriage back into Pola. In the old town centre they wandered around its narrow streets, window shopping.

After a while, Martin said, "What time is it, Veronica?"

She looked at her watch.

"It's 5.35, why?"

"I'm hungry."

Caroline held out her hand.

"Nice to meet you hungry. I'm Caroline."

"Ha, ha!" replied the boy, shaking her hand.

"I think it's time to eat," suggested Veronica.

Manfred then said, "Have you still got that envelope, Veronica?"

"Hopefully"

She added, "To be honest, I'd forgotten about it."

The others all looked at her.

The girl immediately realised what was coming.

"What are you, Veronica?" said Caroline, smiling.

"Forgetful," said everyone, bursting into laughter.

"What's the name of this restaurant we're going to?" asked Martin.

Veronica replied, "Mario's."

"That sounds Italian," said Caroline.

"Ja, it might be. We'll find out when we get there."

Veronica stopped a man, who was passing with his wife.

"Excuse me," she said. "Could you tell me the way to this address, please?"

The man did.

As the children walked down a narrow side street, Manfred spotted the restaurant. It had a small bar terrace outside it.

"There it is," he said, pointing.

"Oh yeah. So it is," added Martin.

As they got closer, Veronica said, "It looks like an Italian restaurant."

"Great!" said Caroline.

Her brother added, "I think, I fancy a pizza."

Some people were sitting outside the restaurant on the bar terrace.

"Can we sit here, Veronica?" asked Manfred.

"Ja, if you like."

The children sat down at a table on the bar terrace.

"It's nice here," said Caroline, as she looked around her.

Veronica got out the envelope with the reservation in it.

A waiter came over.

In a strong Italian accent, he said, "Good evening, Miss."

The girl replied, "Good evening."

The waiter coughed, a little.

"Erm, I'm sorry to say, Miss. We don't normally serve children, who are unaccompanied by an adult, at this restaurant."

"I know," she said, handing him the written note. "But as you can see, my father has made a reservation for us here, knowing this point. He is also one of your top customers."

"I see."

She handed him one of her father's business cards.

The waiter looked at it, as well as the reservation that was written on the paper.

"Just a moment, please"

He went inside, checked his reservation book and then returned to the table, the children sat at.

"I am sorry for any misunderstanding, Miss. You are quite right. Your father, Commander Strauss, has indeed reserved a table for you for 18.00 hours."

Veronica smiled, and said, "Your apology is accepted."

She added, "May I see the menu, please?"

"Si, of course"

The waiter quickly got the menus that he gave everyone.

"Thank you," said Caroline, as she got hers.

"What would you like?" asked Veronica.

Caroline was looking at what was on offer.

"I fancy a pizza."

"Me too," added her brother.

"I thought you were having fish tonight, Caroline?" asked Veronica.

"Seeing these pizzas has made me change my mind."

"Oh, vell. I think I'll stick to having fish."

When the waiter returned, Martin said to him, "Excuse me. Can I ask you something?"

"Si, signore"

"Why's this restaurant called Mario's?"

"Martin," said Veronica, looking at him in her motherly way. "You don't ask questions, like that."

"Why not?"

The waiter laughed.

In his strong Italian accent, he said, "It's called *Mario's,* because it is named after the owner, a signor Mario Milano."

"Is he Italian, by any chance?"

"With a name like that, of course he is," said Caroline.

"He might not be."

Manfred added, "He could be Austro-Hungarian."

Martin looked at the waiter.

"Is he Italian?"

The waiter smiled.

"Si signore. He is Italian. "As a matter of fact Signor Mario comes from Sicily."

"Oh!"

"Would you, er, like to order now?"

"Yes please," replied Veronica, smiling at him.

Later, as the children sat there eating their meal, a five man band walked up the street towards the restaurant. They came up to the bar terrace, where they played a tune for the people sitting at it. A young boy, who was with them, took a cap round to every table. When he got to Veronica, she put some coins in it.

Once the children had finished their meal, the waiter came outside with another man.

"Signori and signore. You were asking earlier about Signor Mario. Well, this is the chef and owner of the restaurant, Signor Mario."

"Good evening," he said, in a strong Italian accent.

"Good evening," replied the surprised children.

"I do hope you liked the pizzas and fish."

Martin replied, "Mine was super, thanks."

Manfred added, "Ja, zo was mine."

"What about you young ladies?"

Veronica replied, "My fish was fine, thank you."

Caroline added, "And my pizza was great, thanks."

"Good, I am so happy."

He added, "Well, have a nice day."

In his cheeky way, Martin replied, "Don't worry. We will."

The waiter and restaurant owner departed.

Veronica then said, "This is perfect, Caroline. I mean, what more do you want, when you go on holiday?"

"Er, not much," she replied, as she sipped her half empty glass of fresh orange juice.

"But it's a pity we have to leave zo soon."

"Yeah, I know what you mean."

"There's always next year," said Manfred.

Caroline and Martin looked at him.

"Well, maybe for you two," said Caroline. "But I'm not sure about us. After all, the magic might not work then."

"That's true," said Veronica.

Manfred added, "If it does work, you can come here again, with us."

"Yeah, that would be really cool," said Martin, as he finished his ice cream.

Veronica put her napkin on the table.

She said, "I think I'll ask for the bill. But first, I need to powder my nose."

Caroline replied, "Oh, me too."

Once the girls had departed, Martin said, "Why do girls always go to the toilet in twos?"

Manfred replied, "No idea."

32

The Sailor and the Harbour

Having departed the restaurant, the children spent a few minutes looking around downtown Pola. It was an old traditional naval town, with narrow cobbled streets. The children did a bit of window shopping. Outside one particular shop that sold a variety of goods, Martin and Manfred stopped to look in its window.

"Can I buy a postcard?" asked Martin.

Veronica replied, "Ja, I think zo."

"I think I might get one, if that's all right, Veronica?" asked Manfred.

"Ja, it is okay."

The children selected one each.

While Veronica paid for them, the others looked around the inside of the shop. Caroline loved the old fashioned things that were dotted around the tourist shop, which to Veronica, of course, was the latest thing. The boys looked at all the different sweets in their large glass jars, on offer. Caroline looked at the souvenirs; Veronica at the clothes.

Having satisfied their curiosity, the children departed the souvenir shop.

Once outside it, Veronica looked at her watch.

"Sorry to rush you, but we need to head towards the rendezvous point. Otherwise, we'll be late."

"Gosh! Is it that time, already?" asked Caroline.

"I'm afraid zo," replied Veronica, nodding.

"Pity."

Just before 19.30, the four children walked towards Pola's Triumph Arch of Sergius.

"Look, Manfred," said Martin, pointing. "There's Lyshka. It looks like he's waiting for us."

"Oh, ja. Zo he is," he replied.

They waved at the sailor, as they walked over to their rendezvous point.

"Evening all," said Lyshka.

As he put out his cigarette, the sailor added, "Did you have a nice time, Miss?"

"Ja, thanks," replied Veronica. "It's been lovely, hasn't it, Martin?"

"Yeah, it's been really good."

"Right!" said Lyshka. "Let's get you children safely back to the dockyard, shall we?"

As the children and Lyshka walked along the harbour wall, near the naval dockyard's entrance, they passed many sailors. Caroline realised, most of them seemed to be heading into several of the bars that ran along the street. Many drunken sailors, drinking wine, beer and spirits, sat outside on the bar terraces at one of the many tables, in the evening sunshine. Many local girls were keeping them company.

"Gosh! There are a lot of drunken sailors here," said Caroline, as they walked past several of the bars.

"I can now see why Lyshka is our escort," replied Veronica.

"Still, it looks fun."

"Ja, I zuppose it does."

"It's a pity we can't join them."

"Caroline," said Veronica, stopping to look at her friend. "We are young ladies."

"Yes, I suppose we are," she replied, disappointedly.

At the naval dockyard gate, Lyshka went over to the guard, who, on seeing them all, opened the gate and let them in. After walking through a part of the dockyard, the children found themselves walking along the harbour front.

"What a beautiful view," said Caroline, as she looked out across the harbour.

"Yes, it is very picturesque," replied Veronica.

A little further up, Lyshka tossed his cigarette butt into the sea.

"Lyshka," said Caroline, enquiringly.

"Yes, Miss," replied the sailor, looking at her.

"How come you're not on shore leave, like the other sailors?"

"Simple," he replied. "Someone has to look after the battleship during the day. This time, it's me."

"Do you not get the night off, like the other sailors?"

"Funny you should say that, Miss. I clock off in an hour. Zo I'll be joining the lads shortly for a few bevvies, in one of those bars we just passed."

"Oh right!" said Caroline, looking at Veronica.

"Most of the crew are on shore leave till 03.00 hours."

"Really," said Veronica.

Lyshka lit himself another cigarette.

"Does that include you?" asked Caroline.

"Probably, Miss"

On the wooden jetty, the children and Lyshka climbed aboard the small motor boat. A couple of other sailors cast off. The motor vessel set off, on its short journey towards *SMS Tegetthoff*.

Once everyone had stepped aboard the dreadnought battleship, Lyshka turned to Veronica, and said, "Vell, that's my mission over."

She replied, "Thanks for collecting us."

"My pleasure, Miss"

"Yes, thank you, Lyshka," added Caroline.

After saying 'goodnight' to the sailor, the children headed straight for the main deck, where they looked out at the panoramic view.

"Wow! That's what I call a good view," said Martin.

"It is," replied Manfred.

As the children looked out across the harbour, the sun was setting. Some fishing boats were leaving the harbour, on their way into the Adriatic Sea to do some night fishing. The children slowly made their way along the deck, looking out at the view.

"You know, Veronica," said Caroline. "It's been a really great holiday, coming down here."

She replied, "Ja, I've loved it."

"It's a pity it's so short."

"Ja, it could have been a bit longer. Never mind, there's always next time."

"Yes, maybe"

After a moment of looking out, Veronica said, "I have this strange feeling inside me, telling me, this feels like the beginning of the end of everything. It's really weird, Caroline."

"Actually, I know what you mean," she replied, adding, "Tonight, my left hand feels odd."

Martin heard the comment.

"Does it?" he said.

He added, "Have you looked at the magic key recently?"

Caroline replied, "No, not for a while."

"Well, you'd better look at it. It might have changed colour again?"

"What here?"

Martin looked around him.

"Well, there's no one about, Caroline."

She looked in her handbag, poked around and then produced the key. Looking at it, she said, "It's still red. I mean, it used to be a normal grey-coloured metal key. This can't be right, surely?"

"Er, no, not really"

"I feel as if it's trying to tell me something. But I don't know what."

"It could be a warning?" suggested Veronica.

"Yes, it could be. But a warning about what?" asked Caroline.

Manfred was thinking.

"Maybe, you might lose your ability to time travel," he said.

223

"Oh don't say things like that, Manfred," said Martin. "Otherwise, we won't be able to see you again."

"I know," he replied. "But nothing lasts forever, does it?"

"True," added Caroline.

The light wind was blowing Veronica's hair.

Changing the subject, she said, "Look at the sunset, Caroline. It's great, isn't it?"

She replied, "Yes, I must admit, it does look pretty good."

The children were now pretty tired, after their day of adventures in Pola. It was time for bed. Veronica made the suggestion. Everyone wanted an early night. Even the boys were happy to go to their bunks. After looking at the harbour one last time, the children walked along the dreadnought battleships deck, before heading back to their cabins and bed.

33

Wakey Wakey Shipmates

On board the dreadnought battleship, in the cabin the girls were staying in, it was now morning. Caroline was in a deep sleep. She was suddenly woken up by Veronica, who had got up and turned on the light in the cabin.

"Good morning, Caroline," she said.

"Morning," Caroline replied, yawning. "What time is it?"

Veronica looked at her watch.

"It's gone nine," she said.

"Gone nine! Really?" said Caroline, surprised. "I didn't realise it was so late."

She sat up, banging her head on the ceiling above.

"Am I going stupid, or was there was no wake-up call this morning?"

"No, you're not going stupid. I didn't hear one either."

"I take it, we're still in Pola?"

Veronica looked through the porthole.

"Looks like it," she said.

Once she had finished brushing her teeth, she added, "We're meant to be departing at 10.00 hours."

"Oh, yes. I forgot," said Caroline.

She added, "I want to watch us depart."

"Vell, you'd better get up then."

"I'll let you finish first," added Caroline, who lay there watching Veronica wash her face.

After a few moments, she said, "That was a great day, yesterday."

"Ja, I enjoyed it," replied Veronica, while using her facecloth.

"Mind you, it was a bit noisy last night, when some of those sailors came back."

"Noisy, it vas terrible. I couldn't sleep a wink."

"Yes, I know what you mean. Actually, I thought it was quite frightening, hearing all those drunken sailors making their way on board."

"I thought one or two would try to attack us," said Veronica.

"The door was locked, so they couldn't. Anyway, they wouldn't dare, not with your father on board."

"You don't know the Austrian Navy."

"True, but I'd like to," said Caroline, smiling.

"Come on. Get up, lazybones," replied Veronica. "I want to go on deck and watch us depart."

"Fine. Just give me a few minutes, will you?"

Caroline suddenly screamed and jumped out of bed, rapidly.

"Ugh, there's a cockroach on my bed."

"Where?"

"There!" she said, pointing and shuddering at the same time.

Veronica got her shoe, hit it, but missed. The cockroach ran across the bed and disappeared under it.

"Where's it gone?" asked Caroline, frantically looking for it.

Veronica put her shoe back on the cabin floor.

"Don't worry about it. It's only a cockroach. It won't hurt you."

"It might."

"You are not going to sleep there any more, Caroline. And I am sure there are hundreds more cockroaches on this battleship."

"Why didn't you tell me? I would never have come aboard, had I known that."

"Caroline," said Veronica, looking at her. "This is a battleship, not a hotel. And even they have hundreds of cockroaches in them."

"Do they?"

"Ja, of course"

"Oh!"

Martin and Manfred had had a lie in. Being boys, they were not the first to surface, if they didn't need to. They were still in bed, when Caroline and Veronica knocked at their cabin door.

After a moment, Martin opened the door.

"Gosh! Are you two still in bed?" said Caroline.

"Not any more, I'm not," replied her brother, yawning.

"Don't tell me, you didn't get to sleep till late?"

"How did you know that?"

"Because we also got to sleep late."

"The sailors kept us awake," said Manfred, yawning.

"Yeah, it was really cool listening to them," added Martin. "Maybe, I'll be a sailor one day. It sounds fun."

"Look, hurry up and get washed and dressed you two," said Veronica, impatiently. "The battleship's about to depart Pola."

"All right," replied Manfred.

"We're going on deck," said Caroline.

"Oh, wait for us please. We won't be long," said Martin, pulling his shorts on.

"It's probably better we see you on deck," added his sister. "You need to brush your teeth and wash your face first, Martin."

"Yes, Caroline!"

The girls went on deck. The sun was shining as they walked along the slightly windy deck of *SMS Tegetthoff*. Some sailors were mopping the decks.

"Good morning, Miss Strauss," said one, winking at her, as the girls passed him.

"Good morning," she replied.

After walking up the deck a bit further, Caroline and Veronica stopped and looked out across the harbour.

As Veronica turned around, she said, "Oh look! There's my father."

"Where?" asked Caroline.

"Over there, by the gun turret," she replied, waving at him.

"Oh, yes. So he is."

They started to walk over to him.

The Commander saw them and started to walk towards the girls. They met next to another gun turret.

"Good morning, girls," said the Commander.

"Good morning," they replied.

"A beautiful morning, wouldn't you say?"

He tried to light his pipe.

"Yes it is, Commander," replied Caroline.

"How did you get on in Pola, yesterday?"

"Fine," replied Veronica.

Caroline added, "It was wonderful."

The Commander, who had been momentarily looking down the deck of the battleship, added, "Ja, I like it. It makes a refreshing change, after the likes of Trieste or Vienna."

Turning to his daughter, he said, "Did Manfred and Martin behave themselves yesterday, Veronica?"

She replied, "Ja, they were fine, Papa."

"By the way, where are the boys?"

Veronica laughed.

"Just getting up," she replied.

"That sounds like Manfred," he added, laughing.

The Commander relit his pipe, as he looked out across the harbour.

"Did you girls manage to get any sleep last night?"

"Not much," replied Caroline. "But we did get some, thanks."

"The crew had last night off. They deserved it, after all their hard work. It's always a bit rowdy, when they return from a night on the tiles. You might have noticed, there was no wake-up call this morning."

"That's true," said Caroline.

"We'll be quietly slipping out of the harbour around 10.00 hours. Most of the crew resume work again at noon."

"Oh, I see."

"They'll then be preparing for some sea trials next week with the German navy."

"The German navy? Sorry, I'm not with you, Commander," said Caroline, who was wondering what he was going on about.

The Commander explained: "We will be undertaking some joint sea trials this week with the German navy, starting in Trieste. The German navy is currently sailing round the Mediterranean, doing their own sea trials. They will be docking in Trieste, on Wednesday. They are coming from Königsberg in the Baltic, having sailed down past France and Spain."

"I see," said Caroline.

She was in her 'make it up as she went along' mode.

She then asked, "Have the Germans got many battleships, Commander?"

The Commander laughed.

"Vell, Caroline," he said. "Let's just say, they've got a few more than us."

The Commander added, "Actually, Caroline. The German navy is a force to be reckoned with."

"Oh!"

Veronica decided to change the subject.

"What time will we get to Trieste, Papa?"

"Vell," he replied. "We should be there around 15.00 hours. Zo there's plenty of time for you girls to relax and enjoy yourselves, here on deck."

Caroline turned to Veronica, and said, "We can do some sunbathing."

The Commander laughed.

"Vell," he said. "There's plenty of space for that."

Caroline replied, "But there are not many chairs for us to sit on, Commander."

He replied, fairly loudly, "That's because this is not a cruise ship. It's a battleship!" After laughing at his own joke, he added, softly, "Ask one of the sailors, Caroline. They'll sort you out with a couple."

"Yes, Commander"

"Vell, I'll leave you girls to it. Enjoy yourselves."

"See you later, Papa," said Veronica, who embraced him.

He waved to the girls, as he walked off along the deck.

As the girls continued their walk towards the aft of the battleship, Martin and Manfred appeared on deck. They ran up to the girls.

"Took your time," said Caroline, smiling.

"I was washing my face," said Martin, smiling sweetly at her. "Anyway, we haven't left port yet."

He stuck his tongue out at her. She responded, likewise.

"Now, now, you two," said Veronica, who was watching them.

Martin then had a thought.

"Caroline," he said, slowly.

His sister looked at him.

"Yes, Martin"

"I've just thought of a good song I could sing, about the sailors who were drunk last night."

Caroline gave him another one of her 'looks'.

She said, "It's a bit early in the morning for songs."

"I know, but…"

"Alright, let's hear it…"

Martin cleared his throat, took a deep breath and started singing…

"What do we do with a drunken sailor?

What do we do with a drunken sailor?

What do we do with a drunken sailor?

Early in the morning

Hoo-ray up she rises

Hoo-ray up she rises

Hoo-ray up she rises

Early in the morning"

The boy, suddenly stopped, singing.

"That's all, I know," he said.

Caroline replied, "Not bad, Martin. That's pretty good for you."

"Ja, it is gut, Martin," added Manfred.

Veronica gave him one of her 'I don't understand you' looks.

"It's an old British sailor's song," said Caroline.

"Oh, I zee," said Veronica, still not fully getting it.

Manfred had noticed a couple of sailors by the anchor chain.

"Look – over there," he said, pointing. "I think we're leaving."

"What are they doing?" asked Caroline.

"They're pulling the anchor chain up."

Some whistles went and the children could hear the engines roaring into life. The dreadnought battleship turned itself around in the centre of Pola harbour and then slowly sailed out into the Adriatic Sea. Throughout all this, the children watched from various viewpoints on the battleships decks.

It was only when they were out at sea, away from the shore, that Manfred said, "What about breakfast, Veronica?"

She looked at her watch.

"Gosh," she said. "I think we're a bit late for breakfast. It's nearly eleven."

"Vell," added Manfred. "I still need something to eat."

"So do I," said Caroline.

"Come on," added Martin. "Let's go down and see what's there."

The children departed the sunlit deck and went inside the dreadnought battleship. They walked down the dark dimly-lit narrow corridors, towards the sailors' mess hall, where they hoped to get something to eat.

34

Battleship at Sea

After eating a late breakfast in the sailor's mess hall, the children returned to the main deck. As they stood there looking out to sea, some whistles blew. Before they knew it, what looked like hundreds of sailors, suddenly appeared from every doorway. All, were heading for the main deck.

"Look, Manfred," said Martin.

"What's going on?" asked Caroline.

"I don't know," replied Veronica.

"They're all lining up," added Manfred.

Out of the corner of her eye, Veronica saw the ship's First Officer, who was walking towards her.

"Excuse me, what going on?" she asked him.

He replied, "Gym practice, Miss."

"Really?" added Caroline.

At that moment, some Austro-Hungarian naval music blasted out of the tannoys on deck. A naval officer yelled some instructions in German and Hungarian. An outdoor gym session then started on the main deck.

The girls were fascinated.

"This is really great," said Caroline to Veronica.

"Vell, I must admit it's different," she replied.

"Let's go over here?" suggested Caroline, who wanted a better view of all the sailors on deck.

As the boys stood watching, the girls began to walk up the deck, by the side of the sailors.

"Manfred, why don't we have a go at the exercises?" suggested Martin.

"Ja, gut idea," he replied. "But let's go up the front."

"Okay"

Whilst the boys joined in, the girls watched the sailors do their gym routines.

"They're very good," said Veronica.

"Yes, I must admit, they are," replied Caroline.

She added, "You know, if I weren't dressed in this long dress, I'd get changed into my gym clothes and join in myself."

Veronica looked at her, in horror.

"Caroline, we are young ladies. We don't do things like this."

"Why not?"

"It's zo unladylike."

"Back in my time it's not."

Veronica rolled her eyes upwards.

Caroline looked at her.

"Veronica, I do this down the gym with my friends," she said. "We call it aerobics. But it's really no different to this."

"I zee."

The gym exercises lasted around twenty minutes, after which the music stopped. The trainer yelled a few words in German and Hungarian. The sailors then began to disappear below deck.

"That was really good," said Caroline.

"Ja, I must admit it was," replied Veronica.

The boys came over to the girls.

"You were good, Martin," said his sister.

"It was fun," he replied.

"Ja, it was," added Manfred.

"We enjoyed it," said Veronica, smiling.

Martin then said, "We're going to explore the battleship, aren't we, Manfred?"

"Ja"

"Have a nice time," replied Caroline.

"See you later," added Martin, waving.

The boys departed. They ran around the decks to burn off a bit more energy, before going below decks to visit the engine room.

In it, Martin shouted, "It's very noisy down here."

"Ja it is," replied Manfred, "And hot."

The boys could see various engines that were in a line from where they stood. Teams of men were shovelling coal into them.

"I wouldn't like to do that job," said Martin.

"Me neither," replied Manfred. "It looks like hard work."

"I'd rather be the Captain."

"Me too"

As the girls looked out to sea, Caroline said, "Veronica, when they were doing those routines, I noticed the battleships crew all seem to speak different languages."

"Yes, that's true. They do," she replied.

"How do they understand each other?"

"Oh, that's easy," Veronica replied. "The officers on board have to speak the four main languages of the Austro-Hungarian Empire, zo that they can communicate with the crew, who in turn have to speak one of these languages."

"Really?" said Caroline.

She added, "How many languages are there that the ordinary sailors speak?"

"Erm, I need to think about that."

After a moment, Veronica said, "I think there are about eleven spoken languages in the Austro-Hungarian Empire."

"Eleven," said Caroline. "So how do the sailors understand each other?"

Veronica looked at Caroline, whilst trying to get her point.

"Simple. They have to speak one of the four main languages."

"No, you are missing my point. What if one of them speaks German, but the other only speaks Hungarian. Then what?"

"Oh, I zee what you mean."

She added, "My father once told me, the crews on the battleships are generally made up by language divide."

"What do you mean?"

"Vell, the German and Czech speakers are generally in the signals. They also do engine room duties. The Hungarians are the gunners, while the Croats and Italians are ordinary seamen or stokers. Does that answer your question?"

"Erm, I think so."

In the bridge, Martin and Manfred were kneeling on some stools, looking out to sea.

"How fast are we going, Captain?" asked Manfred.

He replied, "At the moment, we're doing about ten knots."

"Is that fast?"

"No, the battleship is capable of much higher speeds. However, as we are *not* on any major manoeuvres, we are simply going at a steady rate of knots, back to Trieste."

"Is it good being the Captain?" asked Martin.

The Captain laughed.

"Vell, when you grow up, Martin. You can join your British Empire's navy. You can work your way up through the ranks and then, you'll know."

"Yes sir," replied the boy, grinning up at him.

The girls decided to do a spot of sunbathing on some chairs they had found, in a shady part of the deck.

As they lay there, Caroline said, "I must say, this is really weird lying here, like this. It's not exactly sunbathing, is it?"

Veronica looked over at her.

"What do you mean?" she asked.

"Well," said Caroline. "In my time, I wouldn't be wearing a long dress and thin petticoat, sheltering from the sun. I'd be in my bikini, getting a good tan in the sun."

Veronica was curious.

"You mentioned about this 'bikini' before, when we were sitting on the rocks."

"Yes, that's right. I did."

"But it's vulgar and unladylike, exposing your body and legs, like that."

"No, not at all. Most young women and girls wear them."

"But why?" asked Veronica.

Caroline had to think about that one.

"Dunno," she replied. "It's the fashion, that's all."

"Zo, are you saying, in the future women don't enjoy the sun, like we are now?"

Caroline laughed.

"Definitely not," she replied.

"But this is how ladies enjoy the sun."

"Well," added Caroline. "I'm not much of a lady. Whilst it's nice lying here, like this, it is quite uncomfortable at times, wearing all these clothes in the hot sun. That's why I wear a T-shirt and shorts, back in my own time."

"Do you mean those clothes you wear, when you arrive from the future?"

"Er, yes. That's right."

Caroline added, "I come here wearing my shorts or my jeans. I normally wear a T-shirt with them."

"Why do you call them T-shirts?" asked Veronica.

"Erm," said Caroline, thinking about it. "I think it's because they are shaped like the letter T."

"Oh, I zee."

Caroline was thinking.

"Veronica," she said, smiling. "You and I have different fashion tastes."

"Ja, I gathered that."

She added, "Zo, fashions change?"

"Yes, of course," said Caroline. "Women in my time, don't wear long dresses. In fact, most are quite short and many women wear trousers."

"Trousers. Do they really?"

"Yes, I wear them all the time."

"Zo I have seen. But it is zo unladylike," said Veronica, rolling her eyes upward.

Just then, Martin and Manfred arrived.

"We've found some chalk and a stone," said Manfred.

"Did you?" replied Veronica, sitting up.

"We can have a game of hopscotch, if you like," added Manfred.

"That sounds like a good idea," she replied.

Looking at Caroline, she said, "Can you play hopscotch?"

"Of course, I can play hopscotch," said Caroline. "Mind you, I haven't played it for a few years. I'm a bit old for it now."

"You're never too old," added Veronica. "Come on! Let's give it a go."

After drawing out the games area, the children played several games of hopscotch on the deck of *SMS Tegetthoff*. The children even got a couple of sailors to join in the fun. The boys got themselves a couple more chairs and a table, and played a game of chess, one of the sailors had thoughtfully given them to help pass the time.

Later, the boys chased the girls around the deck, played 'Lookout', and climbed on the guns, with a little help from some of the sailors.

As *SMS Tegetthoff* steamed into Trieste harbour, she blew her horn, indicating her arrival in the Austro-Hungarian port. The children watched, eager eyed, as the dreadnought battleship edged itself towards the shoreline, lining itself up alongside one of the jetties in the harbour. On board ship there was a frenzy of movement, as sailors prepared to go ashore.

A couple of huge ropes were tossed onto the jetty to some waiting sailors, who tied them to a couple of metal bollards. The battleship was now docked. A group of sailors de-berthed down a gangway.

The children, meanwhile, were watching everything from the side deck, fascinated, by what they saw. The port area seemed to be a buzz of naval activity.

As they stood there, Veronica said, "Vell, I suppose it is time for us to go. Shall we get our things, Caroline?"

"Sure," she replied, disappointed to be leaving the battleship.

Looking at her brother, Caroline said, "Come on, Martin. We're leaving."

The boy nodded and replied, "You know, it's been really good fun being on here. Hasn't it, Manfred?"

"I'll say!"

After going down to their cabins to check everything, the children then went to the Commander's cabin. Veronica knocked on the door.

The Commander's First Officer Brano, opened it.

On seeing Veronica, he said, "Oh, good afternoon, Miss Strauss."

"Good afternoon, Brano," she replied, adding, "Is my father there?"

"Yes, of course," he replied. "Er, come in."

The children went in.

The First Officer said, "Wait here a moment, will you? I'll just get the Commander."

After waiting a couple of moments, the door opened and the Commander walked in.

On seeing his children, he said, "Oh, what a lovely surprise."

"Hello, Papa," said Veronica. "You told us to visit you, before we departed. Zo, here we are."

"Yes," replied the Commander. "You are quite right, I did."

"We've come to say goodbye, Papa."

"I zee. Vell, I hope you have all enjoyed yourselves?"

"It's been really great," said Martin.

The Commander then said, "This adventure, might help you consider being in the navy, boys?"

"It might do, Papa," replied Manfred.

"Commander, it's been a real adventure," said Caroline, smiling.

"Gut," he replied. "Vell, I'm glad you enjoyed it."

At that moment, there was a knock at the door. Brano appeared, with Lyshka and another sailor behind him.

"Commander," said Brano. "As requested, sir. I found Lyshka and Maximilian. I'll also get another two sailors, who can help them carry the children's baggage off the ship."

"Thank you, Brano"

The Commander kissed and hugged his daughter and son. He also shook hands with Caroline and Martin.

He said, "I've arranged with Josef to pick you up and look after you, till you get the train home this evening. Have a safe journey back to Vienna, won't you?"

Veronica quickly replied, "We are all going back to the castle, Papa."

"Oh, jolly good"

"Thank you again, Commander," said Caroline, smiling.

As the children departed, Martin turned around and saluted the Commander.

The man smiled at the boy and returned his salute.

The children followed the sailors along the ship's corridors, towards their cabins.

After putting Veronica's suitcase in the corridor, Lyshka said, "Is that everything, Miss?"

"Ja, I think zo."

"Right, let's get you young ladies safely ashore. Shall we?"

"And us," added Manfred, who was waiting in the corridor with Martin.

"Yes of course, young man."

Having collected all the children's luggage, the sailors led the way back along the narrow corridors and down the steep gangway that led everyone onto dry land.

As they stood there, Manfred saw a car approach.

"Look, Martin," he said, "There's Sophie coming towards us."

The cream-coloured motor car pulled up.

Josef, the chauffeur, got out.

"Good afternoon, Miss Strauss," he said.

She replied, "Good afternoon, Josef."

"As arranged, I am here to take you all to the railway station."

"Jolly good," said Veronica.

"Before we do that. Your father suggested that I take you all for afternoon tea at the Savoy. He thought it might help, ahead of the long journey home, Miss."

"Oh, that's thoughtful of him, Josef."

"Your father is always thoughtful, Miss Strauss."

After loading the motor car up, everyone got in. Josef slowly drove off. The children waved at the four sailors, who stood there on the jetty, waving back at them.

Once they were outside the naval dockyard, the motor car gracefully made its way along the seafront, towards the Commander's favourite hotel in Trieste.

35

An Afternoon in Trieste

The chauffeur drove the cream-coloured motor car up to the front of the Savoy Hotel, in Trieste. The elegance of its architecture, there for all to admire. A footman came to open the doors of the motor car. After alighting, the children and Josef followed him into the hotel.

In the foyer, the children looked around them, marvelling at its features.

"Talk about posh and swanky," said Caroline.

"What do you mean?" asked Veronica to Caroline, as they stood there.

"It means you need to be rich to go in a place, like this."

"What sort of place do you normally go in?"

"I don't normally go in places, like this," replied Caroline, looking around.

The girl was stunned by the hotel's beauty.

"Gosh!" she added, "This is amazing. Actually, it's awesome."

"Awesome?" said Veronica, giving her one of her funny looks.

"It's an American phrase, we use. It means really amazing," explained Caroline.

"Oh, I zee," said Veronica.

"This way everyone," said a waiter, beckoning them to all follow him.

The children found themselves in the Grand Dining Room, in the hotel. Huge chandeliers hung down from the ceiling. The waiter sat them down at a table, in the middle of the room. All around them, fellow guests were taking afternoon tea and cakes.

Once they were seated, the waiter returned with some menus, which everyone looked at.

"What would you like, Miss Veronica?" asked the chauffeur.

"I think I'd prefer a proper meal, as opposed to just afternoon tea and cake, Josef."

"Ja, it might be better, as you've a long journey ahead of you."

The children all opted for a full meal and soft drink, each, that they ordered from the hovering waiter.

Once he had departed, the chauffeur said, "Er, will you excuse me a moment, Miss Veronica."

"Ja, of course, Josef."

As he walked towards the exit door, Martin said, "Where's he going, Manfred?"

"I think he's gone to powder his nose."

"Oh!" replied Martin, getting the point and laughing.

As the boy sat there, he was looking around the room.

"It's a bit different to McDonald's, Caroline."

"Just a tad"

"What's McDonald's?" asked Manfred.

"It's a fast food restaurant chain."

"Yeah, you get burgers in there and Happy Meals," beamed Martin.

"Does the meal make you happy?" asked Veronica.

Martin and Caroline laughed.

"No, not exactly," she replied. "They give you free toys with your meal."

"Why do they need to give you toys with your meal?" asked Veronica, not seeing the point. "Surely, you are there to eat a meal?"

Martin didn't know.

"You are," he replied. "But that's was makes it so great – getting a free toy."

"What is fast food?" asked Manfred.

Caroline explained.

"It's food that is served fast – quickly."

"Yeah, it's much quicker than this," said Martin, who was now a bit bored, waiting for his meal to arrive from the hotel kitchen.

"And you eat it with your hands."

"*With your hands,*" said Veronica, raising her eyebrows. "Gosh! How primitive."

Caroline laughed, replying, "It's a bit difficult eating a burger with a knife and fork."

"And I thought the future would be more sophisticated."

"You sound like a bit of a snob."

"No, I am not a snob," said Veronica, a bit annoyed. "It just sounds zo common, eating with your hands."

"Yeah, I take your point," said Caroline, not wishing to offend her friend.

She added, "Veronica, everyone eats burgers with their hands in McDonald's. It's how you eat junk food."

"Junk food?" asked Veronica, not understanding.

"It means, fatty fast quick food," explained Caroline, who was suddenly feeling rather tired.

"I prefer to eat healthy food."

"Me too, actually. I much prefer to eat my mum's home cooking."

Martin looked at his sister.

"Caroline, can you get the magic key out? I want to see if it has changed colour."

His sister picked up her handbag, opened it and looked in it for the key. Picking it out, she put it on the table.

"Look! It's turned orange," said Manfred, excitedly.

"So it has," said Martin, picking it up and looking at it fascinated.

As he replaced the key on the table, Veronica saw Josef reappear in the large dining room. He started to walk towards them.

"Look out!" said the girl, motioning.

Caroline quickly popped the magic key back in her handbag, taking a handkerchief out to wipe her face.

As the chauffeur sat back down at the table, he asked, "Is everything all right?"

"Yes, thanks," replied Caroline, smiling sweetly.

Martin was yawning.

"Are you tired, Martin?" asked Veronica.

"Yes, I'm exhausted."

"I am too," said Manfred.

"We'll soon be on the train," added Veronica.

"What time does the train depart, Josef?" asked Martin, yawning yet again.

He replied, "I believe the Riviera Express to Vienna, departs at 19.00".

"Oh, right," said Martin, nodding.

Josef had had an idea.

"If I may make a suggestion, Miss Veronica?"

"Ja, of course"

"As we have a little time, could I suggest that after we have eaten, we all go for a short walk along the seafront to walk off the food?"

"What an excellent idea, Josef."

Once they had finished their meal, Josef and the children walked along the nearby seafront. They looked out to sea at some of the naval ships and boats that were in the vicinity. The sea air was helping to wake the children up.

Martin and Manfred left the girls to walk along the promenade in a more ladylike way, under their parasols, with their father's chauffeur Josef in attendance.

"I must say, Josef," said Veronica. "This was an excellent idea of yours, to go for a stroll after our meal."

"Thank you, Miss Veronica."

"It's a lovely afternoon," added Caroline, who was enjoying the moment.

"Ja it is," replied Veronica.

They stopped, to look out at some naval ships that were anchored in the harbour.

"You know, Veronica," said Caroline. "I have really enjoyed our visit to Trieste and Pola. It's been a really magical experience."

"Ja, it has. I am so glad, you could come, Caroline. We'll have to do it again, next year."

"Maybe?" she replied, smiling.

Caroline thought it, highly unlikely, she would return to Trieste, certainly not in 1913.

Further up the promenade, the boys were playing a game of Battleships.

"Manfred, I'm attacking your battleship. I've got my guns aimed at it."

"Go ahead – fire – you'll never hit it."

"Sure, I will. I'm firing. Got you!"

"Damn, I'm sinking."

The boys looked out across the harbour.

"You know, Manfred. That was really good of your dad to let us stay on his battleship."

"Ja, it was, wasn't it?"

He added, "But I don't think it was *his* battleship. *SMS Tegetthoff* has its own captain. My father is merely the Commander in Chief of the entire Austro-Hungarian navy. Zo actually, he can go on *all* the battleships."

"Oh right! Well, next time, we'll have to go on more of them."

"Ja, gut idea"

The boys ran up to where some people were watching a naval brass band play, on a round bandstand, on the seafront.

"Can you play an instrument?" asked Martin.

"Of course! I play the violin," replied Manfred.

"Do you really?"

"Ja, but not very vell. I've only just started to learn how to play it."

Manfred added, "What do you play?"

"Me? I play the recorder," replied Martin, adding, "But I want to learn how to play the drums, one day."

"I want to play the trumpet, like that man over there."

The girls had decided to sit on one of the benches that were dotted along the promenade. The chauffeur stood in front of them, smoking a cigarette.

"When will your father be returning to the castle, Veronica?" asked Caroline.

"I am not sure. To be honest, he never tells me. It depends on his job."

"Yes, I suppose it does."

After a moment, she said, "Didn't he say he was going to be going on some naval exercises?"

"Ja that's right, he did. He is due to meet the German navy here this week. They are meant to be doing some naval exercises together. Isn't that right, Josef?"

The chauffeur finished inhaling his cigarette, and then said, "It is, Miss Veronica. I believe, your father will be co-ordinating some joint military training manoeuvres with the Germany navy and our own Austro-Hungarian navy, along the Adriatic coastline and parts of the Mediterranean. But I am not sure where, as I believe that information is classified, Miss Veronica."

"Oh, I zee."

"Veronica, it's top secret information," said Caroline, smiling.

"Erm, not exactly, Miss Caroline," added Josef. "But it's not for our ears and eyes. We are not in the Austro-Hungarian navy, Miss."

"True"

They strolled along the promenade a bit further.

Some gulls flew overhead, landing on the sea wall, near them.

"Will you be staying here, Josef?" asked Veronica.

"Yes, Miss. I will be here, for as long as your father needs me."

"Do you go with him on his battleship journeys?" asked Caroline.

"Not usually, Miss. Sometimes, I drive down to Pola to pick him up from there. I have been with him on several of the battleships, when he needs something in particular delivering. However, I try to avoid any sea travel, as I suffer from seasickness."

Caroline laughed.

"Oh, I suppose that doesn't help, when on board a ship."

"I am his driver, not his naval crew."

"Ja, of course," added Veronica.

The boys ran over to where they stood.

"Any chance of an ice cream?" asked Martin.

"An ice cream?" replied Caroline.

"Yeah, there's an ice cream seller, over there. Near where the band is playing," he said, pointing.

"You've just eaten a big meal, Martin."

"I still fancy an ice cream."

"I'd like one too," added Manfred.

"Can we have one, Veronica?"

"Ja, of course"

She stood up.

"Would you like an ice cream, Josef?"

"That's very kind of you, Miss Veronica. As a matter of fact, I would."

"Come on then, Martin. Let's go and see what they've got. Shall we?"

As they walked towards the ice cream stall, the girls stopped to watch the military band.

"I do love to watch the band play, don't you, Caroline?"

"Erm, yes. But I tend to watch different kinds of bands, to this," she said, smiling sweetly.

"How different?"

"I like to watch rock bands."

"Rock bands?"

She added, "Oh ja. I do seem to remember you saying something about them. But I can't remember, what."

"Erm, well, I can't explain what they are, right now, Veronica, as there are people around. But, let's just say they are different to what you see now."

"Oh, ja. I think I understand you," she replied, getting her drift.

At the ice cream stall, the children and Josef joined a small queue.

"What lovely music," said Veronica, as they waited their turn.

"Er, yes, it sounds alright," replied Caroline.

"Don't tell me, in your country, you don't have brass bands?"

Caroline laughed.

"Oh, we do. Only they're not so popular."

Both girls were careful what they said, in front of the people around them.

The queue moved forward.

"Can I help you, Miss," asked the ice cream seller.

"Oh, yes, good afternoon," Veronica replied. "Could I have five ice creams, please?"

"Certainly, Miss"

The man prepared them and gave the ice creams to her.

"Thanks," she said, handing them out.

Rooting in her handbag for her purse, she paid the ice cream man.

As he gave Veronica her change, he said, "Thank you, Miss. Have a nice day."

"You too"

The children and Josef slowly walked back along the promenade, licking their ice creams.

As they did so, Martin said, "What are we doing next, Josef?"

"I believe we are heading back to the Savoy Hotel, Master Martin."

"What's happening there then?"

"We are taking Sophie to the railway station."

"Oh, right!"

Back at the Savoy, the boys ran up to the motor car.

"Beat you!" said Martin.

"You had a head start," replied Manfred.

After Josef had opened the doors, he said, "Jump in, will you?"

Everyone got in.

Once the car doors were fastened, the chauffeur crank started the motor car and then drove off towards the railway station.

At the station, Josef parked the motor car.

Turning his head towards the children, he said, "Could you all wait here a moment, whilst I organise some porters?"

The chauffeur got out and went and found a couple of porters, to assist him take the luggage from the car to the train. The children walked with them and Josef, along the platform, to the waiting train.

"It's quite busy," said Caroline, as they walked up the platform.

"Ja, it is, isn't it?" replied Veronica.

"Have you got the tickets, Veronica?" asked Manfred.

"Hopefully!" she replied.

As they walked along, the chauffeur asked her, "Which carriage are you in, Miss Veronica?"

"I'm not sure, Josef. I'll need to look in my handbag at the tickets."

They all stopped, whilst she looked.

Having got the tickets out, she read what was written on them.

"We're looking for carriage 4, sleeping compartment 7."

"Very good, Miss," replied the chauffeur, looking for the right carriage.

Having located it, Veronica walked over to the guard on the train, who was organising the sleeping wagon for passengers.

"Good evening," said Veronica, to him.

"Good evening, Miss," he replied.

"We have a reservation in sleeping compartment 7."

"Very good, Miss," he said, smiling at her, while checking her tickets.

Once he had done so, he said, "Could I recommend the porters get your luggage on board first, Miss? Then you can get on."

Veronica replied, "Ja, of course."

Turning to the porters, she said, "Could you load the luggage in sleeping compartment 7, please?"

One replied, "Certainly, Miss."

Turning to the chauffeur, she said, "Vell, Josef. I think it's time to say goodbye."

"Ja, I believe it is, Miss."

"As always, thank you"

"Not at all, Miss Veronica. It is always a pleasure."

With their luggage in the compartment, the children got on the train.

In the corridor, the girls pulled down a window and leant out of it.

"Josef, see you back at the castle," said Veronica, waving.

"Indeed, Miss Veronica," he replied.

He added, "Have a safe journey home."

The chauffeur waited on the platform for the train to depart.

After a few minutes, the stationmaster blew his whistle and raised his flag. A massive amount of steam and smoke was released into the air from the steam engine; its wheels seemed to want to rush forward. Slowly, the locomotive gradually edged its way out of Trieste railway station. As it did, the chauffeur waved to the children, who all madly-waved back.

For a short time, the Riviera Express followed the Adriatic coastline, before heading inland towards the mountains. The children looked out at the countryside. After a short game of cards, they decided to get their heads down.

The long journey back to Vienna was through the night. The children slept. They were all very tired.

36

Return to the Castle

In the morning, the Riviera Express steam train arrived at Vienna South railway terminus. The steam engine pulled up slowly alongside the long platform. Its smoke and steam from the engine rising to the top of the blackened glass-covered overhead roof.

The English children were fascinated by everything around them in the terminus. It was all an eye-opener, as to them, it was really exciting to see a bit of Vienna, in 1912. To the Strauss children, however, it was just another ordinary day at the railway station.

As the four children got off the train, they could see people running here, there and everywhere around the railway terminus. They were still half asleep, as it was quite early.

Veronica summoned a couple of porters.

She said to them, "Could you help us with our luggage?"

One replied, "Certainly, Miss."

Once the luggage was on the trolleys, the children walked down the station terminus's platform, towards the platform's exit.

As they walked along, Veronica said, "Caroline, it might be an idea to have some breakfast?"

"Good idea. I'm starving."

She added, "Do we have time to eat breakfast?"

"Erm," said Veronica. "I think that depends on what time our train to Straussburg departs."

"What time does it depart?"

Veronica looked up at the main train departure and arrivals times' board that towered above them.

She said, "The next train departs at the top of the hour."

Caroline replied, "Oh, right."

"It looks like we have to get the train to Lemberg."

"Lemberg? I thought we were going to Straussburg?"

"We are. The train goes via Budapest and then onto Cracow, before it goes to Lemberg."

"Oh, I see."

Caroline was none the wiser where they were going.

Veronica added, "Unfortunately, our connection home this time, means, we have to get the slow train. We missed getting the express service."

"Did we?"

"Yes, it left about half an hour ago."

"Never mind"

Veronica looked up at the departure board again.

"We need platform 2, Caroline."

"Fine"

Veronica checked the time, by looking at one of the stations big clocks that hung down from the roof, near where they stood.

"We've got half an hour. That's not enough time to eat breakfast. I propose buying something at that food kiosk over there," she added, pointing at it. "Then we can eat it on the train."

"Good idea"

Veronica looked over at the boys

"Manfred, Martin, we're getting some breakfast."

Turning to the porters, she said, "Porter, could we just go over to that food and drink kiosk, over there. Zo I can purchase some cakes?"

One replied, "Yes, Miss."

At the coffee and cake kiosk, Veronica said, "This is where I come, sometimes, on my way to the castle. It's my favourite kiosk."

"Oh, right," replied Caroline, who was looking around.

Veronica ordered a mixture of cakes.

"What about a drink, Caroline?"

"Sure! What have they got?"

"I think they sell coffee."

"That'll do."

"Coffee, Manfred?"

"Ja"

"I'll have a tea," said Martin.

"Three coffees and a black tea, please," said Veronica, to the woman serving them.

"Don't forget the milk," added Martin.

Veronica leaned over the counter.

"Excuse me. Is it possible to have the tea with milk, please?"

"Yes, Miss. Just a minute," replied the woman, as she prepared the order.

Once they had got their food and drink, the children and the porters walked round to the main concourse.

"Can we go round to the platform now, Veronica?" asked Manfred. "I'm really tired."

"Me too," added Martin, yawning.

"Ja, of course," she replied.

Veronica walked up to the porters, who were awaiting her instructions.

"We need to go to platform 2."

One of them replied, "Very good, Miss."

They all walked round to the platform. The stream train and its carriages were already alongside it. After finding a spare first class compartment, the children got on. The porters then loaded their luggage on board.

With everything sorted, Veronica gave them a tip.

"Thank you, Miss," said one of them. "Have a good journey."

In the train compartment, the children looked out at what was going on around them. Another steam train was on the opposite side of the platform.

"I wonder where that train is going?" asked Manfred.

"I think it's going to Prague," replied Veronica.

"Oh, right!"

Ten minutes later, the stationmaster blew his whistle and waved his flag. The steam train conductor waved his flag. The train driver blew the steam engine's whistle, and after releasing the brake, the train slowly edged out of platform 2. Steam and smoke went everywhere, mostly up, into the glass roof above.

The children looked out of the windows, as the steam train chugged its way out of Vienna South railway station. Caroline and Martin were thrilled to be on yet another railway journey. The steam train slowly puffed its way out of the city and into the countryside beyond.

Once they had departed Vienna, the children ate the breakfast they had bought at the railway station. Afterwards, they slept again, as everyone was still very tired. Later, to help pass the time, the children played a few games of cards.

Martin was looking out of the train compartment window, when he turned to his sister.

"Caroline," he said. "What colour is the magic key now?"

"No idea. I need to look."

She rooted in her bag, found the key at the bottom of it and took it out.

"Gosh! It's now green," said a surprised Veronica.

"What does that mean?" asked Manfred.

"I'm not sure," said Martin.

Caroline thought about it briefly, and said, "I think it means, we're out of danger."

"What do you mean?" asked Veronica.

"It's simple," said Caroline. "It's like a traffic light."

"What's a traffic light?" asked Manfred.

"It's something you stop at in a car," said Martin, interrupting. Manfred didn't fully understand him.

Caroline explained: "The point is, red is danger, green is okay and orange, I guess, is something in between."

"Oh, I zee," said Manfred, now getting it.

Veronica then said, "If I understand you, Caroline. What you mean is, the nearer we get to the castle, the better it is for the magic key?"

"It appears so," she replied, pleased with her explanation.

After a moment, she said, "But I am not 100% sure. It is merely a guess. The magic key appears to have a mind of its own. So I am not sure what it will do next."

"Ah zo," said Veronica.

The steam train wound its way across the plains, towards Budapest. After waiting at the platform for half an hour, the train headed north-eastwards towards Straussburg, the Tatra Mountains and Cracow.

During the long train journey, the children had the first class compartment to themselves. It was posh compartment, which Caroline quite liked.

Sometime later, she looked over at her brother.

"Martin," she said. "We need to think about getting back to our own time."

"I know," he replied.

"The thing is," said his sister, thinking aloud. "How do we get back to the castle and up to the attic, without the servants seeing us? Or if they do see us, how do Veronica and Martin then explain our sudden disappearance, after we use the magic key."

"I understand the problem," said Veronica, who had been thinking the situation through.

"What are we going to do?" asked Martin.

After a moment, Veronica said, "I have an idea..."

At Straussburg railway station, the children got off the steam train. They watched, as the stationmaster blew his whistle and waved his flag. The steam train gradually departed the platform. The children watched, as it slowly disappeared into the distance.

"Is everything all right, Miss Strauss?" asked the stationmaster.

Veronica turned to him, and said, "Oh, yes thanks, Mr Prednosta."

"Would you like a lift up to the castle?"

"Oh, that would be great."

The stationmaster loaded the luggage onto his open carriage. The children then hopped on. After taking his seat, the man cracked his whip and the horse and carriage set off for Strauss Castle.

37

The Interruption

The stationmaster drove the horse and carriage down the road, towards the main castle gate. The children were happy to be back at the castle, as everyone was tired after their long railway journey from Trieste. At the gate, Manfred jumped off and opened it for the stationmaster.

As they drove through the gate, Veronica said, pointing, "Mr Prednosta, would it be possible to drop us off, over there, by that corner of the castle, please?"

He replied, "Whatever you want, Miss."

Caroline got the idea.

After dropping them off, the children waved at the stationmaster, who drove off. Manfred, who had waited at the gate, closed it, and ran over to where the others were standing. Veronica, meanwhile, had quickly opened the side door of the castle.

"Quickly, Caroline, Martin," she beckoned. "I don't want any of the servants to zee you." Picking up Caroline's case, she said, "Help me with this, vill you, Manfred?"

Everyone got the idea. Together, they managed to lug Martin's and Caroline's heavy cases up into the attic, leaving Veronica's and Manfred's outside.

Once up there, Caroline collapsed onto the bed.

"I'm exhausted," she said.

"I am too," replied Veronica.

"What about the other suitcases?" asked Manfred.

"We'll get them in a minute," replied Veronica. "First, I need to catch my breath."

"What happens if the servants come?" asked Martin.

"Leave that to me," said Veronica.

Just at that moment, the children heard a voice from below.

"Is that you, Miss Veronica?"

The children fell silent. They then panicked.

"Er, ja. It is," replied the girl. "Oh, just a minute."

She rushed down the stairs, to find Marcel the footman at the bottom.

"Are you all right, Miss Veronica?" he asked. "You look as if you've just seen a ghost?"

"Ja, ja, I am fine, thank you."

The footman continued, "I was walking from the back of the castle, round to the front, when I saw your luggage, Miss."

"Oh! We've only just arrived," said Veronica, flustered. "I was going to bring it up to my room, in a moment."

"I can do that for you."

"Oh, nein! It's all right. I can manage, thanks."

"But it's my job, Miss."

"*Nein*," said Veronica, sternly. "I can manage it, really. Thank you, Marcel."

The footman thought she was acting a bit odd.

He replied, "Very vell, Miss. If you say zo."

"Thank you anyway," said Veronica. "I'll collect my luggage, shortly. After I have rested."

She quickly returned to the attic, closing the doors behind her.

"Phew! That was close."

"So I gather," said Caroline.

Turning to her brother, she added, "Martin, we need to leave. Go and get changed in the train room, will you?"

He followed the plan.

"Veronica," said Caroline. "Will you help me get undressed?"

"Ja, of course"

As Veronica assisted her, she said, "Just a minute, it appears the hook is stuck. Let me try to free it."

Veronica solved the problem.

Caroline slipped out of her dress, quickly changing back into her T-shirt and jeans.

Going into the train room, she said, "I'm ready, Martin."

The boys returned into Veronica's bedroom, where Caroline said, "Thanks for a super holiday, Veronica."

"My pleasure," she replied.

"Yeah, it was really great," said Martin.

"When do we see you again?" asked Manfred.

"Not sure," said Caroline. "Maybe next…"

Before she could finish her sentence, the lower door of the entrance to the attic opened, and a voice could be heard shouting up the stairs.

"Miss Veronica, are you there?"

The children froze again and were instantly silent.

From the bottom of the stairs, Katarina the maid said, "Miss Veronica, afternoon tea is being served."

Veronica tiptoed to the upper door.

Motioning to the others to move to one side, she opened it slightly, and said, "Oh, hello, Katarina."

"Marcel mentioned you were back, Miss Veronica. I wondered if wanted afternoon tea?"

"Oh ja, I do, thank you."

Veronica paused: "Will you give me a few minutes?"

The maid replied, "Certainly, Miss."

"I'll be down shortly."

"Have you seen young master Strauss?"

"Erm, I think he might be in his room," replied Veronica, knowing he was standing behind the attic door.

The maid replied, "Very good, Miss. I'll go and check if he's there. In the meantime, I'll prepare some tea and cake for you both, in the drawing room."

"Oh, thank you, Katarina," replied Veronica, shutting the attic door.

She kept her ear to it.

On hearing the maid walk away, she quickly went down the stairs and locked the lower attic door. Returning to the attic, she locked the upper door.

Caroline rushed over to her handbag.

Reaching in it, she said, "I nearly forgot the magic key."

She pulled it out.

Everyone had their eyes fixed on it.

"Look, Martin," said Manfred. "It's turned back into its normal self."

The boys went over to inspect it.

Caroline passed it over to Manfred, who passed it onto Martin.

As he held it in his hands, he said, "It seems you might have been right, Caroline. The magic key has reverted to its normal colour."

His sister smiled.

Veronica said, "Hurry Caroline. The servants know we are back. Who knows who else might come up here?"

Her friend, understood.

Taking the key, Caroline said, "Come on, Martin. It is time to depart."

She added, "Let's hope the magic actually works, after all our adventures away from the castle."

"Yes, let's hope," Martin replied. "I don't want to be stuck here, no offence, Manfred."

"None taken," he replied.

He added, "I've crossed my fingers for you."

Caroline and Martin embraced Veronica and Manfred.

"Till the next time," said Caroline.

"Which is?" asked Veronica.

"Dunno? We didn't really discuss it, did we?"

"Vell," said Veronica. "Don't forget the forthcoming harvest and the grape harvest, which is in mid-September."

"We'll see, Veronica," said Caroline. "First, we need to try to get back to our own time."

"Ja of course," she replied.

Caroline stood by the attic stairway door.

Turning to Veronica and Manfred, she said, "Let's hope this works."

She unlocked the door, ran down the stairs and unlocked the bottom door. Locking it, she quickly ran back up the stairs and locked the upper attic door.

"I want to return to my own time," she said, giving the day, the month and the year, followed by the time.

At first, nothing happened.

"It's not working," said Martin, as he stood there, next to his sister.

She replied, "Give it a moment."

Sure enough, within moments, the experience of the magic key started to happen. The children could all sense it starting its process. The room suddenly became cold. The white glow began to appear, through the top of the attic's rectangular window. Thunder and lightning, from nowhere, suddenly hit the castle roof. The white glow intensifying, now rushing in, through the rectangular window onto the floor below.

"It's happening," yelled Martin, excitedly.

"Are you ready, Martin?" asked Caroline.

The boy nodded.

Caroline held his hand. Together, they turned and waved at Veronica and Manfred, who waved back. Caroline and her brother stepped into the white glow, undid the door with the magic key and slowly disappeared.

Veronica and Manfred just stood there watching.

The large white glow, which had been hovering in front of the attic door, once it appeared satisfied it had done its work, then rushed through the round window that faced the road, before rapidly disappearing into the air outside.

Suddenly, the room became quiet.

Veronica looked at her brother.

She said, "I think they've gone."

"It appears zo."

She walked across the room and looked out of the round window that the white glow had disappeared through.

"I wonder when they'll be back."

Manfred replied, "Hopefully, next week."

"Let's hope zo."

She turned towards the attic stairway door.

"Come on, Manfred," she said. "Let's go down, and have some afternoon tea and cakes. After all that adventure, I'm starving."

"I am too."

38

Back in the Present

Caroline and Martin walked down the steep attic stairway, in the castle, leaving the white glow and thunder and lightning behind them. After Caroline had locked the lower attic door behind her, she checked the number on the magic key. Nothing on it had changed. Putting it in her pocket, she and her brother then tip-toed towards the castle corridor, where she stuck her head round the door, to double-check no one was there.

She whispered, "I think we're back."

The children quickly sneaked out of Slavo's front door, locking it behind them.

Outside, at the front of the castle, Caroline did a twirl.

"That was really great!" she said, feeling as happy as Larry.

Her brother replied, "Yeah, it was pretty cool."

As they walked round the side of the castle, Caroline said, "I wonder where Dad is?"

"He's probably still cutting the grass."

"Either that or he'll be working on his laptop."

They laughed and walked on.

Martin then stopped and looked at his sister, who walked ahead of him.

"Caroline," he said. "Are you sure we're back, on the same day as when we left?"

She stopped. Turning, to look back at her brother.

"Er," she said. "Well, I'm fairly sure. Why?"

"It's just that…"

"What, Martin?"

"We've been away for nearly a week."

"Yes, I know what you mean. The thought had occurred to me too."

"I mean, if a week has gone by, Dad will have gone crazy looking for us."

Both of them, suddenly realised, the implications of that.

"You have a point, Martin," said Caroline, adding, "But the magic key has always worked, so far…"

Martin added, "That's true. But what about the time?"

Caroline thought about it for a moment. Martin's questions had made her hesitant.

"Actually, I am not sure," she said. "Look, there's only one way to find out. Come on, let's go and find, Dad."

Chris was sitting in the conservatory, typing away into his laptop, when Caroline and Martin came into the room from the garden stairway.

"Ah, what a pleasant surprise," he said, looking up. "I was wondering when you two would show up."

"Hello, Dad," said Caroline, going over to kiss him.

"Hello, Sweetheart," replied her father.

"Alright, Sunny Jim?" he said, patting Martin on the head.

"Yeah I'm alright, Dad, and you?" replied the boy, smiling.

"Moi?" replied Chris. "Your father is fine, thank you."

He added, "Have you had a good day at the lake?"

The Hartley children looked at each other.

"Er, yes, thanks," said Caroline, walking over to the conservatory window and looking out of it.

Her brother decided to sit down at the table.

Chris looked across the table at his daughter. Then with his hands behind his head, he said, "And was the lake alright, today?"

"It was its usual self, why?" replied Caroline, turning to look at him oddly.

"Well, you left your bikes here again."

"Uh-huh," said Caroline, realising what he meant.

"Lucy's grandfather gave us a lift," said Martin, helping her out.

"Did he?"

"Yes! And he gave us a lift back."

"That's very decent of him."

"Yes, I thought so."

Both children were telling their father a white lie.

"I like Lucy," said Caroline. "Her English has improved a lot, since she met us."

"Has it now," replied Chris, knowing that she was probably right.

"She's only here for a few days," added Caroline. "But she goes home soon."

"Oh, what a pity, as she sounds like the sort of girl you could team up with."

Martin was looking across the table at his father in a funny way.

Chris looked at his son, and said, "Martin, what's up?"

"The ceiling," he replied, looking up at it.

"Very good, Martin," said Chris. "You're getting as witty as me."

"By the way," he added. "Did I just hear thunder and what sounded like lightning, outside?"

The children looked at each other. Neither knew quite what to say.

"Yeah, there was a bit," said Martin, looking eerily at his sister.

Chris added, "I didn't see any lightning, but it sounded quite close."

"It was," replied Caroline. "I think it struck somewhere in the village, as opposed to the castle garden side. We were lucky not to get hit."

"Sounds like you were."

Chris added, "It's probably another of these short summer storms, we appear to be having. According to Slavo, it's that time of year again."

265

"Oh I see," said Martin, in his gormless way.

His father decided to change the topic.

He said, "So, what did you two Herberts do at the lake today?"

"Er," said Martin.

The boy wasn't sure what to say.

He and Caroline looked at each other.

"This morning we did some aerobics," said Caroline, helping him out. "This afternoon we were playing hopscotch."

"Hopscotch?" said Chris. "You're a bit old for that, aren't you, Caroline?"

She replied, "You're never too old, Dad."

"True," replied their father, who added, "I must admit, I haven't played it in donkey's years."

Martin and Caroline laughed.

She sat down at the table, next to her brother.

"What time is it?" she asked.

Chris looked at his mobile phone.

"It's just gone six."

After replacing it on the table, Caroline said, "May I?"

Before Chris could answer, she had picked up his mobile. After checking the date on it, she smiled.

Chris and Martin looked at her.

"Is everything alright, Sweetheart?" asked her father.

Caroline replied, "What with no mobile phone, no TV and no watch, I tend to lose track of time, living here in the country. In fact, it's difficult to keep tabs on what day it is, let alone what time it is. Ever since Martin lost my mobile."

"Well, I did get you a new watch that you left in Bratislava."

"Yes, I must admit that was a bit stupid of me."

"I did say I'd get your mother to get you another mobile, once you get home."

"I know you did. It's just that I miss using it. I use it every day in England."

Caroline paused, and then added, "Having said that, I must admit I don't really need it here."

Chris stood up.

"Right, hands up. Who wants a cup of tea?"

Caroline and Martin both raised their hands.

"Okay, three cups of tea coming up," said their father, who headed towards the flat's kitchen.

Chris brought the tea in on a tray. Martin was sitting at the table, looking out at the garden. Caroline had picked up a magazine, she had found on the floor. She was sitting on the laid back chair, they had in the conservatory.

As Chris put the tea on the table, he said, "You two look exhausted. Is everything alright?"

"Yes, I am just a bit tired," said Caroline.

"Me too," added Martin, yawning.

Chris put his hands on his hips.

"Oh, what's caused that?"

"Too much sport," said Martin.

"I didn't think playing hopscotch was tiring."

"Ha, ha!" said Caroline, giving her father a funny face.

He looked at her.

"Well, it wasn't in my day, Sweetheart."

"Sometimes you need to rest, Dad. Even us."

"I'm not Superman," said Martin. "In fact, I'm thinking of having an early night."

His father looked at him, surprised.

"You, an early night," he said. "That'll make a change."

Martin stuck his tongue out at his father.

"I see some things don't change then."

The boy picked up his mug of tea, gulped some down and coughed some out.

"It's hot," he blustered.

"Of course, it's hot," said his father. "I've only just made it. Let it cool down a bit."

There was a moment or two of silence, as they all sat there relaxing. The birds could be heard twittering in the castle garden.

Martin broke the silence.

"Dad," he said. "What do you know about the Austrian navy?"

"Nothing, Martin, why?" replied his father.

Caroline's ears picked up. She looked over at him, giving him 'The Look'.

After a moment, Chris said, "Actually, I didn't know they had one. Wait a minute. They don't have one. I mean, how can they? They don't have a sea."

He added, "They might have a riverboat patrol that they run on the Danube. But I guess, that's about it. What made you ask?"

"Just wondered," replied the boy, smiling.

"Funny thing to be wondering about, Martin."

His father resumed his typing, while curious as to why his son might be asking him about the Austrian navy.

After a moment, Martin said, "What do you know about the Austrian Riviera?"

Caroline, who had been sipping her tea, suddenly coughed on it, violently, before giving her brother another filthy look.

Chris stopped his typing and looked at his son again.

"The Austrian Riviera?" he replied.

"That's right," said Martin.

"Nothing," said Chris. "They haven't got one, unless you mean their resorts on the river Danube." Getting up, he walked over to the window. "Martin, have you been studying Austrian history?"

"Er, sort of," replied the boy, sheepishly.

"I see," said his father. "Well, I'm not an expert on Austrian history. But I believe, the Austrians used to have a coastline. But that was before they lost the Great War, nearly 100 years ago. Does that answer your question?"

"I think so," replied the boy, smiling.

His father sat down again at his laptop. He typed a few things into it.

Martin was looking at his father.

After watching him for a few moments, he said, "Dad, what are you doing on your laptop?"

"Moi?"

"Yes," said Martin.

"Actually," said Chris. "I've just started writing a book."

"A book?" said Martin, surprised.

Caroline looked across at her father. She too was surprised.

"You're writing a book?" she said.

"I am!" her father replied.

"What sort of book?"

"It's a book about this castle."

"Really?" said Caroline, nearly choking in her tea, with surprise. "You never mentioned it, before."

"Well," said Chris. "I've only just started writing it."

"I see."

"What are you going to call it?" asked Martin.

"*The History of Zámočany Castle,* by C.J. Hartley."

"No, I don't believe it," said Caroline, getting up and joining Chris and Martin at the table.

"I am, Sweetheart," said Chris, enthusiastically. "Your father has decided to become a writer."

"Cool!" said Martin.

"What do you know about the castle, Dad?" asked Caroline.

"Er, not much"

"So, how can you write a book about the castle, if you don't know much about it?"

Chris thought about the question for a moment.

"You're right," he said. "I don't know much about it, yet. But ever since we got here, Mr Slavo has been filling me in with a few stories, here and there, about when he grew up and what happened here at the castle during communism. So I thought it might be an idea to write down what he knows about it in English."

"I see," said Caroline, who looked knowingly at Martin.

"What does Mr Slavo know about this castle, Dad?" asked Martin.

"Oh, you'd be surprised," replied his father, smiling.

"Who's going to read your book?" asked Caroline.

"Er, well your mother might," said Chris, not really knowing himself.

He stood up again, and said, "Right! Enough about the book. I can see I'd better go and sort some tea out. Caroline, would you like to give me a hand in the kitchen?"

She looked up at him, and said, "Sure."

As they stood up, Martin said, "What are we having for tea, Dad?"

"Omelette and yogurt"

"What together?"

Caroline looked at her brother, and said, "If you had your way, it would be."

39

Time to do Nothing

The next morning, Caroline woke up late. She was still tired, after her holiday to the Austrian Riviera. Getting up, she went to open the huge white wooden shutters that covered the windows. The sunshine quickly filled the bedroom.

Walking across the room, she decided to check the magic key that was in her jeans pocket. After getting it out, she looked at it. The key still showed 1912 on one side of it. On the other, it still had a big L and a '5' in a circle on it.

"Hum," she said. "Why haven't you changed to a '6'?"

Still in her pyjamas, she walked into the conservatory, where her father was busy typing away into his laptop.

"Morning, Dad," she said, glancing out of the conservatory window.

Chris looked up.

He replied, "Oh, good morning, Sweetheart. Did you sleep well?"

"Like a log, thanks."

Chris looked at his mobile and checked the time.

"Gosh," he said. "You're a bit late getting up this morning. I didn't realise it was that late."

Caroline replied, "I was tired after our long journey from, er…"

She suddenly realised, she couldn't say the Adriatic Sea.

She simply said, "From all the swimming, I did yesterday at the lake."

"Oh!" said Chris, unsure of her comment.

"Anyway, I'm on holiday. So why shouldn't I have a lie in?"

"It's fine with me," said her father, backing off.

Caroline sat down at the table.

"By the way, how's the book going?" she asked, looking over at her father.

"Slowly," said Chris. "Actually, I've barely started it. I have had some extra web work to get done, and unfortunately, that takes priority."

"I see," said Caroline, who wasn't that interested.

For a moment or two, she watched him.

"What are you doing, now?" she asked.

"What I always do," replied her father. "I'm doing some programming."

"Still"

Chris looked at her.

"As you know, Sweetheart. I have to give a presentation of my work at the United Nations, in Vienna."

"Gosh, I'd forgotten about that," replied Caroline. "When is it you are giving it?"

"Well, it should have been a week on Tuesday. However, when you were at the lake on Friday, I got a call from my boss, asking me to bring it forward a week; owing to the fact that some of the department will now be taking the week after next off."

He looked down his glasses at his daughter.

"Sometimes we have to work around change, Sweetheart."

"I see."

"Luckily for me, I'm ahead of myself, for once, which means I don't need to cram a lot of I.T. programming into these next few days, in order to get it done by the new presentation date. Thankfully, my presentation just needs a few final polishes, here and there. Then it's ready."

"Oh!"

"You see, Caroline, I have to try to accommodate my boss, who pays my wages, and also you guys, who are on holiday with me. So frankly, I don't have much choice in the matter."

She looked across at him.

"I understand, Dad."

"All I need to do, is to make sure everything I've done, is ready for me to present at the UN, the day after next."

His daughter had got the picture. However, it took her a few moments to digest the implications…

"Wait a minute," she said. "That means, we're gonna be leaving the castle again?"

Her father looked across the table at her.

"Yes, I'm afraid so, Sweetheart. We'll be heading back to Bratislava on the 15.45 train, this afternoon."

Caroline was shocked.

"But, we've only just arrived back."

Her father looked down at her through his glasses.

"Yes, I know we did. Originally, I thought we would have stayed here for the week. But when I got the call on Friday afternoon, this trip unfortunately changed into just a weekend at the castle."

"But we haven't finished our holiday yet."

"I'm aware of that."

"And I'd rather stay here at the castle."

"I know you would. But I need to sort some bits at the flat, ahead of my presentation. I also think it will be a good idea to have a rest day in Bratislava."

"I see."

"You know how long it takes to get here."

Caroline was thinking about the journey time from Bratislava. She was comparing it, to how long the steam train journey had taken her and her brother, from Vienna South Railway Terminus to the castle, using a different railway line, in 1912. So she knew how tiring the journey actually was. Even so, she was a bit peed off, to be leaving the castle again, so soon.

After a moment, she replied, "I do."

"I want to be reasonably fresh for the presentation."

"I see."

Chris could see his daughter wasn't so happy about it at all.

Caroline was still thinking: "So what are Martin and I going to do, while you're giving your presentation in Vienna?"

Her father was one step ahead of her.

"I thought you both might like to come with me."

"What – go to Vienna?"

Her father nodded.

"Yes! A trip to Vienna. You've not been there before. So I thought I'd show you around."

Caroline knew she couldn't tell her father, she'd already seen glimpses of Vienna, in 1912, having just passed through it yesterday, from Trieste.

"Would you like to visit Vienna?" asked her father.

She replied, "Er…"

She was suddenly in 1912, mode…

Snapping out of it, she said, "Yeah, why not? It could be interesting…"

She was curious, as to what Vienna might look like now.

Chris blew his nose.

"Vienna's a wonderful city," he said. "It was once the heart of the Austro-Hungarian Empire. In fact, it was the seat of the Hapsburg Empire."

"So I've discovered," said Caroline.

Her father looked at her oddly.

Caroline could hardly tell her father, she had met the Emperor Franz W. Joseph, twice. She realised the adventures, she and her brother had had in 1912, had actually gained them nearly a week's extra holiday, because of the time spent in that time period.

She was oddly thinking about her time at Vienna South Railway Terminus.

Chris could see his daughter had her mind on other things.

"Are you alright, Sweetheart?" he asked.

"Sorry," she replied, coming back to the present. "I was in another world."

Caroline tried to remember the earlier conversation.

"You were saying something about the United Nations."

"I was," replied her father.

The girl's mind kept flicking back to 1912. Of the steam train journeys she had taken…

Snapping out of the past, yet again, she reverted to the present.

"The UN's a big worldwide organisation, right, Dad?"

Her father looked at his daughter, oddly.

"Er," he replied. "That's right, Sweetheart."

Caroline tried to act intelligently.

"But I thought the United Nations was in New York?"

"You're right, it is. But they also have offices in many other locations around the world."

"Like where?"

"Erm," said Chris, thinking about it. "Like Nairobi, Paris, Geneva, and the one I'm going to, which is in Vienna."

Chris added, "The presentation I'm doing, is in one of the department's there. I'm showing a few people the web work I have been designing for them. It's what I've been doing for the last few weeks."

"That bit, I was aware of," said Caroline, nodding.

"Actually, it's been a quite a mammoth task."

"I can imagine."

"I was quite lucky to get the work."

"Really?"

"Yes, it was one of my former clients, who now works there. He got me the job."

"That was lucky then."

"Yes, it was."

"But what happens if they don't like it?"

Chris looked at her and smiled.

"Oh, I think they will like what I have created for them."

"How do you know, before you've presented it?" asked Caroline.

"Because I have had to liaise, as I go along. Most of the people I will see, already know what I have been designing. The purpose of the presentation is to unveil the final product and go through it all on a big screen."

"Oh I see," replied Caroline, now getting the full picture.

"Anyway, it beats teaching English."

"Oh, why's that?"

"Because at this time of year, the teaching work dries up. It's non-existent."

Caroline looked at him, funnily.

Chris added, smiling, "It's the school holidays, Sweetheart."

"Oh, I see what you mean," she replied.

"The only difference is, that while teachers in England get six weeks paid holiday. People like me, don't get a penny. So the web work is an important source of additional income."

"Uh-huh"

Chris added, "Anyway, this afternoon, we'll head back to Bratislava, so I can sort a few things there, before going to Vienna."

"How long does it take you to get to Vienna?"

"Well, it's an hour on the train. But then there's the tram journey to the station, plus the underground. So all in all, it takes me three hours, door-to-door."

"Gosh! That's a quite a long time."

"Yes, it is."

"I didn't realise it took so long."

"That's why I prefer to split the journey. Otherwise, it's too much."

Chris got up.

"Well," he said. "That's later. What about a cup of tea and some breakfast, before I do a few more last minute amendments?"

"Good idea," replied Caroline.

"Tell you what," added Chris. "Go and get your brother out of bed, and in the meantime, I'll put the kettle on."

"Okay," said Caroline, smiling.

Martin was still in bed, when Caroline went to wake him up. After knocking at his door, she went in.

"Rise and shine, Martin," she said, going to open the shutters.

"I'm already awake," he replied, lying there looking at her.

"Well, it's time to get up."

He sat up.

"I am not rushing today," he said. "I'm still tired, after all that travelling."

Caroline replied, "Me too."

She added, "You'll be even more tired tomorrow, though."

Her brother looked at her.

"Oh, why's that?"

"Because we're going back to Bratislava this afternoon."

"This afternoon? You're joking?"

"I'm not," said Caroline, nodding.

Martin was shocked.

"Are we really going back?"

"Yeah, Dad's just told me."

There were a few moments of silence.

Martin then said, "But I thought we had another week or so at the castle?"

"So, did I."

"Umgh, so why are we going back now?"

"Dad's presentation at the UN in Vienna, has been brought forward a week."

"Really?"

"Yeah, really!"

"What about the magic key?"

"What about it?"

"Has it changed its number?"

"Not yet"

The boy was horrified about leaving the castle, yet again, and so soon.

"But I want to see Veronica and Manfred again."

"Me too," replied his sister.

"Will we see them again?"

"I don't know, Martin. Judging by the fact that we're leaving this afternoon. I doubt it."

"We could try to go back, after breakfast?"

Caroline looked at her brother.

"Martin, the number on the key hasn't changed, so we can't."

"Pity"

"Anyway, I'm tired. I want to chill."

She stood up.

"Look, get yourself washed and dressed and I'll get breakfast ready."

"Oh alright," replied her brother, wearily.

Once they had all had eaten breakfast, Chris said, "Well, I'll leave you two Herberts to do the washing up. After that, you can do whatever you want. Is that alright?"

"Yes, Dad," replied Caroline, a bit fed up.

Chris looked at her.

"I need to get this I.T. work completed, Sweetheart."

"I know! You've already told me a hundred times."

"Well, I'm running a bit behind."

He added, "Who's doing the washing up this morning?"

"I am," said Martin, going over to the sink.

"That means I'll have to dry up," said Caroline. "I hate drying up."

"So do I. That's why I volunteered to wash."

"Right," said Chris. "I'll leave you two Herberts to it. Try not to argue too much."

He left his kids in the kitchen and went and sat in the conservatory, where he worked on his presentation.

Once their task was completed, Martin sat down at the kitchen table. He looked at his sister, who was now wiping the table with a cloth.

She said, "You could have done this, Martin."

He replied, "That's a girl's job."

"No, it's not. You need to learn."

The boy chose to ignore her comment.

After a moment, he said, "What are we going to do today?"

"Nothing," said Caroline.

"What about a game of football, out the front?"

"Alright, Martin. But nothing too strenuous. I am still tired, after all that travelling."

40

The Castle Visitors

At the front of the castle, on the overgrown grass driveway, Caroline and Martin kicked a ball about. They took it in turns to be in goal. During this, their friend and neighbour Mr Slavo suddenly appeared at the main gate.

After entering the castle, he said, waving, "Morning, Caroline, Martin."

"Good morning, Mr Slavo," they replied.

Caroline added, "Did you have a good journey back?"

"Yes, thanks," he replied, adding, "I decided to get the early train from Bratislava, so I can enjoy the day in the garden."

"Oh! Good idea," said Caroline, passing the ball to Martin.

Slavo left the children to their game of football and walked towards his flat.

The children were pleased to see him. They liked their new friend 'Mr Slavo'. There was something about him that made him a nice person. He was always polite and he never seemed to lose his temper.

Just then, Mike and Lucy arrived on their bikes.

"Hey, Martin, Caroline," yelled Mike, waving.

He blasted his horn on his bike.

The children looked up.

Caroline shouted to her friend and neighbour.

"Mr Slavo," she said, waving. "Have you got a minute?"

He was just about to unlock his front door.

Returning to the children, he saw Mike and his friend at the castle gate.

Caroline said, "Sorry to bother you, but is it possible you could let our friend Mike in, please?"

"Yes, of course," he replied. "But I thought you had a key?"

"We have," said Caroline, cheekily. "But it's inside and you happen to be here."

She smiled sweetly, in her girly way, at him.

Slavo got the idea.

"No problem, Caroline," he said.

Walking over to the gate, he saw the two children sitting on their bikes, leaning on the entrance gate.

"Hello, Mike," said Slavo, opening it.

"Hi, Mr Slavo"

"How are you?"

"Fine, thanks"

"Er, do come in."

Once Slavo had closed the gate, he walked over to where everyone was grouped.

He said, "I haven't seen you for a while, Mike. Where've you been hiding?"

The boy laughed.

"Oh, I've been doing a bit of this and that. Keeping myself busy, you know."

"I see some things don't change."

"By the way, this is Lucy," said Mike, introducing her to him.

"Good morning," said Slavo, to her.

She replied, "Good morning."

The man could see they hadn't come to see him.

"Well," he said. "I'll leave you all to it. Have fun."

"We will," replied Martin.

Slavo waved, as he walked over to his flat.

Mike and Lucy got off their bikes.

"How are you, Mike?" asked Caroline.

"So, so," he replied.

"Lucy?"

"Yes, I am okay, thanks.

She added, "Are you coming down to the lake, today?"

"Yeah, we could do. But only for a short time."

"Oh, why's that?"

"We're leaving again this afternoon."

"Are you?" said Mike.

"Yes, unfortunately, my dad's decided to go back a bit earlier than I thought we would."

"Oh"

"But we can still come down now. We've got a couple of hours, before we depart."

"Great!"

"Actually," said Lucy. "I thought you were both coming to see us at the lake, yesterday?"

Caroline and Martin looked at her.

"Oh yes, we were," replied Caroline, adding, "Sorry about that. We spent yesterday at the castle. Didn't we, Martin?"

"Er, yes," he replied, sheepishly.

"Oh, I see," replied Lucy.

She added, "Well you said to call in. So here we are."

"I'm pleased to see you," said Caroline.

"Can we join you?" asked Mike.

"Yes, of course. Park your bikes, over there," she said, pointing. "Then we can have a game of football."

The children kicked the ball around, passing it to each other.

As they did so, Caroline said to Mike, "I didn't know you knew Mr Slavo?"

Mike laughed, as he passed the ball.

"We go back a long way," he replied, smiling.

"I see."

After passing the ball about, he added, "Lucy wanted to see the castle. Is that alright?"

"Yes, of course, it's alright," said Caroline. "I did say, come round."

The four of them played football, until they had exhausted themselves, in the hot sunshine.

After a while, Caroline said, "Hang on guys. Let's have a drink."

"Oh, that's a good idea," replied Martin.

"Lucy, Mike, bring your bikes," said Caroline. "We'll park them round the back."

As they walked round one side of the castle, they chatted.

"This looks an amazing place," said Lucy.

"That's because it is," replied Martin.

"Mike's told me so much about it. I really wanted to see it, before I went home."

"Well," said Caroline. "The garden's rather overgrown."

"It's like a jungle," said Martin.

"My dad's spent half the summer cutting the grass."

"He's still cutting it. It'll take him a month of Sundays to finish it."

"Yes, and when he does, he'll have to cut it all again."

The children laughed.

They had reached the back of the conservatory.

"You can leave your bikes here," said Caroline.

Mike and Lucy parked their bikes.

"This way for the drinks," said Caroline.

The children went up the rear steps of the castle into the conservatory.

"I thought I heard footsteps," said Chris, looking up, as they walked in.

On seeing her and Martin's friends, he said, "Oh, hello, Mike. Hello, Lucy. How are you?"

"Fine, thanks," they replied, shaking hands with him.

"Lucy wants to have a look round the castle, Dad," said Caroline.

"Sure," he replied. "Be our guest."

Lucy was looking around her.

"Wow," she said. "What a lovely room."

"This is where we hang out," said Caroline.

"What a great place to hang out."

"We call it the conservatory."

Martin changed the subject.

"I thought we were getting a drink, Caroline?"

"We are."

She added, "Come on, Lucy. Let's leave Dad to it. He's got a presentation to prepare."

"Yes, okay"

The children walked into the next room.

Looking around her, Lucy said, "There's no furniture in here."

"That's true, there's not," said Caroline.

"I thought this castle would be full of old furniture."

"So did I, before I looked inside."

Caroline added, "I guess, when the castle was split into flats, it must have been sold off."

"No, that's not true," said Mike. "The Russians and socialists stole it, when they took over the castle."

"Did they?"

The boy nodded.

"That's terrible. Why?"

"It's how it was."

"I think Mike's right," said Lucy. "As it confirms what my father told me, last year?"

"What did he tell you?" asked Martin, who was trying to act a tad intelligent.

"He said that the socialists stole furniture, land and property, from many of the big houses and castles in Czechoslovakia. I guess they did that here, as well."

"Really?" said Caroline. "What a bunch of thieves."

Lucy was walking around the room.

"I bet in the old days, they used to have lots of Balls and banquets in here."

"Yes, it's true. They did," said Mike. "The room has been used by many people over the years. People even got married in here. I think they still get their photos taken in the castle gardens."

"That's really interesting, Mike," said Caroline.

Lucy added, "The castle is much bigger than I thought it was."

"It's *our* secret castle," said Martin, smiling.

Caroline laughed.

"Yes, that's one way to describe it," she said.

In the kitchen, Caroline went to the fridge and got them some Kofola to drink.

Pouring it into some glasses, she said, "This is what my dad calls Communist Coke."

"Communist Coke?" said Lucy. "Sorry, I'm not with you."

"It's our dad's stupid name for it," said Martin. "Something about the communists in Czechoslovakia banned Coca Cola and they invented their own version."

"That's true, they did."

"I quite like it," said Caroline.

"Oh, so do I," added Martin.

"It's refreshing."

The children quickly finished their drinks.

"Let me show you the garden, Lucy?" suggested Caroline.

"Okay"

As the girls walked out of the kitchen, Martin said to Mike, "Looks like we're going round the garden."

"Nice," he replied, before laughing in his funny way.

41

Another History Lesson

Caroline led her friend's, and brother, through the conservatory, down the rear castle steps next to it and into the castle garden. She led them over to the old broken stone fountain that was located nearby. Some of the long grass, Caroline noted, had now been cut.

Lucy was looking around her.

"This is an amazing garden," she said.

"We like it," said Martin.

Mike was looking around him.

"This used to be a really nice garden," he said, to Caroline.

"Really?"

"There used to be lots of garden parties held here."

"Did there?"

"Yes," said Mike. "The socialists used to have them. It was *the* place to come in the summer. The mine used to have an annual garden party here, for its workers."

"Oh, I didn't know that," said Caroline.

Further down, Lucy pointed, and said, "Can we go and look at the garden, over there, Caroline?"

"Sure"

The four of them walked down the main lawn.

Mike said to Caroline, "The castle has always had garden parties in it. It's only since the castle was turned into flats that they stopped."

"Really?"

"It's a pity, as they used to be really great. You know, the best ones were in the castle's early days?"

"What do you mean, in the early days?" asked Caroline.

"In the period before the Great War, when this area was a part of the Austro-Hungarian Empire. There used to be many garden parties held here. That was when the castle was owned by Commander Strauss and his family. They were a lovely family."

"Uh-huh"

She turned and looked at him.

"How do you know that?" she asked.

"Er," he replied. "It's something we learnt at school."

Martin added, "Funny thing to learn at school."

Lucy turned to Mike: "I never learnt that in school."

The boy smiled: "We go to different schools, Lucy. And, we're in different classes…"

She replied, "Yes, that's true."

They walked on …

As the children walked along an overgrown path, Caroline led the way, followed by Lucy. Martin was at the rear. His mind was wandering…

"I see what you mean about a jungle, Martin," said Lucy.

Caroline remarked, "I don't think my father has got round to pruning this part of the garden, yet."

Martin, suddenly remembered, walking through where they now were, with Manfred, L'ubor, and himself, during the afternoon of the 1912 Strauss summer garden party…

Ahead was an old bench that the girls decided to sit down on.

"You could spend hours in this garden, Caroline," said Lucy.

"Don't worry. I do!"

…the boy also remembered an earlier conversation Caroline had had with Veronica, about Mike looking like L'ubor.

"Mike," said Martin. "Ask a stupid question, but did you have a grandfather called L'ubor?"

"L'ubor?" he replied. "No, not that I'm aware of, why?"

"Caroline met someone, she thought might have been your grandfather."

His sister gave him a filthy look, then realised the comment might not be so bad after all.

"No," replied Mike. "My grandfather was called Vladimir."

"Oh, right," said Martin.

"Is he still alive?" asked Caroline.

"No," replied Mike. "He died last year."

The girls sat there for a while, listening to the birds in the trees.

After a while, Martin got bored standing there.

"Come on," he said, walking on a bit. "We can go to the meadow, Lucy."

Everyone got up and walked on along the overgrown pathway.

As they walked, Mike said, "I love this garden. I grew up here."

"Did you?" said Caroline.

"My grandfather used to be the head gardener here."

"Did he?"

"You seem to know a lot about this castle, Mike," said Martin.

He laughed. "One of my relatives built it."

"Really?" replied Caroline.

After a moment, she stopped and looked at him.

"Wait a minute," she said. "You just said your grandfather wasn't called L'ubor."

"That's right," said Mike. "My great grandfather was called L'ubor. But there are many L'ubor's in this village. So it might not be him."

"I see," said Caroline, intrigued.

They walked on…

Further up, Lucy said, "You seem to be quite interested in history, Caroline."

"Not really," she replied, looking at her friend. "What makes you ask that?"

"You seem to know a lot about the history of this castle."

Caroline laughed.

"Hardly."

She added, "I just heard about it from my dad, Mr Slavo, and Mike."

"I see."

"History is not really my cup of tea…"

"What is then?"

Caroline thought about the question.

"Dunno really. At school, I like geography and media studies."

"Oh, right," replied Lucy.

She was thinking of her own likes at school.

"I like maths and chemistry."

"Maths is hard, and as for Chemistry…I hate it. I came third from bottom in my class."

"Really?"

Caroline nodded.

"Really!"

The girls walked on…

The boys waited for the girls, who were just behind them, to catch up.

"Here we are," said Martin. "This is the meadow."

Everyone stopped, to look around them.

"It's really nice," said Lucy.

Martin added, "I used to call this the football pitch. But then I found out it was called the meadow. Mind you, now my dad's cut the grass, it looks like a football pitch."

After wandering around it, Caroline said, "Come on, Lucy. Let's head back to the castle, shall we?"

"Yes, okay."

The children started to make their way back towards it.

As they walked, Lucy said, "Shall we go down to the lake now, Caroline?"

"Yeah, why not? It seems like a good idea."

"Great."

Lucy added, "Have you still got your bikes?"

"Yep," said Caroline, nodding.

"Super," replied Lucy.

Further up, she said, "It's a pity you're leaving, Caroline."

"Tell me about it."

"What time did you say your train goes?"

"Erm, I think Dad said it departs around 15.45."

Lucy looked at her watch.

"Oh that's okay. We've got plenty of time."

Caroline was pleased how Lucy's English had improved, since meeting her.

"Let's tell the boys."

The girls ran a few paces, to catch up with the boys.

"Martin, Mike," said Caroline. "Lucy and I are gonna go down to the lake. Are you coming with us?"

Martin replied, "Yeah, okay."

"What about you, Mike?" asked Caroline.

"Fine," he replied, laughing in his usual way.

Back at the bikes, Caroline spoke to Lucy and Mike.

"If you two wait here, we'll get our bikes."

"Fine," replied Mike.

In the conservatory, Chris looked up from his laptop, as he heard his kids walk in the room.

"Dad," said Caroline. "We're going for a quick bike ride, down to the lake, with Mike and Lucy. Is that alright?"

"Yeah, it's fine, Sweetheart. But remember to be back by one thirty at the latest, will you?"

"Okay"

Caroline and Martin wheeled their bikes down the conservatory stairs.

After getting on her bike, she said, "Right, let's go then."

Leading the way, she set off towards the castle's main gate.

"Race you!" said Martin to Mike.

A speedy race by the boys towards the gate followed.

42

The Bike Ride

After leaving the castle, the children set off on their bikes, towards the lake. Martin led the way. Once they reached the nearby hill, the boys raced down it. They were closely followed by the girls, who then decided to take their bike ride at a more leisurely rate.

A short while later, as the girls cycled along the long flat straight road, Lucy said, "I love cycling along here. It's so peaceful."

"Yes," replied Caroline. "I suppose it is."

A bit further along the road, Lucy said, "Is the scenery in England different to Slovakia?"

"Yes of course it is," replied Caroline. "But I think you've got higher mountains than us."

"Oh!"

"The scenery round here is much the same as back home. The only difference, I suppose is, we cycle on the left."

Lucy looked at Caroline.

"I see."

She added, "I can't imagine cycling on the left."

Caroline looked around her. No traffic was coming.

"Let's try it," she suggested.

She switched sides of the road. After checking the road situation, Lucy followed. The girls rode up the road for about 100 metres.

Seeing a car in the distance, they switched back to the right hand side of the road.

"That was fun," said Lucy.

"Yeah it was," replied Caroline. "For a moment, I felt like I was back in England."

"When do you go back there?"

"In about a week or so"

"Oh, right!"

They cycled on…

Mike and Martin were riding along, further up the road…

"Mike," said Martin, while trying to keep up with him. "Can I ask you something?"

"Sure"

"Do you live in Zámočany?"

"Yes, I do."

"Whereabouts?"

"I live in a house near the river."

"How long have you lived there?"

Mike thought about it.

"Since my father moved there, why?"

"Just wondered."

Martin's mind was thinking about when he had met L'ubor on his bike, the first time…

"And you said your father was one of the gardeners in the castle?"

Mike replied, "No, my grandfather used to be the head gardener at the castle."

"Oh right. Sorry."

He added, "So what about your father? What does he do?"

"He's a history teacher."

Martin looked at his friend.

"Is he?"

"Yes, he is."

The boys arrived at the road junction.

"We'd better wait here for Caroline and Lucy," suggested Martin.

"Okay," replied Mike, laughing.

Martin liked his friend's easy going way. He wasn't sure if it was because of the simple English he used, or whether it was just Mike's casual attitude to life…

The girls arrived at the junction.

"Caroline," said Martin. "If we don't have long, instead of just going down to the beach, why don't we cycle around the lake?"

"Good idea"

"See, I'm not just a pretty face."

"I'm not answering that."

Mike then said, "In that case, why don't we go the other way around it?"

"Alright," replied Caroline, brushing her hair backwards.

They set off…

When the girls reached the field next to the camping site, Caroline stopped.

"Lucy," she said. "That's where Martin, Mike, and I went to the M Festival."

"Oh, I went to that."

"Did you?"

"Sure! I go every year."

"I didn't see you there."

The girls laughed.

Lucy added, "I'm not surprised. There were thousands of people there."

"Exactly!"

"Anyway, I didn't know you then."

"True"

Caroline set off again.

"Come on," she said. "Let's catch the boys up."

The girls raced each other to catch them up.

On the long road that looked out above the lake, the children looked out across it. Caroline was now cycling with Mike.

"Have you ever swum across the lake, from this side to the other?"

He looked at her.

"No, why?"

"Well, when I was in France, last year, I swam across a similar sized lake?"

"You must be a good swimmer?"

"I am, and I'm a good runner."

A car beeped on its horn and then passed them.

"What sports do you like, Mike?"

"Me? I like many sports."

"Like what?"

He thought about it.

"Ice hockey, skiing…"

"You can't play those in summer."

"True! Well, I also like football, volleyball, and horse riding."

"Oh, that's different."

"Yes, I suppose it is."

They cycled on…

A bit further up, Caroline said, "Mike, do you visit the castle a lot?"

He looked at her.

"It depends. I like to look around the castle garden."

"Oh, me too"

Caroline thought about it.

"But are you allowed?"

Mike replied, "When Mr Slavo is at the castle, he lets me visit."

"I see."

"What do you think of the garden?"

"Not much. When my grandfather was the head gardener, I am told, it used to look really great."

"Really?"

"Sure"

"How you do you know that?"

Mike thought about it.

"He showed me photographs of it."

"Oh right!" replied Caroline, suddenly feeling like a lemon. She cycled on…

When the children reached 'the beach', on the opposite side of the lake, they stopped.

Martin looked at his sister: "Have we got time for a drink, Caroline?"

She replied, "I don't know, Martin. I haven't got my mobile phone any more, have I?"

"Where is it?" asked Lucy.

"My dear brother dropped it in the lake."

"Really?"

"Yes, so I have to wait till I get home, in order to get a new one."

"I see."

Martin added, "Dad bought you a new watch."

Caroline replied, "Yes, he did. But stupidly, I left it in Bratislava."

"That's your fault."

"Alright clever clogs. I didn't lose the phone, remember."

Lucy looked at her watch.

"Caroline, if you're interested, it's just gone one."

"In that case," she said. "We haven't got time for a drink, Martin."

"Pity"

"You can have one, once we get back to the castle. I think we need to head back now. Dad's expecting us back by one thirty."

"Oh alright," said the boy, despondently.

"We'd better go," suggested Mike.

Caroline replied, "Yeah, we'd better."

The children set off round the lake, on their bikes. They passed quite a few holidaymakers, who were staying at the different cottages that were dotted around the lakes edge.

The girls crossed the dam first. Closely followed by the boys. The four of them then raced down the steep dam hill and up the hill beyond it; so as to avoid the climb that followed. A fun leisurely ride along the long straight road, back to the castle, followed.

At the castle gates, the children stopped to get their breath.

"I enjoyed that bike ride," said Caroline, smugly.

"So did I," replied Lucy. "We must do it again."

"That sounds like a good idea."

Mike was peering through the castle railings.

"What are you looking at, Mike?" asked Caroline.

"Oh, nothing. Just checking the castle is alright."

Caroline was surprised by his comment.

She said, "We need to go in, Lucy. Catch you next time."

"See you," she replied, getting on her bike.

"Catch you later, Mike," added Martin, who had got off his bike and was now standing by the castle gate.

"Bye," replied the boy, in Slovak.

Mike and Lucy began to cycle away.

"Bye," said Caroline, waving.

"Hello," said Lucy, returning the wave.

43

Departure

The English children were glad to be back at the castle. They had worked up a bit of an appetite, after all the cycling they had done, down to the lake and back. Both had wanted to burn off a bit of energy.

After parking their bikes round the back of the castle, by the conservatory, Caroline and Martin returned to their flat, where their father had thoughtfully prepared them lunch. In the kitchen, everyone sat eating it.

"Have you enjoyed your second visit to the castle?" asked Chris.

"Of course," replied Caroline.

"It's been brilliant," added Martin. "But I'm looking forward to coming back."

"Oh, we'll have to see about that," said Chris.

"Are we coming back?" asked Caroline.

The children stared at their father.

He thought about it for a moment, and then said, "I need to think about it."

"There's nothing to think about," replied Caroline. "We've still got another week or so here."

"Maybe, Sweetheart. First, I need to do my presentation at the UN. Then we can decide, eh?"

"I see."

"Actually, I thought you two might like to go somewhere else, once we get back to Bratislava."

"Like where?"

"I thought we could visit Budapest for the day."

"Budapest?" said a surprised Martin.

"Sure," said Chris. "We can always come here next year."

The boy spat out his drink.

"Next year"

"Oh, that's no good," said Caroline.

She looked at her brother in horror.

"Why not?" asked their surprised father

Martin replied, "'Cause we like it here."

"So do I. Nevertheless, there's more to see of this region than just this castle."

Caroline added, "I know there is. But we like the castle, Dad."

"I just thought we might try something different."

Neither of his kids wished to go anywhere other than the castle.

Caroline then said, "It's a pity we can't stay here and you go off to Vienna, to do your presentation."

Her father looked at her.

"Nice idea, Caroline. But I'm afraid it's just not practical."

"Pity"

The children wished to return to the castle. Neither, could contemplate the thought of not returning. Both Caroline and Martin wanted to use the magic key at least one more time, *if*, it would allow them to. The question on their minds, was, *would it work again*? And, *when was the number on it, going to change*?

"Right," said Chris. "Who's going to do the last lot of washing up?"

"I will," said Caroline, volunteering.

She got up and threw Martin a dish cloth.

"What's this?" he asked her.

"It's called a dish cloth."

"I know it is. Why've you chucked it at me?"

"Because it's your turn to do the drying up."

"Is it?"

"Yes, it is."

"Oh alright"

Chris stood up. He could see everything was tickety-boo.

"Right," he said. "I'll leave you two to it. Don't forget, we have to be ready to leave at three thirty, alright. Oh, and we'll need to drop the bikes back, in about half an hour."

He started to walk out of the kitchen.

"Where are you going?" asked Caroline.

"I'm going to pack my bag. Is that okay?"

She laughed.

"Of course!"

Caroline was packing her bag in her room, when her brother walked in.

"Where's dad?"

"I think he's just popped next door to see Mr Slavo."

"Oh, right"

The boy sat on the bed.

"Have you still got the magic key?" he asked.

His sister replied, "Of course I've still got it."

"What are you going to do with it?"

"I'm going to keep it. What do you think I was going to do with it?"

The boy didn't have an answer to that.

Caroline continued to pack.

After a moment, Martin said, "Can I see it?"

His sister got the key out.

"Look! One key," she said, a bit annoyed.

"Alright, keep your hair on. I just wanted to see whether the number on it has changed?"

"Oh, I see," said Caroline, calming down.

They looked at it.

"Well, it's still got 1912 on this side of it."

She turned it over.

Looking at it closely, her brother said, "And it's still got a big L and a '5, in a circle, on the other."

"So, to answer your question, Martin. I don't think it has."

The boy was disappointed.

"Pity"

Caroline replied, "Yeah, I know what you mean?"

"Do you think it still works?"

"Well, hopefully, it does."

"Shall we try?"

His sister looked at him.

"Martin, not now. We haven't got time. We're leaving, remember."

"Yes, I know we are."

"Anyway, I need to pack and so do you."

The boy remained downcast.

Caroline added, "Look, there's always next time."

"Yeah, I know there is. But it might not work then."

His sister thought about it for a moment.

"Umm, you have a point. But seeing as the number '5' in the circle on the key, hasn't changed, I don't think we can go back in time, till it does change."

"Uh-huh. I'd forgotten about that."

Caroline looked at her brother. He knew what was coming…

"What are you?"

"Forgetful," they said together, laughing and doing a high five after.

"But we didn't say goodbye to Veronica and Manfred," he added, going to sit on a chair.

"Yeah, I know we didn't. But if you remember, we were in a bit of a rush."

"True"

"Look, even if we don't come back after Dad's presentation, we can always try again, next year."

"Next year? We might never come here again."

"Oh don't say things like that, Martin. Otherwise, we won't."

"I like it here."

"Me too"

Caroline zipped up her travel bag.

"Anyway, we can only go back in time, if the magic key will let us."

"But the number on it hasn't changed yet."

"I know it hasn't." she replied, double-checking the magic key's number, as it lay on top of her bed. Nothing on it had changed.

As she popped it in her jeans pocket, she said, "However, I have this feeling, it might."

This time, she was merely saying this, to keep her brother happy. Martin looked up at her.

"You have many feelings, Caroline."

"Yeah, I do," she said, adding, "But only time will tell…"

"Humm…"

After a moment of silence, the boy said, "Caroline, I've got two other things you might like to think about."

She looked across at him.

"Yeah, go on."

"What are you gonna do with Mr Slavo's front door key?"

"Oh, that's a good point."

After quickly thinking about it, she said, "Erm, probably nothing. Why?"

"Well, he might need it?"

"Yes, he might. But seeing as he's in his flat, makes it impossible for me to return it, right now."

"Yeah, I take your point. But isn't that stealing?"

"No! I have only *borrowed* his spare key."

This was a bit of a white lie, but it was the only thing Caroline could say, to defend her actions.

"I take it you want to go back to 1912, again?"

"Yes of course I do. But couldn't you give it back to him, then borrow it again, next time?"

"And how are we going to get in his flat, if he's not here, next time we're here?"

"Erm, that's a good point."

"Tell you what, Martin. Just to keep you happy. Next time we're at the castle, I'll try and return it. Is that alright?"

"Yeah, it's alright," he said, nodding his head slowly.

Caroline walked across to the window.

After looking out of it, she turned, and said, "And what was your other thought, on this fine sunny afternoon, eh?"

"Erm, it's about Mr Slavo's other key."

"Other key? What do you mean?"

"He's got the same attic key as you, right?"

Caroline looked oddly at her brother, giving him one of her famous faces.

"Er, well, now you come to mention it. Yes, he has."

"That's how we first got to go back to 1912, remember?"

"Erm that and a few other things in between and before, but yes, now you come to mention it, I do remember."

"Perhaps *his* key is magic."

Caroline thought about it for a moment.

"Erm, yeah, it could be. But probably not, Martin."

Caroline added, "I think Mr Slavo is more into cutting the grass and doing repairs around the castle with Dad, than time travelling back to 1912, like us."

"True"

"I mean, he's not exactly said anything to us about time travel, or anything related, has he?"

"Er, no. But it was just a thought."

"Well, it was a good thought."

"Yeah, I know it was."

"You know, Mr Slavo is more likely to have a copy of our key, or perhaps his is the original key."

"It could even be a spare key."

"Er, yes, it could. On the other hand, perhaps I've got the spare key, or a copy of it, or even the original. Look, who knows, Martin."

"Yeah, who knows?"

Just after three thirty, Caroline, Martin, and their father, departed the castle.

"Well, this is it. Time to go," said Chris, as he locked the main door of the castle.

"Pity," said Caroline, adding, "Still, all good things come to an end."

"You said we were coming back," added Martin, as they walked towards the fountain.

"Hopefully, we are," said his father.

A few paces further, he said, "Just a minute."

He went over to Slavo's flat and rang the bell.

After a moment, Slavo came to the door.

"Good afternoon, Chris. Are you all packed?"

"Yes, we're ready to leave."

"Good! Well, let's head down to the station. You don't want to miss your train."

They walked back to where the children were waiting.

"Good afternoon, Caroline, Martin."

They replied, "Good afternoon, Mr Slavo."

"I mentioned to Chris that I'd see you off at the station."

"Really?" said Martin.

"Your father thought it might be a good surprise."

"Yes, it is," said Caroline.

"Come on then," added Chris.

They all walked across the main front entrance of the castle to the main gate. Once they had passed through it, the children looked through the metal railings one last time.

"Well, this is it," said Caroline.

"Yeah, time to go," replied Martin.

They stood there for a moment.

"Happy memories," said Caroline.

"Come on you two," shouted their father, who was ahead of them, talking with Slavo.

As they walked down the road next to the castle, Martin said, "Do you think we will come back?"

Caroline whispered, "Well I hope so, as I think I've still got the power of the magic key."

She added quietly, "But the funny thing is, I still don't know why I've got it."

"Yes, I must admit it is all very odd."

The boy added, "I think I'm going to miss Manfred and Veronica."

"Ssh, Martin," said his sister, putting her hand to her mouth.

Speaking quietly, Caroline said, "You can't say that here or anywhere. It's top secret, remember."

"Yes, I know."

"Anyway, no one will believe you, if you do talk about it. But we might not be able to go back in time again, if we say anything to anyone."

"Oh, that's a good point. I hadn't thought of that."

"You want to go back to 1912, again, don't you?"

He stopped and looked at her.

"Of course. Don't you?"

"Definitely!"

Just before they rounded the bend, Caroline suddenly stopped. She looked at her hand. Martin looked back at his sister.

"Why have you stopped?" he asked.

"Because I've just had a funny feeling."

"What now? Just as we're leaving."

"Martin, it's the same feeling I get, when we go up to the attic, to go back to 1912."

"Really?"

Caroline's hand mysteriously moved a little.

"Did you see that?"

"I did."

"My hand just moved of its own accord."

"Are you sure?"

Caroline looked at her brother.

"Of course, I'm sure."

She added, "Why would I tell you otherwise?"

The boy didn't have an answer for that.

"It was a sort of twitch feeling. I get it every time we go back in time, when we're at the bottom of the attic stairs."

"But, we're not at the bottom of the attic stairs."

"I can see that."

"Maybe the key's trying to talk to you."

His sister stood there, in the hot afternoon sun.

"Martin, keys don't talk to you."

"It's a magic key."

"Yes, I know it is."

"Well, why don't you look at it?"

She rooted in her pocket and got the key out.

Both of them looked at it.

"Nothing," said Caroline, despondently.

As she was about to put it back in her pocket, she suddenly felt another twitch in her lower arm and hand.

"Oh my God, Martin. I've just had another twitch."

"Really?"

Both of them looked at her arm and hand.

They looked at the key closely again.

As they did so, the circle with the '5' in it, suddenly flashed at them in green.

"Look, Caroline!" said Martin. "The '5' has just changed to a '6'."

She looked at it closely.

"Gosh! So it has. And right in front of our very eyes."

"Wow! This is really cool."

The children were ecstatic.

"What do you think it means?" asked Martin.

Caroline instantly knew the answer.

"It means, we've another chance to go back to 1912."

They both yelled "*Yes*" with excitement, before jumping in the air and hugging each other with delight.

When Martin had landed, he said, "But when?"

"That's the question," replied Caroline, smiling.

"We've definitely got to go back," said Martin.

"Yes, I know we have," she said, adding, "It looks like there *is* going to be a next time, after all."

"Brilliant!"

Realising they had a train to catch, Caroline said, "Come on, we'd better catch up with dad and Mr Slavo."

They walked on, with Caroline helping her brother carry his travel bag.

He sang, "We're going back to 1912. We're going back to 1912."

"Shush, Martin," replied his sister. "It's meant to be a secret, remember?"

"Sorry, Caroline"

They walked on, down the lane…

44

Time to Say Goodbye

At the railway station, the children walked across to where their father stood chatting to Slavo. The men were standing in front of the Zámočany station booking office. Some other train travellers stood nearby.

Looking up, Chris saw his kids walking toward him.

He said, "Everything alright back there?"

Caroline and Martin were grinning like Cheshire cats.

"Yes, everything's fine," replied Caroline.

She and her brother were suddenly feeling as happy as Larry.

Chris looked at them.

"We wondered where you two had got to," he said.

"We were just looking at the animals in that house back there," said Martin.

"Oh, I see."

"Are you looking forward to going back to Bratislava again, Caroline?" asked Slavo.

"Not really. I much prefer being here."

She added, "We're only going back, this time, because dad's presentation at the UN, in Vienna, was suddenly brought forward a week."

"Yes, so I gather."

"I'm going to miss the castle," added Martin.

306

"Well, there's always next time."

"You're right, Mr Slavo," said Caroline, beaming. "There's always next time."

She added, "If we don't come back next week, I'd like to come back here at Christmas."

"Christmas?" replied Slavo, looking at Chris.

"Oh I'm not sure about that, Caroline," said Chris. "Maybe next summer, Sweetheart?"

"Pity"

"Have you got the tickets, Dad?" asked Martin.

"No, as Slavo suggested I get them on the train."

"Oh, right"

At that moment, two people on white horses, rode across the railway crossing. One of them, a girl, was waving at them.

"Look, Martin," exclaimed Caroline. "There's Mike and Lucy."

"Oh, yes. So it is."

Their friends rode over to them.

"Hello," said Mike, happily.

"Is that you, Mike, under that hat?" asked Chris, jokingly.

"Yes, it's me," he replied, laughing.

"I didn't know you could ride a horse?"

"Oh, I can do many things," he added, smiling.

Lucy and Mike demounted.

"This is an unexpected pleasure," added Chris.

"We wanted to say goodbye," said Lucy.

"That's very nice of you."

"Yes, it is," added Caroline. "I didn't think you'd come."

"Life is full of surprises," said Mike, smiling.

"What a lovely white horse," said Caroline, going up to stroke it.

"Do you like her?"

"She's beautiful," said Martin.

"They're both beautiful," said Caroline, stroking the other horse.

As Mike gave the horses some lumps of sugar, Chris and Slavo walked along the platform chatting.

"You didn't tell me you were going horse riding this afternoon, Mike," said Caroline.

He replied, "We had a change of plan."

"Oh, I see."

"Where did you get the horses from?" asked Martin.

"They're my uncle's," said Mike.

Caroline replied, "Really?"

"Yes. He's got a stud farm in the next village."

"Has he? Oh, I'd like to see that."

"These white horses are famous."

"Are they really?"

"Yes," said Mike. "These are some of the descendants of the famous Lipizzaner horses that you can see in Vienna."

"Oh, right!"

"The stud farm has been here for about a hundred years or so. One of my great grandfathers used to look after some of the horses, as a boy, up at the castle, when the land was owned by the castle."

"Did he?" said Caroline, intrigued.

Lucy decided to change the subject.

"Do you know when you're coming back to the castle, Caroline?"

"I don't. It depends on what my dad decides."

"I see."

"When are you leaving?"

Lucy replied, "I'm going home tomorrow."

Mike was stroking his horse.

"Caroline," he said. "I think you will come back here."

The girl was surprised by his comment.

"Oh!" she replied. "What makes you think that?"

"You told me you like it here."

"Uh-huh"

"When you come back, I'm sure you'll have many more adventures in Zámočany."

"Maybe"

The two girls looked at each other, in an odd girlie way.

Just then, they could all hear the sound of a diesel train approaching. It hooted its horn, as it rounded the bend.

Slavo and Chris walked over to where the horses and his kids were standing.

"Looks like our train," he said.

Slavo added, "Well, have a safe journey back everyone."

"Don't worry, we will," said Martin, smiling.

They watched, as the diesel train pulled up opposite them.

"This really is it. Time to go," said Caroline.

"Yes," replied Lucy.

She added, "See you, Caroline, Martin. Take care."

The children embraced each other.

Caroline and Martin ran across from where they were standing and got onto the train. Chris pulled down a couple of windows, so they could all look out.

The train guard looked down towards where the stationmaster was standing. With everyone on board, he waved his red flag and blew his whistle.

Slavo now stood next to Mike and Lucy, as the diesel train slowly edged itself away from the station. It sounded its hooter again. Everyone waved madly at each other.

"Bye," shouted Caroline.

"Hello," said Lucy.

"See you," yelled Martin, waving madly.

"Well, there they go," said Slavo.

"Yes, it's another adventure over for them," added Mike.

Lucy cocked her head and looked at him oddly.

Slavo then said, "Well, I must be off. See you another time, Mike."

"Yes, see you, Mr Slavo."

"Nice to meet you, Lucy."

"You too, Mr Slavo"

After mounting their horses, Mike and Lucy started to ride away from the railway station.

As they rode, Lucy said, "Do you think they will come back, Mike?"

He replied, "Sure they will. Caroline's got a magic key. So she's got to come back."

Lucy looked at him in astonishment.

"A magic key? Really? How can that be possible?"

"Ah, well…"

He laughed in his funny way, adding, "Well, it is."

"Caroline never mentioned it."

The train tooted its hooter.

Mike's horse reared up.

Once it had settled, he added, "I think Caroline and Martin will definitely return to the castle. It's *their* secret castle."

"Really?" said a surprised Lucy, looking at him.

"Sure"

"How do you know that?"

"Caroline told me it was."

"Oh!"

Mike winked at her, laughed, and then galloped on ahead.

None the wiser to the boy's comments, she rapidly followed…

Caroline Hartley will return in...

Caroline Hartley

and the Secret Castle Adventure

Acknowledgements

I would like to thank the following people for their help when writing this mini-series of Caroline Hartley adventures:-

Cover drawings - Veronika Begánova

My late mother, Peter Martin, Liam Higgins, Brian Killeen, Martin Somora, Katarina Hindrová and many of my students.

About the Castle

The castle, gardens and castle estate described
in this book are purely fictional.

The real castle and gardens that inspired
this book can be located at
Podrečany, Slovakia

About the Author

D.J. Robinson is a native British English teacher
who lives in Bratislava, Slovakia.

D.J. Robinson writes British English lesson plans for
teachers and students worldwide who are learning English.
The webpage is www.newsflashenglish.com

Lightning Source UK Ltd.
Milton Keynes UK
UKHW04n0705240818
327701UK00001B/3/P